DATE DUE

Always a River

Always a River

BY

DRAYTON MAYRANT

APPLETON-CENTURY-CROFTS, INC.
NEW YORK

Foreword

FOR THIS STORY I HAVE GONE TWO HUNDRED AND SIXTY years back into the past of a ghost town of today. All through my childhood and youth the site of Dorchester-on-the-Ashley was a rendezvous for picnickers and for horseback riders. But it was then and it is now no more than a site, and it is in danger of being lost even to memory. For the Carolina woodlands, which Sandy Purbeck found to be semitropical, are swift in taking back their own. The busy little Puritan town of Dorchester the Third is no more. Before the War of the American Revolution it was abandoned by its New England settlers, who moved in a body to Liberty County, Georgia. Only a few of them remained, to marry and settle in Summerville nearby. The Presbyterian Church in Summerville is heir to the Old White Meeting House where Sandy Purbeck worshiped. Only a fragment of its tabby wall still stands; but names in its graveyard commemorate families from the Bay Colony. The site of the village should be a shrine. It gave its name to the county. But it lies neglected and overgrown upon the riverbank where Cusabo Indians moored their dugouts when they came to the trading post. In spring the wild swamp lilies bloom, and the Carolina jessamine—more kind than men in remembering—garlands the few ruins which remain of a Puritan town in a southern colony.

D. M.

Part One

DORCHESTER THE SECOND

WEST AND ACROSS the narrow bend of the frozen river, a wall of opaque cloud hid the horizon. It rose swiftly, as if to meet the cold fire of the sinking sun. For minutes the naked, ice-sheathed trees of the forest glittered against it like diamonds on the black velvet of a jewel case. Jagged ice piled high along both banks of the Neponset gave off a flicker here and there, then darkened sullenly.

From a thicket on the southeast bank the two young men were watching. As the last arc of the pale sun slipped from sight, Sandy Purbeck began to rise from the ground where he lay on his stomach.

"Down," his older brother commanded in a whisper. "Get down behind the log again—and keep perfectly still!"

Sandy obeyed, but protested, also in a whisper: "The sun is down. You can't shoot."

"The sun is down but it hasn't set. Those clouds are hiding it."

3

"You mean you'll dare?"

"Of course I will. We're miles upstream from the village—and, I tell you, the sun hasn't *set*."

Sandy lay motionless, cupping the powder horn in his hands. The long, dark barrel of the smoothbore musket lay across the fallen log, absolutely steady in Peregrine's hands. In their home was also a short-barreled bellmouth weapon, but this newer one was the pride of both their hearts. It was the early model of the Brown Bess, just come into use in England, and it had been sent to their father by a kinsman in Dorsetshire. Being a clever man with his hands, he had carved into its stock a peregrine falcon to mark it for his cousin Peregrine Purbeck. And for that reason the older son and namesake had preempted it since his father's death.

The old bellmouth musket fell to Sandy's lot, but he had not even brought it along on this hunt. Nor had he brought the forked stick which served as gun rest, for this target could be sighted from the lower rest of a log. The log, too, would furnish an ambush when the prey approached. They were both careful hunters who killed just enough for their need, and their need this afternoon was just one dinner.

The older brother spoke under his breath. "Here they come! Give me the powder!"

One by one the wild turkeys were fluttering into the thicket to roost. It offered a little more shelter than other parts of the wood, for its boughs although bare of leaves were thickly interlaced overhead. The great birds, too heavy and clumsy for migrant flight, alighted upon the ground or settled on low branches with plaintive guttural croonings. Sandy pitied them briefly as he thought of

4

arrowheads of wild geese driving south, too high for a bullet to reach.

Just then his brother fired. An enormous gobbler leaped high, somersaulted to the ground, rolled over and lay still.

He was quite dead when they picked him up, his bronze-and-iris plumage wet with blood from Peregrine's bullet. All around them the terrified flock flapped and rustled and gobbled, as they made their escape from the noisy death of the white man. Peregrine was jubilant.

"It's even bigger than ours! Won't Ness and her granddam be surprised?"

Thought of Ness's surprise and pleasure allayed Sandy's misgivings at the destruction of the bright and beautiful bird. Now Ness and her grandmother would have a turkey dinner. Hosea Goodman had shot and hung a turkey before his departure on business for New York. But it had been stolen from the hook in the lean-to wall—presumably by a prowling Pequot.

It was Sandy who carried the turkey all the long way back. They recrossed the river where it narrowed at the bend. There it was solid enough to give footing, and they knew that nearer Dorchester Bay the salt tides kept it open. Its ice and its current were both as dark as the dark sky and dark woods. Now it was running northeast, and they followed its northwest shore. Flakes from the snow cloud began to fall before they reached the village. Its streets were unlighted and empty, and only a few shutterless windows framed rectangles of unsteady yellow candlelight. The hunters proceeded directly to the Goodman house, and Ness Goodman opened the door to them. Peregrine stepped in, leaned the long gun

5

against the wall, took the bird from Sandy and held it out to her.

She shrank back—a small, fair girl only as tall as his shoulder—and her eyes went from him to Sandy.

"Oh, no! I can't let you give me your dinner and you go without!"

Sandy opened his mouth to explain, but his brother spoke first.

"What makes you think we've brought you *our* turkey?"

"It's just the kind of thing Sandy would do. Grandmother told him this morning that ours had been taken. I heard her telling him at the gate while I was sweeping the house."

Peregrine said sharply: "Well, Sandy didn't do it— even if it's the kind of thing he would do. We have our own turkey, and we got another for you."

"Peregrine shot it," Sandy put in, "—shot it with a single bullet."

It gave him a twinge of jealousy every time she raised her grave eyes to Peregine's face. Yet he not only had to give his brother the credit deserved, he wished to do so and took a fierce pride in his brother's achievements.

Ness was exclaiming with delight and calling to her grandmother. The turkey was hung in the lean-to, which served as kitchen and storeroom for food.

"I'll never leave anything out again," Mrs. Tompson lamented. "But Hosea killed that one so far ahead of time that he warned me I'd better leave it to freeze."

She insisted upon giving them a bowl of baked Indian pudding to take home for supper.

6

"I don't see how you boys make out. I wouldn't trust any man's cooking."

Peregrine eyed the sweet greedily. Molasses was a treat.

"Old Mag bakes our bread when she comes to clean the house." His bold, laughing eyes came to rest on Ness's face above her crossed white kerchief. "And who knows but that someday I may get a wife?"

Ness dropped her eyes before his, but her white skin never flushed. It was exquisitely fair and of the fine texture of a very young and very blond child's complexion. Near the left corner of her mouth, a small dark mole set it off like a beauty patch. She was neither beautiful nor even pretty; but there was charm in her delicacy, her wistful expression, and her low voice. Her baptismal name was Gentleness, and she embodied the virtue.

Outside the snow was thickening. It slid with soft rustlings from the steep-pitched roofs designed to spill it. As they went through their gate, Peregrine and Sandy perceived a vertical bar of light between bowed shutters. Without misgivings they pushed open the door. Any friend who had come in and waited to see them would, they knew, have lighted a taper.

Three middle-aged, black-clad men rose from the bench in the narrow hall. Under their hats, knitted scarves protected their ears and tied beneath their chins. Thick capes made them shapeless, for the house was bitterly cold. But the eyes of all three went in accusation to the Brown Bess in Peregrine's hands. Elder Pratt spoke.

"Evil is the day for me when I must come to chastise the sons of my old friend for desecrating the Sabbath by hunting after sunset."

COLD WITH APPREHENSION, Sandy stepped aside and against the wall. Profaning the Sabbath was punishable by hours or even days in the stocks. He was remembering men he had seen locked helplessly there, enduring pain and exposure and humiliation. Even as a boy, he had never pelted them with refuse as many of his friends had done. Were he and his brother—sons of honored Schoolmaster Peregrine Purbeck—to suffer that indignity before all of Dorchester village?

But Peregrine was closing the door and turning, at perfect ease, to look his three accusers in the face.

"Sit you down, my father's friends," he invited.

And as they did so his eyes lit at this first advantage he gained by standing over them. Yet his face remained grave and his tone was respectful.

"It is true, Mr. Pratt, that I shot a turkey gobbler in a river thicket this afternoon."

He removed his hat, contriving to make the gesture a token of respect, and set it on a table nearby. Sandy hastily did the same, but with less grace. He jerked his own hat from his head with an abruptness that rumpled his thick light hair. For he heard the redoubtable Mr. Cornwall speaking.

"And you forgot, young Purbeck, that the river would carry the sound of your gunshot."

An expression of patient reproach came over Peregrine's features. There was both reproach and surprise in his voice.

"Mr. Cornwall, you are making a serious charge against me—but, fortunately for me, a charge I have witnesses to refute. I am sure your own sons and daughters will tell you that they learned from me recently in school how the river carries sound. I devoted a lesson to it, explaining to my pupils that many primitive tribes communicated by shouting or beating drums close to the surface of water. Even if guilty of the evil intention you ascribe, my intelligence would prevent the making of such a mistake."

Sandy had listened, with his apprehension growing into amazement. Now his amazement grew into admiration. Peregrine had completely reversed the role of accused and accuser. In fact he was subtly charging one of his judges of bringing an accusation which was false. Elder Pratt saw it and spoke sharply.

"I will do the examining. There is need for only one of us to question. Peregrine Purbeck, where is the bird you shot?"

"Sandy and I have just given it to Dame Tompson and her granddaughter. It was for them I shot it, since an Indian stole theirs."

"The giving was a kindness. I had heard of the good woman's loss. But by shooting it after sunset, you broke a law."

"I ask you, Elder, with all respect: *Who charges I shot after sunset?*"

"Mr. Lord heard the gunshot, and so did several others. They went at once to look west, and they saw that the sun was down."

"If they looked west, they must have seen the snow cloud above the horizon. Sunset, as taught in the schools, is the dropping of the sun below the earth's horizon. It is not the covering of the sun by a cloud."

Although his view was narrow, the elder was just. Too,

9

he had the Puritan's respect for education. The young schoolmaster seemed to know what he was doing; but what he was doing was putting three churchmen in the position of having brought unfounded and foolish charges.

"Then you mean—"

"That the snow cloud engulfed the sun while it was still well above the horizon."

To Sandy it had seemed that the cloud was only just above the trees, and he knew how fast the sun sank when it reached that level. But his brother's logic entranced him, as a snake entrances a bird. He knew that Peregrine had always wished to study law instead of being a teacher as he, Sandy, wished to be. Now he realized how well qualified Peregrine was for the profession of law.

Mr. Pierce, smallest and least dangerous of the three inquisitors, was nodding.

"My wife warned me that the cloud would bring snow. We fed and housed our stock early."

Elder Pratt frowned. "How early, Mr. Pierce?"

"That I cannot rightly tell. But it was earlier than we usually do so."

Neither could Sandy tell. He was lost in a maze of argument. He knew that the cloud had engulfed the sun before the sun reached the horizon, but he recalled that he had been lying on the ground for some time after that meeting of cloud and sun. He could not prove how long —and, what was more to the point, neither could the elders.

Mr. Pratt was frowning at Peregrine, who met his gaze fully and with apparent frankness. In fact he advanced a step, resting his gun butt on the floor and circling its barrel with mittened fingers. But he kept silence, clever enough to know that the man forced to speak first had the disadvantage of attack against defense.

Mr. Pratt realized it too, and that was why he frowned. He looked from one to the other of his intended victims. There was no likeness between them in features or coloring. Peregrine had his mother's thin face and mahogany-colored hair. Sandy's mouth was wide, his nose straight and blunt, and his hair the same shade of tow blond his father's had been. Thin but broad of shoulder, he slouched, while Peregrine held his narrower shoulders so erect that he appeared tall. He stood as straight as a ramrod now, looking Elder Pratt in the face confidently and calmly.

But the three older men were neither confident nor calm. They had come, thinking themselves secure in their charge, to denounce an offender and announce his punishment. It seemed they had acted in haste upon a report which might not be true. This was not in the tradition of severe yet careful Puritan judgment. Mr. Pierce fidgeted and Mr. Cornwall fumed. Mr. Pratt spoke at last, and his words were slow and thoughtful.

"I saw the cloud, but I cannot in truth say that I timed its progress. How long, Peregrine Purbeck, after the sun went under, was it that you fired and killed your quarry?"

"Like you, Mr. Pratt, I did not time the movement of the cloud. It was rising fast enough to bring snow from overhead before my brother and I reached our home. I can only leave my case in your hands. The training of our church makes me more ready to suffer undeserved punishment than to make to you a statement of which I am not certain."

Elder Pratt—hands securely tied by that expression of trust and that reminder of the sanctity of proof—admonished them both to be more careful in future, and then withdrew his defeated forces. Peregrine's gravity turned at once into laughter.

"Fasten the door, Sandy. Old Cornwall might come back. Did you see the sour expression on his face when he realized he couldn't prove that shot was fired after sunset?"

Sandy fixed the wooden bar in its slots. His face was troubled as he turned to his brother.

"It seemed to me that after the sun disappeared we waited a long time before the turkeys came."

"We were lying on frozen ground, and that made it seem longer. I haven't thawed yet—and I'm hungry. Get the loaf and the meat."

Sandy brought the bread and cold venison. Along with the pudding it made a feast, and its flavor would be sweeter because of the defeat of the elders. Yet Sandy frowned.

"I believe the sun had set before the turkeys came."

"To tell you the truth, I think so too; but—*can you prove it?*"

"No."

"Neither can Elder Pratt. And that's all that matters."

"Still, I'd like to know the truth."

He stopped at the look on his brother's face.

"I don't mean I'm not thankful to you for arguing and defending us."

"Then, since my argument persuaded them, I don't see why you're foolish enough to want to know any more."

"Perhaps I'm foolish," said Sandy.

And as he spoke he was half convinced in his heart that he was foolish.

But at the same time his mind told him that Peregrine had again won: Won a double victory, against him as well as the elders.

ALL NIGHT THE snow slid from the roof. But, where angles allowed it a purchase, it piled in deep, disguising drifts as if to hide all things unbeautiful. It concealed dirt and lack of paint and ugliness and bleakness. It transformed the small bare town into enchanted country.

Peregrine snored softly, on his back with his arms flung out. Sandy tossed as his dreams brought back the events of the evening.

In his dreams he saw more clearly than consciousness would have allowed the fallacy of his brother's argument. It was not that he objected to fooling the opposition. It was that he could not bring himself to fool himself. A lawyer might play with words and hide the bare boards of reality in the manner the snow hid cowsheds and middens. But a teacher could not afford to do so. To a teacher was entrusted the truth; and the truth was a thing too precious to permit of deviation.

He admired and envied Peregrine—in consciousness and in dreams—and he reminded himself that he could never have done what Peregrine had done. Without Peregrine's quickness they would both have been disgraced and punished. Yet, in spite of that realization, he wanted to know the truth: Whether or not the sun behind the snow cloud had reached its setting before the gunshot.

Whatever he learned in the years ahead, he would never, he realized, learn that. That *yes* or *no*, so precious to him, was engulfed in eternity as completely as the sun had been engulfed in the snow cloud.

Daybreak came like a rose-tinged lamp which is lighted above white damask. From his window he could see long fields of unscarred snow stretching into distance and reaching for the Heights. From their drifts buildings emerged like unfinished sculptures not yet free of their marble's formlessness.

The first drumbeat came early and clear across the stillness from Meeting House Hill, causing Sandy and Peregrine to seize cloaks and hats and mittens and snatch their two guns from the wall. King Philip's War was over and the time had passed when every man took his musket to church with him; but two armed men served as guards at every meeting, and this day was the turn of the Purbeck brothers. Peregrine carried the Brown Bess and Sandy the bellmouth. As he turned to close the gate, he saw Ness and her grandmother come from their own house farther along the street. But he dared not delay for more than a wave of the hand. The guards on duty were supposed to arrive early and stand upon either side of the step while the congregation entered the church. Then they themselves went in, closed and barred the door and took up the same position upon two hard benches at the back.

Once at their stations they dared not even relax. They sat upright and chilly through a talk two hours long. An ordained pastor would have preached even longer. Mr. Lord was one of the lecturers, younger and less repetitious. As headmaster of the Dorchester Free School, where Peregrine assisted by instructing the younger pupils, he was well known to both Purbecks. They knew, as did all the rest of the town, that even stronger than his interest in education was his ardor to spread his faith by establishing missions in other colonies.

He caught Sandy's attention at once; for not only did Sandy long to teach, he longed to travel. He did not realize that he also wished subconsciously to escape from the domination of a handsome and brilliant older brother. Now he sat listening and wondering what place would be chosen for the mission. Would it go far west to the boundaries of New York, or even farther—into the southern wilderness?

Mr. Lord said the mission was a duty they owed to their past. Had not their forefathers, he demanded, crossed an ocean to give them the freedom of worship they now enjoyed? Those forefathers, he reminded, were of sturdy stock and had behind them a history which dated from before the Roman conquest of Britain. At a time so far back that the Britons were savage tribesmen who painted their bodies blue with wode, worshiped the oak and the mistletoe and wore skins of wild beasts, the ancestors of Dorchester men had lived in Britain's forests a day's march from Britain's channel. There, upon a hill, they had practiced their pagan Druid rites and at the same time fortified themselves against attack by hostile tribes.

It sounded to Sandy as if war and religion went hand in hand. Yet, perhaps it was profane to call Druidism religion. More likely it was devil worship—like the outbreak of witchcraft which had occurred in Salem two years before. The horror still persisted, and it was suppressed by punishment more dreadful than any death in war. But, he reminded himself, had it not been suppressed, some kind of black mass might now be taking the place of this beloved and accustomed service.

Judging by the pastor's words, drastic methods bore fruit. He was telling them that the Roman invasion had brought Christianity to Britain. In the invading legions were men who had served in the Holy Land or who had witnessed the courage and devotion of martyrs in Rome.

Meanwhile, near that Druid hill, at the crossing of two Roman roads, a town the Romans called Durnovaria had sprung up.

Peregrine covered his mouth with a hand, trying to hide a yawn. Then he motioned with his head to Sandy. Sandy, turning his own head and frowning in reproof, saw Forbearance White looking over her shoulder at him. Her prominent nose showed even larger in profile. He glared again at Peregrine and fixed his eyes straight ahead. Although he gazed at the pulpit he could see halfway up the aisle the neat back of Ness Goodman's bonnet. She was sitting as still as he and listening as intently. Their pastor had leapt the centuries to a village in Dorsetshire. It lay on the banks of the river Frome, on the site of ancient Durnovaria, and its name was Dorchester, which meant *gate to a fort*.

That was the Dorchester from which their forefathers had sailed to New England, leaving Plymouth in the spring of 1630 upon a ship called *The Mary and John*. Its captain had set them ashore upon bleak Nantasket Point, and from there they had made their way to that part of the mainland the red men called Mattapan. To honor the Reverend John White of Trinity Parish, Dorchester, England, who was the inspiration of all Puritan emigrations from Dorsetshire, their settlement in the New World was named Dorchester the Second.

Sandy's father had often told his sons the story, and Sandy had read the diary of Mr. Roger Clap. On the passenger list of *The Mary and John*, he had seen his grandfather's name: *A. Purbeck*. Sandy, his namesake, took the mere initial as proof that he too had disliked his unusual appellation.

From these reflections he came back to hear Mr. Lord's conclusion.

"With this determination of spreading and strengthening our faith, some of us are asking dismissal from the Church in Dorchester of Massachusetts, in order to carry the Church to the British colony of South Carolina."

UNTIL THE MEETINGHOUSE had been closed and the congregation dispersed, the two young men who were the day's guards stood by to assist. Then, spurred by the same desire, they started as fast as the snow allowed to overtake Ness Goodman.

Her home was a short way beyond their own on the long road that threaded the settlement. The outline of its buildings could be seen through bare trees from any small rise of terrain they crossed. Men who kept its records likened it to a cockatrice; Sandy compared it rather to

Cygnus. Its more than two hundred houses followed the design of a swan's long-stretched neck and body with two wings extended. It was now a little more than sixty years old, and unpretentious country-colonial dwellings had replaced the original thatched log cabins. Most of them stood behind fences or low walls of native stone. Their façades rose with a clean austerity. In spite of the northern climate, their builders had been lavish with windows, for windows were in the New World an un-taxed luxury. Each sharp-slanting roof was pierced by one or more chimneys. Lean-tos and low-built ells were characteristic additions. Every home had its kitchen garden, now a plot of frozen earth absorbing ammonia from the snow, but carefully cultivated in season. Stark, twisted apple trees etched themselves in orchards. The elm and the Indian mulberry grew wild in yard and field.

Mrs. Tompson went into the house, but Ness saw them and waited. With her gray cloak and white bonnet and mittens, she was a small neutral figure which blended into a background of winter and snow. Peregrine often teased her, saying she should wear a cherry-colored ribbon in her hair or at her throat, else he might pass her without seeing her. She always took him in earnest and lifted wide, honest eyes, answering: "Nay, for that would be vanity."

Sandy had looked at no other girl than this one next door. To him she seemed perfection of Puritan woman-hood: her voice like muted music, her dove's eyes and dove plumage of coloring and dress.

She invited them into the house and Peregrine would have accepted; but Sandy knew that to do so would be to beg an invitation to dinner. So they dallied in the snowy street and talked. A message had come, Ness told them, that her father was delayed in New York.

"Perhaps he's enjoying himself," suggested Peregrine. "I'd like to visit there myself."

Ness was shocked at the very idea. "Oh, no! He will stay only so long as his business obliges him to. But I'm hoping he will come soon. Since my mother's death, he and I have always spent the Sabbath day together. Now he will be absent for still another Sunday."

She looked so troubled that Sandy tried to reassure her.

"Don't give up hope, Ness. There is still time, and ships come in almost every day from New York."

Ness shook her head doubtfully and said, "Captain Tolman, who brought the message, does not know of any ships from the port of New York which are expected in Dorchester Bay."

"He may sail into Boston harbor," Peregrine suggested, "and come overland from Trimountaine."

Because of deeper water more ships made port there, and the town of Boston—formerly Trimountaine—was growing faster than Dorchester although it had been settled shortly after Dorchester's settlement. Ness brightened at the suggestion.

"That may be. I know my father will do all he can to be here to sit by me in church next Sunday."

"If he fails," said Peregrine, "I'll sit by you instead."

He added, half in teasing and half in malice: "That will leave Sandy free to sit by Forbearance White."

Sandy started angrily. "You know perfectly well—"

He stopped as Ness's eyes met his with a look of distress.

19

"Brothers should not quarrel," she told them gently. "I have no brothers, but my father is closer and kinder to me than most fathers are to a daughter. You are a true friend, Neighbor Peregrine—but you are not my father."

"Nor do I wish to be," he told her.

She tried to meet his laughter and failed, in embarrassment. Sandy saw her small hands clasp each other tightly in their thick mittens. In order to help her he changed the subject for one which had occupied his mind all the way home from meeting.

"Mr. Lord gave us a fine address. It would be wonderful to carry the Church into the wilderness—as our grandfathers brought it here."

She lifted her eyes to him then, and he saw that they were shining.

"I should admire those who went—but I would be afraid to go myself."

He had been thinking about it—longing—wondering. Her words brought about his decision. She would never care for him while Peregrine cared for her. His admiration for Peregrine was so great that he could not believe even she would refuse him. And his own love for his brother was great enough to prevent any rivalry. He could never have Ness, but he could make her admire him. When she was Peregrine's wife she might sometimes think proudly of their brother who had gone into the wilderness to teach. He would be happier teaching—even in a strange land—than staying to clerk as he did at the trading post and seeing Ness and Peregrine. . . .

He opened his mouth to tell her, but Peregrine spoke first.

"I'm sure you wouldn't be afraid, Ness. In fact I'll wager that you go someday."

Mrs. Tompson had come to the door. She called in a tone of distress: "Peregrine Purbeck, I cannot believe my ears! Do I hear you making a wager on the Sabbath Day?"

He laughed at her. "No, it was only words. I meant to say I was convinced that someday Ness would go into a new country to help carry the Gospel."

"Ness will do nothing of the sort. She will stay in her father's house with her father and me. What gave you such a wild idea, and what do you mean?"

"I mean," said Peregrine brazenly, "that *I* intend to go south as schoolmaster of Mr. Lord's mission."

In spite of brotherly thoughts and plans, Sandy's feeling for Ness was not that of a brother. This was too much from Peregrine for him to endure. His voice was hoarse with anger.

"Not if I can stop you, you won't!"

The other three gazed at him in surprise. Peregrine began: "But, Sandy, why—"

"Because I'm going myself. Even if I were not, I'd not let you drag Ness into a wilderness where she's afraid to go."

They faced each other, Peregrine startled and Sandy enraged. From childhood they had fought, and in childhood the older had thrashed the younger. Then had come a time when Sandy won. For that reason as well as because of the dignity of maturity, neither was so anxious to start a quarrel. Now Mrs. Tompson's voice, sharp and commanding, checked Peregrine's placating reply.

"I opened this door to invite you both to come in and

share our dinner. But it is unseemly that you brawl on the Sabbath—and that you dare speak of dragging my grand-daughter anywhere. Go to your own home! And don't come back here until you can behave like Christians!"

Sandy turned on his heel and strode away. Peregrine, who always led, was left to follow; for Mrs. Tompson pulled Ness into the house and slammed the door. Her outburst had merely amused him, but he was bewildered by the rebellion of his younger brother. In his own selfish way he was fond of Sandy, and since their father's death he had enjoyed playing the role of older brother. It had never once occurred to him that Sandy might not be content to remain secondary in all things.

Ahead of him now Sandy kicked open their wooden gate. As it swung inward it hit Ness's huge gray cat, which had been crouched to spring upon a bird hunting for food in the snowy walk. With a yell of frustration and fright, the animal leapt over the fence and galloped for the sanctuary of the Goodman house.

Sandy paused to look after it, hoping he had not hurt it. For he knew that Ness loved it tenderly and petted and spoiled it, although it was only an ash cat the color of dirty snow. When in early summer it climbed the apple trees and stole baby warblers from their nests, he did no more than shout and clap his hands to drive it away. Peregrine had once knocked it out of a tree with a rock, but Ness never learned why it limped for a week. When

Sandy reproached Peregrine on her account, Peregrine, unrepentant, replied that he wished he had killed it.

Peregrine was laughing now as he watched the cat's retreat, and Sandy wheeled and went into the house and up to his room. He was already beginning to feel ashamed. His conscience reminded him that his brother had no idea either that he, Sandy, cared anything for Ness or that he had set his heart on going with Mr. Lord's mission. His brother had senior claim both on the girl and on the profession of schoolmastering. He was not to blame for what he had said to the one and about the other.

When only a few minutes later Peregrine called him to share the cold Sunday meal, he was glad to go downstairs. But something told him this was the time to have a plain talk with his brother.

"I'm sorry I shouted at you—but I still don't like what you said."

Peregrine was as prone to forgive as are most people accustomed to having their own way.

"You injured no feelings—except the ash cat's and Goody Tompson's."

"The dame is Ness's grandmother and the cat is her pet."

"It's a horrible cat," said Peregrine. "It's just the cat a witch would choose to carry her messages to Satan. On nights when Ness is searching for it, I'm sure it's howling and capering with a coven on one of the Blue Hills."

"You know quite well that it is not. An animal cannot be a witch."

"It can be a familiar. In Salem a dog was condemned and executed for witchcraft."

23

"You and I talked of that at the time, and you didn't believe it any more than I did."

"Better not say that to the elders."

"I'm not saying anything to them. What I say, I'll say here and now to you."

Peregrine was chewing on the same loaf and cold haunch of the night before. The meat was almost frozen, so that the carving knife chipped rather than cut it.

"I don't see why we can't warm this up and make some gravy."

"Have you lost your mind, Peregrine? You know that no one's allowed to cook between sunset of Saturday and sunset of Sunday."

"What harm would it do?"

"I don't know—but it's against the law. Anyway, you're just trying to change the subject."

"I'm not. But I still have no idea what I did to make you angry."

"You take everything for granted."

"For example, what?"

"Ness Goodman," said Sandy.

Peregrine tried to digest his brother's accusation along with the rock-hard venison.

"Ness and I are not betrothed."

"You've made her love you. Surely you intend—"

"I'm fond enough of her, and she'll make any man a good wife. If she'll have me I'll marry her. But I had no idea that you—"

"I'm not talking about that. I'm talking about your leaving a schoolmaster's post—the same position our father used to hold—to go into the wilderness."

"Oh, that? I have no idea . . . I was only teasing Ness."

24

"You don't intend to ask Mr. Lord to take you?"

"Of course not. I have no desire to go into some colony I know nothing about."

"You're just saying that because you now know that *I* want to go."

"I'm doing nothing of the kind. Life's dull here, but it could be worse. As for your wishing to go, I think you're foolish; but if you're determined on it, I'll go with you to Mr. Lord and tell him you're a better teacher than I am."

Sandy felt no gratitude, but rather a helpless rage. He recognized the pattern. All this had happened before in regard to other matters. Peregrine was being generous, but he was giving up nothing he really wanted.

To leave Dorchester, to go south with the new Church —that, Sandy told himself, is the only solution.

"I'm in earnest. Will you ask Mr. Lord tomorrow?"

"Right after school," Peregrine promised him.

But they did not talk with Mr. Lord the next day or the next. For horror crept into the village that night on werewolf paws.

ALTHOUGH GOSSIP WAS punishable by law, news was a commodity exchanged daily at the trading post where Sandy clerked for Mr. Rox. The death of Mr. Purbeck just a year before had cut short his younger son's education. Lacking the diploma that Peregrine had won, Sandy was obliged to take any work he could get. On this early winter morning Mrs. Bridgham hurried in.

"Good day to you, Sandy Purbeck. I hear you have China tea brought by that brigantine lying in Boston roads."

"The brig didn't drop anchor until Saturday afternoon, so it couldn't be unloaded before the Sabbath, Mrs. Bridgham. Mr. Rox has gone in Dyer's cart to get the tea and other merchandise."

"Well, it doesn't matter. I'm not yet out of tea." She caught her breath as though she could no longer contain the news she had come to spread. "Have you heard about Minnie Freely?"

Sandy shook his head. He knew the widow Freely and her half-grown twin daughters. Mrs. Bridgham was rushing on.

"The girls sickened some days ago. The mother says their limbs ached as if they had been beaten, and they were hot to the touch and cried out they were being burned."

"It sounds like a strange disease. What does Dr. Blake say?"

"Widow Freely did not call him. You know she is poor—and timid and ignorant."

All that was true. The Freelys were not Massachusetts Bay colonists. They had come from the lonely forests northeast, where the husband and father—a trapper—had been killed by Indians. Traders on a journey south had brought mother and daughters to Dorchester and left them to be a thorn in the flesh of the orderly Puritans. Mr. Minot let them have a small house rent free, and they planted Indian corn in its field and gathered wild fruit and berries. The Free School Board forced the daughters to

26

attend school, and a few charitable neighbors paid the mother to scrub floors or wash blankets.

"Dr. Blake attends the poor without payment."

"The woman did not send for him, and Minnie died last night—died begging her mother to remove from her chest a thing she insisted was crouched there and smothering her."

Mrs. Pierce and Mrs. Tolman came in just then, and Mrs. Bridgham hurried to compare notes with them.

Mr. Rox's absence gave Sandy double work to do, and he hardly had time to think of Minnie's death. It was late afternoon before trade slacked and Dr. Blake came in. He ordered meal and salt meat and eggs sent to the Freelys and charged to the township's poor fund.

"Leave them on the doorstep, Sandy. Do not set foot in that house. I'm sure the disease is catching."

"Widow Freely told Mrs. Bridgham something sat on Minnie and smothered her."

Dr. Blake gave an exclamation of anger.

"The woman is a fool—a criminal fool if she is saying such things. Her daughter died of a rare and horrible disease which may paralyze any and all parts of the body."

"Her mother told Mrs. Bridgham she suffocated."

"She did—when the paralysis reached her lungs and she could no longer breathe. I have read of this and heard other doctors discuss it, but until now I hadn't heard of a case in the New World."

"Then it's new—as well as rare?"

"It is older than history. Long before the birth of Christ it—or something like it—struck ancient eastern cities, killing and crippling children by the score. For some reason young people are more prone to develop it."

"It sounds like a plague, if it can go from one victim to another."

"It is a plague—and so far no cure has been found for it. This is the first case I've seen, and of course I wasn't called until one girl was dead and the other in extremity. But, even had I been called, I have no treatment for it."

"Will Moll Freely die too?"

"How can I tell? Only God knows that—and only God can cure her."

He turned and stamped out, leaving Sandy to close the post and shoulder the sack of provisions.

The Freely woman opened the door and asked as he backed away from her: "Be you not comin' in to see how sufferin' is my Moll?"

"Not now. I just brought you the food Dr. Blake sent."

She gathered it up eagerly, and his heart reproached him for his refusal.

"I'm sorry about Minnie. I hope Moll will get well."

"Likely she will—if the thing doesn't come back."

"What thing?" he asked in horrid fascination.

"The thing sat on Minnie's chest and smothered her. Moll be beggin' me all day to keep it off her."

A faint cry came from within the house, and the widow pulled in the sack and began to close the door.

" 'Tis the night I fear," she told him through the crack. "Things of evil be loose in the dark, and they slip past you like shadows."

Sandy knew that nothing he could say would pierce her armor of ignorance. As he walked away, he heard her shutting and barring doors and windows. When he

28

got within sight of his own house, he saw Mrs. Tompson and Ness standing in the twilit street with Peregrine. Either his brother's persuasiveness had earned them both forgiveness, or else the dame's curiosity was stronger than her indignation.

Peregrine called: "I've been promising Dame Tompson you'd bring her the latest news from your customers."

He told them all he had heard. The older woman's face was stern. Ness raised a hand to touch his sleeve.

"I think you were brave, as well as kind, Sandy."

Peregrine jeered. "And why is my brother heroic?"

There was vexation in Ness's voice. "Sandy went to the Freely house after the doctor told him the sickness was a plague."

"I didn't go in the house," Sandy told her honestly. "The doctor sent them provisions, and the least I could do was carry them to the door."

Peregrine said scornfully: "The Freely woman is half-witted. If she ever had any sense, the Indians scared it out of her head."

Ness defended her softly. "If I saw someone I loved killed, or if anyone I loved were threatened even, I—I just don't know what I'd do."

Sandy put his hand over the cold little hand on his arm.

"If anyone troubles you, just let me know."

"And don't forget me," teased Peregrine. "You may need two defenders."

"She needs neither one of you," Mrs. Tompson told them tartly. "Why should anyone threaten her? Besides, her father will soon be home."

Ness's face lit with joy.

"Yes, we had a letter today. He says that most important affairs are keeping him longer away, but that he will be here in a week—and will bring a surprise for me."

IN THE LITTLE village the long white week went by. Drumbeat summoned its folk to meeting on days of prayer; but there was no observance of Christmas. On Holy Night the long meadows sloped away from the settlement in a stillness as deep as that which lay upon the hills of Bethlehem. Above, amid flaming northern stars, the heavenly Swan looked down where candlelight outlined palely the town of Dorchester in the slender symmetry of a spread swan on the snow.

Its people had come into quiet years. There had been a time of famine for those first hardy ones brought by *The Mary and John*. Then their cattle had fattened on the chosen grazing ground, and they had raised their houses and church and school. Although the settlements at Salem and Plymouth were a few years older, the Dorchester School Board was the first free school board in America. Its teachers were, next to its preachers, its men of most importance; and all its ordained preachers were university men.

First of that long line had been the Reverend John Warham and the Reverend John Maverick. They believed so deeply in discarding all ceremony and holding only to the pure word of God that they led their small band of adherents from old England to a New England.

They called their faith Independent—other men called them Puritans—and from their meetinghouses spread through the New World the form of worship known as Congregationalist.

The Massachusetts colony of which they were a part claimed, in addition to Salem, Plymouth, and Boston, all lands on to and including Nova Scotia north and east and all lands west to the south sea. The port of New York, the Connecticut valleys, Rhode Island and the Providence Plantations were mere cutouts from the pattern of this map.

The verdant Connecticut river valleys had already lured men from Dorchester to farm or trade. The village trading post was the heart of Dorchester town, although the location of the settlement had been determined by the richness of surrounding pasture land. Grass was abundant, but the ground was stony and its stones frequently hid dens of rattlesnakes. These were dangerous to beast as well as man and were systematically hunted out and destroyed. But many still remained; Sandy had killed more than one in his own orchard, sunning after winter hibernation. In the township limits was a small hill called in the Indian tongue *Mos-Wachuset*, and said by some to have given the name Massachusetts to the Indian tribe and the European colony. Its rocky sides were pocked by nests of the great pit vipers, and for that reason it was avoided.

Snakes in the fields, wild beasts in the forests, and the ever-present danger of the red man had made life uneasy for the first settlers. They were first except for a few adventurers who had arrived before them and lived in solitude. One of these was a maternal ancestor of Gentleness Goodman: David Tompson, who had settled upon the small island named for him.

By the year 1695 these hardships had been for the greater part overcome, but not yet completely disposed of. Sandy and Ness and Peregrine were of the same generation as the two Minot children who were saved by a valiant servant. Dorchester knew that story by heart. The three had been alone in the house when an Indian raider, war-painted and armed, attempted to break in. While he attacked the barred door, the maidservant hid the babies under two enormous brass cooking kettles, then ran for her master's musket. Through the window she and the angry savage exchanged shots. She was apparently the better marksman, for he missed her while she wounded him and sent him running back to the woods.

Now, except for what the French called *la petite guerre*, which they and their Indian allies kept up on the colony's borders, life was for the colonists easier and far safer. A Dorchester man, Chief Justice William Stoughton, had succeeded Governor Phips. Other men of Dorchester had, like him, gone on to Harvard College from the Dorchester Free School.

There was one threat, however, for which no defense had been found. Privateers still harried the coast and the coastwise ships. Ness was now tormenting herself with fears about her father and the vessel upon which he was returning. Sandy tried to comfort her as he walked home with her one afternoon when she had come to the post to buy tea and molasses.

"You know how Father loves his tea, and he likes it sweet. He always stirs several spoonfuls of molasses in the saucer. I'm going to brew a pot for his supper. Grandmother has had the Indian pudding in the oven since morning."

She cast an anxious glance toward Dorchester Bay.

"I hope his ship comes in before nightfall."

"Stop worrying," Sandy ordered. "He may be at home when you get there—with the surprise he's bringing you."

She began at once to walk faster, making him regret his words.

"Perhaps he will be—in time to go with me to prayer meeting tonight. We'll see you there, and I'll whisper to you what was the surprise he brought. I'm hoping *so much* that it's a Hollandish apron with ruffles around the hem."

They were approaching the Purbeck gate and she tried to take her packages, but Sandy refused to yield them.

"I'll go on with you and see for myself. Look! There's Samson Dyer's cart—and your father's in it—and—"

Ness had stopped short and was staring. She said breathlessly: "And a woman—a woman in a striped cloak."

The vehicle had come to a halt in front of the Goodman house. Hosea Goodman jumped down and helped the woman alight. Sandy drew Ness on toward the group.

"Can she be the surprise he meant? Have you some kinswoman who might visit you?"

Ness's father saw her just then and came to meet her, drawing the brightly clad stranger along with him. As they came nearer, Sandy saw that the woman was young, although probably ten years older than Ness. She was tall, with a figure rounded enough to manifest its curves even under the long wrap she wore. On her black hair

33

was a hat instead of a bonnet or coif. Her red mouth laughed, and her tawny eyes sparkled at Sandy.

Ness cried, "*Father*," and threw herself into his arms.

He embraced her tenderly and did not hurry about it, while Sandy glanced nervously from them to the woman with the smiling red mouth. Then Hosea Goodman released his daughter and spoke.

"This is the surprise of which I wrote you, my dear. She was Rosa Zuider when I met her at the Trimountaine Inn of New York."

Sandy had not until then seen Goody Tompson. She was suddenly with them, hands on her hips. She faced Rosa Zuider.

"Woman, were you a barmaid at the Trimountaine?"

The stranger did not answer. Goodman answered for her. But in that second Sandy saw the change in the face he had thought handsome. Its eyes narrowed to slits of rage and its curved red mouth drew thin. Ness stepped back and toward him, and he put a hand on her shoulder.

Goodman answered.

"Whatever she was has nothing to do with what she now is. She is now my wife and the mistress of my home. You will all remember that and treat her in accordance."

WHEN SANDY BURST through the door shouting his brother's name, Peregrine looked up from the lessons he was preparing.

"Ness's father has just come home!"

"Is that all? The way you look, I was afraid he had been captured by a privateer."

"I think he has been," said Sandy—and told of the New York woman.

Peregrine closed his textbooks.

"I'd like to see her. She must be worth seeing if she caught old Goodman. What did you think of her?"

"I didn't think of her. I was thinking about Ness."

"She may do Ness good. Ness needs livening up."

"Ness doesn't need anything. She's right just as she is. But this woman is all wrong. Goody Tompson saw that at once."

"Goody Tompson's tongue is as sharp as her eyes. I'm anxious to get over there and get a look at old Hosea's Rose."

He insisted, despite Sandy's argument, that they should go together for a neighborly visit next day. Ness admitted them, her sweet face wearing the stricken look they had seen on it at meeting the previous night. All four of that household had attended church, Hosea Goodman sitting between his daughter and his new wife, and Mrs. Tompson rigid and disapproving on the other side of Ness.

This evening the older woman was not present. As if to set the seal of her disapproval, she had disappeared from the family living room. Hosea Goodman, a thin, straight-featured man, sat in a straight-backed chair on one side of the chimney and his bride sat demurely next to him.

Her dress was bronze-colored, and its bodice lacked the kerchief of Puritan women. Her hair, as glossy as a crow's wing, was fastened on top of her head in blue-black whorls. Under her skirt appeared soft black slippers. They moved restlessly, revealing the fact that they were far larger than Ness's small shoes. Occasionally their movement revealed a glimpse of white-stockinged ankle.

Her eyes lit at the sight of the two young men. Ness introduced Peregrine, and Hosea asked them to be seated. Peregrine immediately took a chair by Rose, and his eyes surveyed her boldly. Sandy sat on the other side of the hearth by Ness, while all waited for the man of the house to speak. He rubbed thin hands together in satisfaction.

"How good it is to be home," he said contentedly.

The young woman beside him lifted her eyes. Her lashes were stubby but thick. She smiled the same feline smile Sandy had seen on the day of her arrival. Her voice was deep to the point of huskiness.

"Home with your daughter," she said.

There was no offense in the words, and yet they offended Sandy. Peregrine was still looking at the woman, while Ness sat gazing into the fire. Goodman continued to rub his hands as he nodded agreement.

"The streets of New York are slippery with mud and sleet, and a reeling intoxicated man is not an uncommon sight. Here there is a truer cold and the snow is deep and dry. In our village there is peace and dignity."

His eyes went trustfully to the woman at his side.

"Yes, my wife and I are glad to reach home. Is that not so, my dear?"

She inclined her head and smiled at him, but there was mockery in her smile. Sandy and Peregrine saw it. The former was indignant, the latter amused.

"Even if they are slippery," he suggested, "the streets

of New York are lantern-lit and there are all manner of shops and taverns and other diversions."

"Neither my wife nor I," Hosea Goodman said, "set store by such worldliness. Before I married her she told me she longed to be the wife of an honest man in a small and quiet village."

Peregrine stared hard at Rose, but she cast down her eyes.

"Dorchester," he told her, "is no small town. We are a day's ride from Salem, and we are close to Boston—which is not so old as we. Roads four rods wide have been built from here to neighboring towns. Dorchester is the most important town in Massachusetts colony."

None of them contradicted him. Rose's eyes were fixed on the red ash in the fireplace. The logs on the andirons had burned almost across. Half on the brick hearth and half in the chimney, Ness's cat lay curled—as gray as the dead ashes.

Hosea Goodman arose from his chair, picked up a stout length of oak and threw it well back in the chimney. The dying back log broke into a cascade of sparks which fountained out and upward. Some of them fell on the ash cat's fur, awakening it rudely and causing it to leap with a squall of terror back into the room.

Ness cried: "Oh, Father, I fear you've singed True Thomas!"

Goodman was regretful. "I didn't mean to. I hope he's not injured."

Meanwhile, Ness had picked up the snarling, spitting animal. Sandy tried to help her, but the cat raked savagely at him with a taloned paw. He withdrew his hand, recalling that he had once suggested the cat's name because of its romantic Old English flavor. They had all three been younger then, and Peregrine had shouted with mirth.

"Why are you laughing like that?"

"Because, although Thomas is suitable, I wouldn't call any tomcat true," Peregrine had replied.

That had been years before. Now the ash cat was scorched and Ness was stroking it and laying her cheek against it. Sandy grieved for her grief, and even Peregrine tried to reassure her.

"Only its fur is singed. It isn't burned, Ness."

"No," agreed Mr. Goodman, "it's more frightened than hurt. If I'd seen it I wouldn't have thrown the log; but when it curls there in the ash it seems to become invisible. Forget it now, Ness. I want to hear this plan of Sandy's about going to the South to take the Church."

Sandy saw a look of distress cross Ness's face. He told himself that she was deeply troubled about her pet. Her eyes met his, then fell. She turned and crossed the room and put the cat outside. When she returned he saw that her face was composed. He heard Peregrine answer for him—as Peregrine so often did.

"It's a fine thing to do. I'm proud of my little brother."

"He's as big as you are—and stronger, I hear," said Mr. Goodman drily.

Peregrine flushed, and Sandy heard Rose give a little mewing laugh like a wordless taunt.

"Of the two of you," Goodman went on, "I'd say *you* were the rover."

Peregrine's eyes grew warmer brown as they came to rest upon Ness.

38

"I have my reasons for staying, as Sandy has his for going. He's not only stronger than I am, he's a better teacher."

Goodman had the Puritan quality of frankness.

"You have a diploma. He has none."

In spite of his selfishness, Peregrine could be honest.

"It takes more than a diploma to make a teacher, Mr. Goodman. When I went to Mr. Lord and began setting forth Sandy's qualifications, he said: 'You needn't tell me. Ever since that week you were ill and Sandy taught in your place for me, I've known the boy was a born teacher. I'll gladly take him.'"

Peregrine smiled at the young women, both of whom had fixed admiring eyes on him during his speech. Goodman, too, nodded approval.

"I recall your sickness. Was it anything like what killed the Freely girl?"

"No, it was pleurisy. Minnie died of a plague, and others might have caught it had Dr. Blake not kept them away from the house."

"It happened while I was away, but I have heard rumors. Has young Moll recovered completely?"

"No," said Peregrine, "and I don't think she ever will."

"She has lost the use of her arm," said Ness. "She cannot even raise it."

Her eyes darkened with sympathy. "As soon as the doctor lets me go to the house, I shall go to see her and try to help her. I'm sure Grandmother will make her a pie, and it might amuse her if I took True Thomas."

Hosea's bride said scornfully: "Amuse her to see a cat?"

"Oh, yes. I've taught him several tricks. If I hold up a piece of something he likes, he'll stand on his hind feet and walk several steps for it."

I<small>N SPRING THE</small> leaf buds opened on elms and maples and oaks, and the wild mulberries came into succulent foliage. Where the long meadows had slept under a white quilting of snow, grass now sprang between the field stones, and dogtooth violets blossomed. The cows were again put to pasture, the wheel of the water mill creaked. The willows, heavy with pale, long-fingered leaves, leaned from the Neponset's banks until they touched its tide.

Afternoons were longer and young people strolled along Chickataubut or Pond Road and out toward Mos-Wauchuset. Young men rowed on Dorchester Bay to examine the fort called a castle and fitted with guns to serve against attack by the Dutch. In spite of Goody Tompson's objections, Sandy dared take Ness out to it in this last spring with her. While the sunset reddened its ruined brick, he described to her the violent storm of 1665 during which Captain Richard Davenport, commander of the castle in the bay, had been killed by lightning.

Since childhood he and Ness had been accustomed to gather the wild herbs in season. Like most Dorchester women, her grandmother used them for seasoning and for simple medication. In recent years Peregrine had joined these excursions. But he cared nothing for young woods or early flowers and only teased the other two because they loved such things.

He was poring over a textbook when Sandy came in and spoke excitedly.

"Has Goody Tompson talked to you yet?"

Peregrine looked startled.

"No. Why should she?"

"She said she was sure she saw you in their orchard this afternoon, and she called to you but you disappeared."

"Why shouldn't I go in their orchard? That old woman is a scold, and she has a suspicious mind."

Sandy, surprised at his vehemence, tried to explain. But his brother went on heatedly.

"You know the birds are beginning to nest and that tomcat catches them when he can."

"I know. I told Goody Tompson I thought you were chasing the cat. She wanted to ask us to go gather herbs with Ness. She says the wild leeks are early this year, and she needs wild ginger and wintergreen."

Peregrine drew a deep breath, expelled it and began to laugh.

"Is that all she wanted me for?"

"Of course. What else should it be?"

"Oh, nothing—nothing at all. But she's always finding fault with me. You were here last Sunday when she heard me whistling and preached me a sermon about respect for the Sabbath."

Sandy said impatiently: "You ought to be grateful to her. If one of the elders had come by and heard you whistling a jig, you'd have got more than just a sermon. But, listen to what I'm telling you! I work only a half day tomorrow. As soon as you get home from school, you and Ness and I can start out."

Peregrine blurted: "I can't go. I've something else to do."

"What?"

The young teacher put his hand on the open book on the table.

"I told you I was doing some translation of Virgil. It's time just now for the School Board to visit. I shall not only have to make the pupils recite. You know well enough they will call on me for translations and explanations."

Sandy knew that, and he knew also that he was overjoyed at the chance of an afternoon alone with Ness. She would be disappointed, he told himself. But he was still glad next day when he took her big basket at the gate and they started out through the woods toward the river.

Ness showed no disappointment, either by word or expression. Along with the covered basket she gave him her faint shy smile, and every now and then she skipped —joyously and childishly—to catch up with his longer steps. She saw he was trying to shorten them.

"Please don't! I love to skip. I forgot and did one day on my way home from church. Grandmother was horrified, but Rose only laughed."

"Do you like her, Ness? Is she kind to you?"

"She has never been unkind to me, and I try to like her—for Father's sake. She's good-natured, and she doesn't object to Grandmother's taking charge of the house as she has always done."

"Maybe Rose is just lazy, and willing to let you and your grandmother do the work."

"She has never been taught to keep a house or cook or spin. But I wouldn't say she's lazy. She takes long walks by herself, and she strolls for hours in the orchard."

Sandy was thinking that Hosea Goodman's buxom wife would do better to expend her energy in sweeping and scrubbing for him. But just then Ness cried out with delight and went down on her knees.

"Look! It's the first anemone I've seen this year."

He took the fragile stem from her and laid it in the basket. The flower petals were so white that they appeared unreal.

"They seem afraid to open wide," Ness told him, "as if they were shy."

He thought: It's shy and lovely and fragile, as she is. But he only said: "I've heard people call it a windflower."

"That's another name for it. Oh, Sandy—" She lifted wide eyes to his face and he thought he saw grief in them. "Oh, Sandy, next spring I'll be coming here—*all by myself*—to find herbs."

For the first time, his eyes fell before hers did. What could he say? Peregrine would be with her. So he began to search for other flowers: trailing arbutus and Solomon's-seal and wild ginger with small pale blossoms and heart-shaped leaves. Down on his knees, Sandy dug the roots with his knife. In the next hollow they discovered striped wintergreen and the lily-bladed, deep-rooted leeks.

When they judged the basket full enough to satisfy Dame Tompson, they sat together on the riverbank and watched the turn of the mill which Israel Stoughton had built long years before. For decades now, Dorchester farmers and farmers from other townships had brought their grain here to be ground. The great wheel groaned in its labor and in every revolution spilled small cascades of the Neponset's water. Above, the weir lay swollen and still in the pale blue afternoon.

Sandy sat beside Ness in complete contentment. He looked at her pure, clear profile and thought of other girls. She was superior to them all, and for that reason her choice must fall upon a man superior to others. His brother fitted the role. He took a strange pride in the thought, in spite of his affection for Ness and his realization of Peregrine's faults. Any girl whom Peregrine loved must love Peregrine. Conversely, with such a girl for his wife Peregrine would certainly develop his better side.

Just then Ness said: "Sandy—" and he felt her hand touch his.

But he did not grasp it. He waited for her to speak, while the willows trailed their silvery leaves and the water wheel creaked on.

"Sandy—" she repeated diffidently and stopped again on the word.

He looked up, and her eyes met his. They were big and bright, but troubled.

"What is it, Ness?" he asked her.

"It—it's none of my business. But—after all—we're old friends."

"Of course we are—and will always be. Is it something you wish to ask me?"

"Yes. But you needn't answer if—if you'd rather not."

44

"I'll answer anything you ask me, Ness."

"Perhaps you won't want to, if it's secret and sacred to you. I asked Peregrine; but he just laughed and said, 'Probably so.' "

She would, of course, have asked Peregrine first. He, Sandy, took second place. And it was certainly something about Peregrine that she wished to know. She faltered but spoke the words.

"Are you betrothed to Forbearance White?"

His astonishment was so violent that he could hardly reply.

"No. Of course not. Why should you think us betrothed?"

"It's just the way she looks—and acts—if other girls ask her about you. And then Peregrine—Peregrine did not deny it. Sandy, why do you look that way? Are you angry because I asked you?"

He shook his head, wondering why she had asked the question. The only answer to that could be that she loved Peregrine and for that reason wished to know about Peregrine's brother.

So, when he helped her to her feet, he released her hand too quickly, and they walked side by side but alone back to Dorchester village. They approached it by way of the Pierce house, and all Sandy could think to discuss was the "remainder biscuit" brought by Robert Pierce from England.

Both of them knew, of course, that it was a sea biscuit picked up on the channel coast before *The Mary and John* set sail. But the legend had become a joke in the little Puritan village. Strangers were taken to see it, and most especially young lovers gazed upon it as if upon a charm. Sandy thought, with a small heartache, how much he would have liked to stop and knock on the Pierce door and with Ness go in to see it.

But the sun had set and he felt quite sure that Ness would prefer to go and look at it with his brother rather than with him.

"Ness," he asked her, "has Peregrine ever taken you to see the remainder biscuit Mr. Pierce brought from England?"

She moved a step nearer him and he felt her hand slip into the crook of his arm.

"Never," she told him. "Sandy, will you take me to see it now?"

And as he stood there uncertain with joy at her request, the door of the Pierce house opened and Rose Goodman came out. She descended the steps alone and stood alone on the walkway—until Peregrine Purbeck stepped from the shadows and joined her.

Instinctively sandy reached out and drew Ness against him. He caught her tight, as if holding her away from all that might hurt her. Never before had he held her so, but she did not pull away. She yielded, clasped so close to him that her cheek was on his shoulder and he felt the warm, quick breath from her parted lips on his throat.

Standing so in the shadow of a low-branched elm, they were not seen by the two who turned toward the

46

village. Rose had taken Peregrine's arm while her other hand lifted her long skirt. Sandy heard her throaty laughter blend with his brother's teasing voice, until the sound died and their figures were lost in the twilight.

Ness's whole body was trembling as he drew her along after them. He would have liked to stop and hold her in his arms and comfort her; but he knew he must not for her sake, and also it was not seemly for them to walk alone after nightfall. At her gate he gave her the basket.

"Ness, shall I go in with you?"

"No, Sandy. I'd rather—be by myself—until I can think what to do."

He was sure that her grief was for Peregrine, and he felt his clenched fists tighten with desire to hammer his brother's handsome jaw. But she put a hand on his arm just then.

"Sandy, promise me that you'll never tell about her."

"You mean about Rose—Rosa Zuider?"

"She is now Rose Goodman. She is my father's wife."

"Ness, how can you care what happens to her? I'd like to see her in the stocks—and Peregrine there beside her."

Peregrine's name did not appear even to catch her attention.

"I don't care for Rose. I care for my father. Disgrace and punishment to his wife would disgrace and punish him."

Sandy thought that over, but still he could not believe that her only anxiety was for Hosea Goodman.

"I'll do as you ask. But—about you and Peregrine—"

Her fingers tightened on his arm. "What about me and Peregrine?"

"I thought you—you loved him, Ness. If he hurt you, I could kill him!"

"Do not speak such rash words! Peregrine cannot hurt me."

"What do you mean, Ness?"

"I mean he cannot hurt me because I do not love him."

Sandy reached for the basket that kept them at arm's length, took it from her and put it on the ground. Even so, the new wonder made him afraid to go nearer. He put both hands on her shoulders.

"But, Ness, I thought—all these years—"

He saw her face as a small, pale blur, and her voice was only a whisper.

"I know you thought so, Sandy—and I often wondered why."

"What do you mean?"

"I mean what I said. If you don't understand I cannot explain."

"I thought you loved Peregrine because he is handsome and clever and bold." Bitterness crept into his voice. "It's been that way all my life. All my life I've seen that people liked him better than they liked me."

"Then you were blind, Sandy Purbeck. You let your own worship for your brother blind your eyes. Anyone would have to be both blind and foolish to choose Peregrine if they could have you."

The wonder of it was still with him as he drew her into his arms, but fear and uncertainty had gone and left only joy. Between their kisses they whispered things they had kept unspoken too long.

"You're just like the white anemone, Ness. I thought of that when you found it."

48

"You're far more clever than Peregrine, but you're modest and he is not. Nahum Wales told me that you could throw Peregrine in a wrestling match, and that you could swim the Neponset while he was afraid of water."

"Peregrine is so clever," Sandy defended him. "He teaches Latin while I'm still studying it." Even greater than the wonder of Ness's love for him was the wonder of being preferred to Peregrine. He drew her to him again. "But, Ness—dear Ness—I'm glad it's *me* you love!"

Just then Rose Goodman laughed softly outside the gate. Ness jerked from Sandy's arms.

"I thought you were in the house, Rose!"

"If I'm not in the house, I'm at least alone in the night. Mr. Rox will bear witness I've been to the post to buy meal for Mrs. Tompson."

Bold in her certainty that she had not been seen, she added: "Don't be afraid. I won't tell on you."

The candlelight haloed Ness's fair hair. To Sandy she looked helpless and small, facing the dark, tall woman.

"How dare you think you have anything to tell?" he asked her furiously.

She laughed again. "Village gossip says that Ness is your brother's girl and Forbearance White is yours."

"That is untrue," Ness told her, certainty in her voice. "Sandy Purbeck and I are betrothed. Nothing you tell can hurt us. But—except for my father's sake—I would tonight tell enough to destroy *you*."

Ness had advanced as she spoke, and Sandy stepped up beside her. "That is true. And I too saw my brother join you outside Mr. Pierce's house."

"So," said Rosa Zuider. For seconds she stood very still. Then she repeated: "So! What will you do about it?"

"I'll have to think first," said Ness, "—to think about my father."

"If you tell, who will believe you—after I tell I've seen you—here—in the arms of your lover?"

"Hold your tongue!" ordered Sandy. "We are betrothed, Ness told you! You are an evil and slanderous woman!"

She smiled at him, a sly feline smile which drew her full mouth narrow.

"I have heard Hollanders in New York say that you Puritans thrive on slander."

"That's not true. We search out evil in order to uproot it, but we love good. Ness and I will soon be married— and, besides, no one has ever cast a slur on her character."

The woman's eyes appeared to him quite yellow in the candleshine. He saw the outline of her face, broadening from the soft, pointed chin in a triangle to the domed brow like that of a cat.

"Not *yet*," she said deep in her throat, so deep that the threat seemed almost a growl. Then she turned away from them and went into her husband's house.

W ITH A CANDLE on the table beside his Latin text, Peregrine was sitting exactly as he had been when Sandy asked him the day before to go to the lower falls. Now he looked up and, seeing his brother, started to his feet.

"What's the matter? I thought at first you were going to hit me."

"I ought to," said Sandy; "and I'd do so if I hadn't found out Ness doesn't love you."

"What are you talking about? What makes you think Ness doesn't love me?"

"She just told me herself. So you and Rosa Zuider can't hurt her. But you can hurt her father—and hurt yourselves even more."

"You sound like one of the elders. Rose and I have done nothing wrong."

"You've been sneaking and meeting her after dark. I saw you join her outside Mr. Pierce's house tonight."

"So you've been spying on me?"

"No, I haven't. I went to the falls with Ness and happened to come back that way."

"You needn't have come back that way. There's a shorter path through the woods."

"Ness and I talked of the biscuit brought from England. She wanted to see it, but by that time night had fallen."

"In that case you and Ness were walking together at an hour just as late as Rose and I."

"You were with another man's wife. I was bringing home the girl I'm going to marry."

Peregrine flushed an ugly red.

"So you turned her against me? You spied on me and caught me at a disadvantage and used that to turn Ness against me?"

"I did nothing of the kind, and she never loved you. If she had and you'd hurt her, I'd be giving you a thrashing now instead of wasting words."

Although angry, Peregrine eyed his younger brother with new respect.

"You're suddenly very self-righteous, and high and mighty too—telling me you're going to marry Ness and calling me to account for walking down the street with Rose."

"It wasn't accidental. You refused to go with Ness and me in order to meet her. You've been meeting in the orchard too, pretending to chase the cat."

Peregrine laughed brazenly.

"It's the first good turn that cat has ever done anyone."

"Haven't you the decency to feel ashamed of what you've done to humiliate Ness's father?"

"I haven't done anything except snatch a squeeze or a pinch now and then. Hosea Goodman is old enough to have known just what he was bringing back from New York."

"He knew she was a barmaid. But she told him she wanted a good husband and a quiet home."

This time Peregrine roared with laughter.

"Rose wanted a quiet home and a good elderly husband? What she wants is a hug and a buss under a tree in the dark. If she doesn't get it from me she'll get it from somebody else. Any man fool enough to marry her deserves to be fooled by her."

Sandy's rage was mounting.

"I don't care about you and Rose. But I won't have Ness's father made a laughingstock. Nor will I have *my* father's name disgraced by your lewdness. The law could punish Rose with death and be almost as severe with you."

"It hasn't come to that. I've taken care not to let it. What do I care for her? She's nothing but a trollop."

52

"Well, take your trollops elsewhere! You'll find a plenty of them on Boston water front. Don't insult a godly town and respectable families with them."

"It's an idea," said Peregrine. "Especially since you've stolen my girl."

"I didn't steal her. You took her for granted—just as you've taken me for granted all my life."

"It's your own fault. You've always seemed to enjoy playing second fiddle."

"I'm not doing it any more. It was because I thought you so fine—but you've taught me better sense."

"Then I've done you a favor. Independence becomes you. As for Ness, she appeared to enjoy my company. And didn't you yourself tell me I'd made her love me and should marry her?"

"I thought so then, but I know better now. I'm going to marry her. And meanwhile, if you do anything to distress her or her father, I shall not hesitate to have you before the Church."

"Oh, no, little brother," said Peregrine. "You'll never do that to me."

Sandy took a step toward him.

"Are you trying to make me hit you?"

"No, I'm perfectly serious. I know you're too loyal to do anything of the kind."

"You're clever at argument, but you can't dissuade me that way."

"I'm not trying to. I've known all along you're a better man than I. You're strong and I'm weak. But you took me for granted as surely as I took you. Somebody had to take the lead, and you stood back and waited for me to do so."

Peregrine's wits and Peregrine's charm were softening

Sandy again. He was aware of it and it irritated him. He moved toward the door. He would not eat with his brother until his anger had cooled.

"Good night. I'm going to bed. But I meant every word I said."

"You may sleep peacefully. I'll leave Rose Goodman alone."

Sandy spoke shortly, turning away. "You'd better."

But as he crossed the threshold Peregrine said: "There's just one thing. . . ."

Sandy looked over his shoulder. "What?"

Peregrine said annoyingly: "In fact there are two things. The first—although to me the least important—is: What will Forbearance White and her father say about your marrying Ness?"

"I don't care what they say. What have they to do with me?"

"Mr. White tells me repeatedly what a fine young man you are. The girl has shown her preference for you."

"She has done nothing of the kind. Don't slander her!"

"She has—and in a most inconvenient way. I didn't tell you when it occurred, but I feel now that I should."

Sandy stared in surprise and amazement.

"In the graduating class last spring, each pupil was told to write either a story which was not true or her —or his—true plans for life. Forbearance handed in to me a story in which *you* wooed and married her."

"I don't believe it! How could you tell it was I?"

"The hero was Andy Burbeck, brother to the schoolmaster. The girl was tall and blond—with a Grecian nose."

"It's Roman, not Grecian. Is she crazy?"

54

"I think she is—with a dangerous craziness. She's a religious fanatic, yet hot-blooded, and she's not attractive enough to have yet found a suitor. Consequently those feelings are bottled inside her. When they reach boiling point, something will happen."

"I don't believe she meant me. I think you're crazy too. But—did Mr. Lord see her story?"

"No. I took care he didn't. I tore it up and reproved her."

"Thanks for that. But I still don't think—"

"All right then. I won't even mention the second thing I had in mind."

Hardly able to keep his temper, Sandy turned again. "Oh, no! Come out with it!"

"Are you going to marry Ness and take her with you into tropical jungles where she is afraid to go?"

Sandy put a hand on a chair to steady himself. With the other hand he pushed back his thick, rumpled hair. Peregrine's face was quite grave but his eyes glinted with laughter.

"Had you forgotten your mission? We talked with Mr. Lord."

"I—I had forgotten. I'll talk with Ness."

"Ness is unselfish. I know that—although I'm selfish myself. No matter how afraid she is she'll tell you to go—and go with you."

"I know," said Sandy.

He dropped into the chair, put his elbows on his knees and rested his head in his hands.

"But I can't let her do it. I can't take her to a place where she'll be unhappy and afraid—and probably suffer hardships."

"I thought you'd see it that way," said Peregrine.

He was enjoying himself, but his brother was too deep in misery to realize that.

"Mr. Lord accepted you. Do you recall what he said when I went with you to apply for the schoolmastership?"

"Not—not exactly. But I do recall that he accepted my application. I know I'm obligated—and I don't know what to do."

"Well, I know," said Peregrine.

His voice grew hard.

"I'm not like you and Ness. I'm not so unselfish that I'd ruin my life to keep my word."

"Peregrine, I can't break—"

"I know you can't. So I'll remind you of Mr. Lord's words. He said, 'Sandy, of course you shall have the position. I feel myself fortunate to get either of the Purbeck brothers for my assistant schoolmaster of the new Church.'"

"I know what you mean; but I can't let you make such a sacrifice. You said—not long ago—that you had no desire to go to this new place."

"Since then I've read and heard a little more about it. Also, it would put me more than an orchard's length from Rose. Thirdly, since I'm the Ishmael whose hand is against every woman, I'm the one to go out into the wilderness."

"You mean you really would—"

"Take your place with Mr. Lord's mission, while you stay here and marry Ness."

Sandy got to his feet and started: "Peregrine, I can't thank—"

But his brother interrupted him roughly.

"Just don't thank me, whatever you do! I'm selfish. I do nothing I don't want to do."

SUMMER WAS SWEET in Dorchester. The apple blossoms opened and fell, and the wide streets were shady with New England elms. Life in the village was busy, yet quiet. It moved with a calmness and dignity which was not usually found in other towns.

Only Ness and Sandy knew of Peregrine's fall from grace. He was to all others the beloved young schoolmaster who fulfilled his duties with intelligence and integrity. He had long since gone to Mr. Joseph Lord and arranged for himself and Sandy to change places. Sandy marveled at the ease with which it was accomplished.

"What did you tell him?"

"The truth: that we both loved Ness Goodman and I had hoped for her. But that when I discovered you were the one she loved, I suggested you stay here and I go with him."

"He was willing?"

"Not only willing, he sympathized with me and patted me on the back. He said he was glad to have a teacher of youth who had nobility of character as well as brilliance of mind."

"Don't make fun of yourself! You did a fine, generous thing. And I wasn't asking you if he was willing to take you in my place, I was asking if the Free School Board members were willing to let me replace you here."

"I know you were—and they are. But I'd advise you

to go to Harvard this summer for three months' intensive study on your Latin."

Sandy went over to Cambridge and made arrangements to enter the Latin class in August. Until then he would continue to work at the trading post and to enjoy the springtime of his love for Ness. Her father and grandmother had been pleased when he asked for her formally; and Rose, sitting dutifully at Hosea's side, had smiled out of her cat's eyes and wished them blessings.

She appeared to be behaving herself and making her husband content. Sandy reminded himself of that, and told himself that Mr. Goodman might not have been so willing to let his daughter go if he had not married again. Ness reported that she and Rose were polite to each other and that Peregrine's name had never been mentioned.

"But Grandmother shows she doesn't like her. I'm sure Rose is aware of it and holds it against us. I have a feeling she'd do us a mischief if she could."

"Well, she can't. And what's more, she knows that unless she behaves herself we can and will do her serious mischief."

So they put Rose and all else from their minds in the new happiness they had found. They shared a gentle, tranquil love which satisfied them both. Sandy had never really cared for any other girl. He was partly flattered and partly annoyed by the preference Forbearance White showed for him and the consequent teasing he got from Peregrine and his friends. In contrast with the big-boned, thick-set girl, Ness's demure sweetness and goodness were emphasized.

He took her to see the biscuit brought from the channel coast and now kept sacredly in a box in the Pierce house.

58

Her ancestors as well as his had been with the man who brought it across the sea from English Dorchester. They were of the same Saxon stock, and they walked by the Neponset as men and women of their blood had walked long since by the river Frome. Romance was for them kindly as well as beautiful, but a thing lacking all excitement or opposition. Word of their betrothal had spread and the village approved it. While they walked hand in hand across the grassy meadows, she told him of small attentions that pleased her.

"Mistress Pratt came to see Grandmother yesterday and offered to help us with quilting and sewing. Mistress Poole told me on the street that she was stitching for our home a sampler with the words: *Marriage is Honorable*."

Sandy was duly impressed. They talked of where the sampler should hang; for they would live in the Purbeck house after Peregrine went away. They planned to be married just before his departure. He had said he wished to carry the memory of that into the wilderness with him. He had been gay and kind and brotherly, and had said he looked forward to the adventure.

"My name means a stranger or exile. Perhaps all this was predestined. We cannot escape destiny."

He had looked sad and handsome, and Sandy hated himself because it flashed across his mind that his brother was good at play-acting. He dismissed the thought and turned to pleasanter ones.

Even a creature as humble as the widow Freely came to him in the trading post to offer her mite.

"Ye knows, Master Purbeck, that I has nought to give. But I'd take it kindly would ye and your lass let me come scrub your house top to bottom before ye wed."

Her voice made Irish music and her deep-sunk eyes were eager to be allowed to share in what others were doing.

But, being a man, it had not occurred to him that anything should be done to the house. It was true that old Mag left dust in corners, and she flatly refused to go in Peregrine's room. He had frightened her by shouting at her that he'd put Cromwell's curse on her if she disturbed his books.

Fearing his hesitation meant refusal, Jennie Freely still gazed anxiously into his face.

"Never a week since my Min was took but the Goodman lass has come to the house to bring summat for my Moll and me. Now 'tis a fresh-made loaf of bread with a jar of the apple jelly, now 'tis a dress of warm wool that she and her granddam had made. More times than one while Moll was still in the bed has she brought the cat in a basket so Moll might play with the creature."

He had not known, and he burned with pride to hear of Ness's good deeds.

"My brother tells me that Moll is able to walk and at school again."

"She be—but she be not happy there."

The woman's pale, tired eyes were still imploring him.

"Will ye then let me clean the house for the lass before ye bring her home?"

"I will, Mistress Freely, and thank you for the gift of your labor. Ness will thank you too when I tell her of your kindness. But why is your Moll not happy at the school?"

"The children torment her because her left arm be lifeless."

60

Sandy frowned and made a note to use his cane unsparingly on any child who mocked another because of affliction. Jennie Freely was still talking, with no resentment in her voice, only a tragic hopelessness because of her daughter's distress.

"Doctor says 'tis paralyzed by the sickness that killed Minnie. But the children keeps tellin' Moll that the reason 'tis withered is that a witch has looked on her with the evil eye."

Yet, now that his dreams appeared realized, it sometimes seemed to Sandy that everything was still a dream. Forgetting, he would find himself planning for Peregrine and Ness—content in that lapse of memory to look on her as a sister. It troubled him and made him moody, and Peregrine saw and seized the chance to jeer.

"For a prospective bridegroom, you're not enthusiastic. Are you already regretting our bargain?"

"Don't dare call it a bargain! It's not respectful to Ness."

"Don't be a prig! And as for respect, Ness gets her full quota from you. In fact I'm wondering if the poor girl gets anything else."

"Peregrine, are you trying to start a fight?"

"By no means. As your older brother, I'm merely sorry to see you regretful."

"Of course I'm not regretful. But marriage is a—a pretty serious thing."

"Too serious for me, I've come to believe. I shall remain a lonely bachelor—my life ruined by the fact that the girl I chose preferred my brother to me."

"What makes you talk that way? Mr. Lord himself told you that you did a noble thing in giving up Ness and taking my place in the mission."

"Maybe it's not noble. And maybe I'm trying to warn you."

"To warn me of what?"

"That you're in love with a dream as frail as a windflower. Love and marriage, Sandy, need something stronger—something warmer and more earthy."

"Something like your feeling for another man's wife?"

"Yes. It's honest enough if directed to your own wife."

"You make me think of the tomcat," Sandy yelled in rage. "And all my life I've admired you and tried to do what you did."

"Exactly," said Peregrine, his voice and his face now grave. "I may be a tomcat, but you're a copycat. What's troubling me now is the fear that you merely copied me in making yourself believe you were in love with Ness Goodman."

That had been too much, and Sandy had stamped out, slamming the door hard behind him. Even that gesture could not relieve his feelings. They boiled in his heart like the lower falls of the Neponset River as he went next door to Ness.

He found her bubbling over with joy, her small face almost pretty. For her there were no doubts; she loved him completely. She wondered at his preoccupation as they walked out of town on the Boston road. Perhaps he was sad at leaving her to go and study at Harvard. She tried to cheer him.

"By the time the ponds freeze over, you will be home again with me."

He only nodded and walked on, so fast that she had to skip to keep up. Could Peregrine be right in saying that he, Sandy, wanted Ness only because he thought Peregrine wanted her? That would be an offense against both her and his brother. No, he was very fond of her. It was true she was like a windflower—but he preferred windflowers to brilliant tropical blossoms. In fact he had never seen or even thought of such blossoms. . . .

He felt Ness's gentle touch on his arm. They had come to an outcrop of field stone.

"Let's sit here and talk awhile," she suggested.

In the meadows on either side cattle were grazing. Within sight were the fresh-water ponds of whose freezing she had spoken. It was still summer and they were circled with wild blue iris and the yellow star grass. Sandy spoke abruptly.

"I'm to take over the school on the first of December. Mr. Lord will be ordained to the ministry before then, and he wishes to sail before Christmas. Ness, are you— are you sure you're willing to marry me?"

Without words she laid her head against his shoulder. He leaned and kissed her on the cheek. It was soft and cool and smelled faintly of lavender. She was dear and sweet and good and all a woman should be. Peregrine had always enjoyed making trouble.

Ness said: "Mistress Mason is glad you will teach her children. She says she hears you are a born teacher."

63

That pleased him. And he told himself that Ness would take a wifely interest in all that concerned him.

"Mistress Calicot came yesterday from the water mill. I was making Thomas stand on his hind feet for a piece of cheese, and she said he was the cleverest cat she had ever seen. She came to bring me a length of dark-green wool she had woven. It is not bright enough to be unseemly for wear, and green and white are my favorite colors."

"They are your colors," he told her, "—colors of the windflower and of young apple leaves."

They sat in silence, holding hands and thinking of the green dress. He knew that she would not wear it to church or in the street. For such occasions Puritan women wore dark gray or black, relieved only by white cuffs and collars. Rose Goodman was the exception. She, alone, dared appear in public in gaudy attire. She was criticized for it; but so long as she did not desecrate the meetinghouse with her vanity, sympathy for her husband saved her a reprimand. Sandy assured himself that his wife would never be reprimanded. He was fortunate to get such a girl.

She continued happily: "Grandmother admired the green stuff. She says she's going to send a pie to Mistress Calicot."

"That will give us another chance for a walk through the woods," he told her.

And as he spoke he told himself that then they would recapture the magic Peregrine had threatened to dispel.

It seemed as if that hope had come true when they started a few days later. His conscious mind had forgotten all the nagging worry that had beset him after his talk with his brother. In Mrs. Tompson's basket they carried a blueberry pie, green apples for preserves, sour milk biscuits, and cottage cheese.

The woods were thick with foliage. Tawny meadow lilies grew in open places, their clustered blossoms drooping from graceful peduncles. Too soon for them both, their path came out on the riverbank.

They could now hear the sound of the falls. The Calicots lived on the farther side, so Sandy rowed Ness across the river in the small boat always left moored to the nearer bank. He pointed out to her the place where he and Peregrine had crossed after shooting the turkey on that Sabbath eve last winter.

"It was hard weather, and the river was frozen there."

"But it was dangerous," she said fearfully. "The current was running beneath and you might have broken through."

"It's dangerous unless the ice is unusually thick. Nobody should try to cross unless sure of that. But, you remember, a bitter freeze came at just that time."

"I remember. You brought us the turkey—and I saw there was snow all over your cloak and hat."

He too recalled that visit, and he had thought—with a pang of jealousy—that she was looking at Peregrine, not at him. He had loved her then, he assured himself. He would not now allow Peregrine to destroy their love by words which blighted like an evil eye.

Mrs. Calicot welcomed them loudly. She was apple-cheeked and plump as a robin. Only three topics concerned her: marriage and birth and death. She would have hurried their wedding.

"Why, Master Sandy, do you wait? Why go to school?"

"Because I must master the Latin as well as my brother does."

She shook her head. "You will be going and coming between Dorchester town and Trimountaine. That is not well—because of the voices."

The matter of which she spoke had occurred too long ago for Sandy or Ness to have known of it. She told them how, as a little child living in Dorchester village, she had heard the voices crying across the long meadows at night. They had never been explained, and reputable people swore they had heard the repeated call of: "*Come away, boy! Boy, come away! Come away!*"

Sandy laughed at her. "It was only someone bringing a cow home after dark."

That gave Mrs. Calicot a turn to laugh. She chuckled plumply.

"Never yet, young schoolmaster, have I seen a cow was a boy."

"Then it may have been a cat," he said in embarrassment. "I've often heard Ness call True Thomas 'boy.'"

"Ah," said Mrs. Calicot, "but there you have a cat! When I last saw the brave beast, he had between his jaws a rat almost as large as himself. There are rats in the water mill so fierce they frighten my tabbies. Come the day, Ness Goodman, when you wish to give up your tomcat, a good home will await him in Calicot's mill."

They told her good-by, and she stood in her door calling after them: "Let nothing hinder your marriage! Love's more important than Latin!"

For some reason Sandy was annoyed by the unasked

advice. Did the woman, he wondered, think him a laggard lover?

"Her lungs are good enough for her to call across the meadows herself."

Ness managed a faint smile, but there was real fear in her voice.

"Mistress Calicot was a baby when it happened. Oh, Sandy, *what* can those strange voices have been?"

He kissed her cheek as he helped her out of the row-boat.

"Nothing more than some man calling his wife's cat— as I shall call True Thomas for you after we are married."

Then he forgot both irritation and amusement, and he pulled her close to him.

"But, Ness, you're cold! You're shivering! Why?"

"It makes me shiver to think of—of voices without bodies!"

"That's superstitious nonsense! I told you some man was calling something—a child or a pet animal."

"Mistress Calicot said the matter was discussed in open meeting, and every man in Dorchester denied having called."

"It could have been a man from Boston or from Milton. Citizens of those towns pasture cattle in these commons."

"But, Sandy, the meadows of these commons run on to the Blue Hills."

"I know they do. What of it?"

"Haven't you heard—I've heard—very old women say that, in the Blue Hills on Walpurgis Night, witches and their familiars meet and invoke Satan, and he joins them to make the coven thirteen?"

AUGUST WAS DRAWING near, and Ness dreaded the parting.

"I know you must go and I want you to go. But, for some reason, Sandy, I'm afraid to say good-by."

"It will not really be good-by. Cambridge is near enough for me to walk home Saturday night, be with you on Sunday and go back Sunday night. Since I'm returning to attend my own church, there's no objection to travel on the Sabbath."

"But you'll be walking alone over the same country where the voices called 'Come away, boy!'"

"Ness, that's superstition!"

"Witchcraft is not superstition. The greatest of our churchmen and judges found witches among us in this colony. Sandy, I've wondered if—if Rose could be a witch."

She had bewitched both his brother and Ness's father, Sandy thought to himself; but his mind was just and rational. "I cannot believe there are witches."

"There must be; because they all confessed to it before being hanged. That is, all except the one man who was pressed to death because he refused either to confess or to stand trial before a jury."

"There's your answer," he told her. "The other poor wretches confessed to something they hadn't done because they feared torture."

"The Bible says 'Thou shalt not suffer a witch to live.'"

"I know," said Sandy. "I've thought about that. In the Beginning there may have been things which do not exist today."

68

She slipped a hand in his. "I'll try to think as you do. But nothing could make me go near the place where the voices were heard."

Sandy knew she must have spoken so at home; for shortly after that Rose Goodman came to the post. There was mud on her long skirts, and he glimpsed a yellow bodice through the thin summer shawl she held around her.

"I've been walking where Ness says voices are heard. All I heard or saw was those two stupid girls."

"What girls?" he asked, totally unexpecting.

"Forbearance and Thankful White. They were walking over the meadow. They told me they had seen you and Ness sitting on a field stone, and they asked me if Ness was going to marry you."

He stared at her in horror.

"When I told them yes, the big one ran to the field stone and threw herself down upon it. The little one shook her fist at me, burst into tears and ran after her cousin."

"I swear to you I've neither said nor done—"

She laughed at him, roughly but kindly.

"I know you haven't. Pay no attention to them. The older one is crazy for a husband, and the younger is crazy about her. God knows why we aren't all crazy—living in this dead town!"

He was grateful for her support.

"I don't let them trouble me, but I'm afraid for Ness. You know how sensitive she is—how timid and fearful."

"I know," she said.

Her tone was scornful and her red mouth curled. She seated herself on a bench and looked sideways at Sandy.

"You're fortunate to be going to Boston."

"The college is in Cambridge."

"It's the same thing. There'll be street lanterns and laughing—and a pint now and then."

He did not doubt she would drink ale like a man, for he knew she had come from the bar of an inn. As if reading his mind, she continued.

"There are fine taverns in Boston, and the Harvard students visit them after dark."

"But I shall not have time. I'm going to get my certificate for Latin and come home and marry Ness."

"And live the rest of your life in a village that's dead?"

"Why did you come here then?" he asked her angrily. "You made Mr. Goodman marry you. Until you talked to him about wanting a home and a husband, he didn't seem anxious to marry again."

She laughed. "He wasn't. But neither was he hard to persuade. That's the way with you Puritans. You're easier to fool than men who know the ways of the world."

"We aren't so easy to fool as you think. Why did you marry Mr. Goodman?"

"I had my reasons," she said sullenly. "I'm not so young as I was, and I thought it would be an easy living. More than one time I've wished I was back in the Trimountaine bar."

"Why don't you sew and cook as Dorchester women do? There are sick people you could visit."

She laughed huskily and scornfully. "Go to see half-witted children, taking a cat in a basket?"

He was angered, because she made Ness's charity sound ridiculous.

70

"Do as you choose. You're not my wife. But be careful what you do or say to Ness."

"I have no grudge against Ness. It's the old woman I hate."

She rose to her feet and her shawl opened, showing the bright bodice stretched too tight over her bosom.

"So long as she doesn't trouble me I'll not trouble her. What I came for was a ribbon the color of my bodice—and a bit of lace, just enough for a collar."

"You know the trading post is forbidden by law to sell our people lace and other frivolous clothing."

"I'd heard it; but I thought you might have a small piece put by. I'd not tell."

"I haven't. And if I had, I wouldn't risk punishment just because you are a vain and worldly woman."

"Maybe you'll learn better," she said. "Maybe you'll yet learn."

Her eyes shot yellow sparks at him and she turned and went out, trailing her long, muddy skirts like a slattern.

He did not tell Ness about that meeting. They had other things of which to talk in the few days before parting.

Their favorite walk was still the path to the lower falls. While they sat those midsummer afternoons on the Neponset's bank, he read to her from treasured books which his grandfather had brought from England.

"Along the shore of silver-streaming Thames,
Whose rutty bank, the which his river hems,
Was painted with all variable flowers—"

"It's beautiful, Sandy. Who wrote it?"

71

"A poet named Edmund Spenser."

"What I like most about it is that he could be describing the Neponset this afternoon. It streams like silver under the willows, and the wet meadow along the shore is 'painted with variable flowers.' "

"That's the way with great writing, Ness. It belongs to all time and all places."

"He mentions daisy and violet and lily and primrose and vermeil rose. There are daisies and Canady lilies in our fields now. We picked violets right here in the spring. But I don't know what a vermeil rose is."

"It's just a red rose."

"We have red roses and primroses in the village gardens. The poem sounds as if it was written for us."

"That's why I brought it to read to you. Listen to this part, Ness.

"And make your joys redound
Upon your bridal day, which is not long—"

"I don't want it to be long! Sandy, come back to me soon!"

She snuggled shyly against him, and he put his arm around her.

"I'll come soon. You know I must take the school before Christmas."

And, he was telling himself, I'll have a wife who will be a helpmate. Not only is she gentle and domestic, she likes the same things I do. She is enjoying poetry with me.

As if in answer to the thought, she asked: "When you're not too busy, will you read to me—winter nights —from the books your grandfather brought in *The Mary and John?*"

72

"Of course I will—by the fire, with snow falling outside."

"Do you think your grandfather read from them—in Dorsetshire—to the girl who was afterward your grandmother?"

"I think he did—in that first Dorchester—in a meadow of cowslips, on the bank of the river Frome."

"Was there a river by that first Dorchester?"

"There was. There should be a river for all towns—and for all lovers. For our forefathers it was the Frome; for us it is the Neponset; for Edmund Spenser:

"Sweet Thames! run softly, till I end my song."

As HE TRUDGED north on the Boston road Sandy heard no voices. The fields were mauve and yellow with asters and goldenrod. Leaves were already beginning to fall and the grass was withering brown. He noticed that the cattle in their grazing sought ponds and water meadows in order to find it. The landscape was changing color and fading with the summer. The red cedars on Savin Hill stood out in their evergreen.

At noon he broke stride and sat on a field stone. Wishing for Ness beside him, he opened the lunch she had given him when he went to say good-by. He ate the cold sausage, cheese, bread, and apple, then picked up again the small bundle he carried. Samson Dyer's cart would next day bring his box of books and clothes. It made semiweekly deliveries between Dorchester and Boston. To ride in it he would either have had to leave a day earlier or be a day late for opening of the semester.

"Calm was the day," he told himself; for the poem he had read to Ness was still with him. The salt breeze was blowing inland and delaying hot Titan's beams. Looking around on either side he found "meads adorned with dainty gems." Autumn would soon be upon the Massachusetts colony. Ness had said, "By the time the ponds freeze you'll be home again with me." By mid-November he should have earned his Latin certificate. The "meadow by the river's side" would still be waiting for him—and Ness.

The road stretched longer in order to skirt pools and salt-water inlets. He recognized it as terrain similar to that around Dorchester. When that first valiant little band had made their way to the mainland, they had found these mud creeks and water meadows with blue hills climbing farther inland. They had made use of the pastures and set their homes in the groves and proved themselves tougher than the terrible Pequots.

He was thinking about it with love and pride as Boston came in sight. He found the town bigger and noisier and dirtier than he recalled it. He passed the old landmarks he knew: Blaxton's Common, the Frog Pond, and the Parade Ground, and saw buildings which had been erected since his last visit. Above the low rooftops to the east was a tracery of masts and spars—of ships which brought the tea and spice and cloth for the trading posts.

Carts and carriages clattered over the cobbled streets, and he saw men and women in what seemed to him elegant dress. He was passing shop after shop with shutters open and wares displayed: bright stuffs and shining glassware and brass hoops for seamen's ears, and the eastern silks not approved for sale in Dorchester. As he looked he made a mental note to describe it all to Ness.

Across the Charles and in Cambridge he reported at the Latin hall and was registered and directed to his living quarters. These consisted of one small room shared with another student. The boy, younger than Sandy and more slenderly built, gave him a handclasp which hurt, clapped a tall glossy hat on his head and bolted down the stairs, calling back that his evening was engaged.

As he put away the few belongings he had brought, Sandy sighed with relief at being alone. He planned to write a long letter to Ness and then to get a long night's sleep after his journey. He looked around the room in which he expected to spend ten weeks or more with a stranger, then went to lean from the window and gaze out on the twilight.

The grave brick buildings were etched with vines, some of which were green and some beginning to redden. Over the parasol tops of the elms the river shone dully metallic.

He lighted a candle, sharpened a new quill and seated himself in a high-backed chair at the wooden table.

My beloved and respected Ness, he wrote, *having arrived this late afternoon, I cannot yet tell you of Harvard College. There are elms in its yards, and a creeper which I take to be ivy clings to its "bricky towers." All day long I wished for you, recalling lines of that poem we read. It is one of my favorites, so I am glad you liked it. I quoted it while I sat on a stone to eat the lunch you gave me. The sausage which you yourself made was uncommonly tasty. The fields on my way were full, I observed, of late*

75

summer flowers. Yet I love the spring flowers best, your white windflower the most of all. In Boston's bay I saw many ships and wondered whence they came. I did not delay in that city but crossed direct to Cambridge, which is set upon ground between the Charles and the Mystic.

The student with whom I share this room appears agreeable. His manners are good and his clothes fine, but his speech has not our accent. He was leaving upon some errand just as I arrived. I shall have little time for him or other company, as I intend to study hard and return to you as soon as I can. The week will be long until Sunday, but you will be in my thoughts. Kindly tell Widow Freely that I asked Mr. Rox at the trading post to save for her the potato culls, as I have been doing. I will now close, having written in haste so as to send you this letter by Mr. Dyer when he brings my effects tomorrow. Present my respects to your father and to Mistress Tompson. To you I send my tender love as well as respect, and remain

Your obedient Sandy
(signed) A. Purbeck

WHEN SANDY'S ROOMMATE came in that night Sandy was asleep. When Sandy went out the next morning the roommate was asleep. For several days they saw no more of each other than that; then the dark-haired boy arrived early one evening.

He smoothed the beaver of his fine hat carefully with a forearm, then set it on the wardrobe top and turned and stared.

"That's what I should be doing: wrestling with Horace's Odes—nymphs and Latona and Tempe and all that kind of thing. But I've been watching the Boston Bull wrestle Jamaica's Jungle John."

Sandy's interest was aroused. "You mean you've been to a real wrestling match?"

"Best match I ever saw. The Bull was still unconscious when I left. I think the black man broke his neck. I'm sure I heard it crack."

Sandy both boxed and wrestled, and he longed to have seen the fight; but he was not bloodthirsty.

"I hope not."

"I hope he did. The scoundrel was fighting foul. By the way, what's your name? Mine's Shannon Couturier."

Sandy hesitated. He knew this had to come. His Puritan conscience told him that nothing short of a full name was a name. But he hushed it and answered: "Sandy Purbeck."

As he spoke he saw the other's eyes go to the box in a corner, the box which had been brought in Samson Dyer's cart. It was of oak, leather-hinged and brassbound, and brass studs driven into its top printed A. PURBECK.

Their glances met and Couturier spoke quickly.

"I didn't mean to pry. It's a handsome traveling trunk."

Sandy said bitterly: "I'm ashamed of my real name."

"Oh, come now! Purbeck sounds to me like stout West County English."

"It is—Dorsetshire—and I'm proud of it. My baptismal

name is the one I hate. My ancestors were all school-masters."

By his low whistle the other managed to express both amazement and admiration.

"No wonder you've got such a brain then and study all the time! There are no teachers in my family; but," he added proudly, "my mother's father in Ireland wrote a book."

"Wrote a book? That's a fine thing to do. Is it in Latin or English—poetry or history?"

"It's in English, but I heard my father say it had a lot of words in it the printer had to delete. It's on two subjects: horse racing and cock fighting."

It was Sandy's turn to be amazed. He suggested: "It must be exciting."

"As a matter of fact it's quite dull. Do you care for racing or cocking?"

Sandy took refuge in a good old Yankee custom and answered that with another question.

"Is it the custom to race horses and raise cocks where you live?"

"You bet! At New London on the Edisto River."

"I'm afraid I don't know where that is."

"It's pretty far south of here—in the lower section of the colony of South Carolina."

Sandy cried out: "But that's the place where my brother is going in December!"

"Fine! I'd like to meet him. Is he in the racing business?"

Horrified, Sandy exclaimed: "Oh, no! He's going with a mission, to establish the Independent faith in the wilderness."

78

"It's not exactly a wilderness. The governor and the other toffs have balls and levees in Charles Town."

It crossed Sandy's mind that Peregrine would not object to either balls or horse races. But he put the thought away as disloyal. His new friend was continuing.

"Your brother must be a pious fellow. If he's going near New London, I'll give him a letter to my father. Chances are by that time I'll have been booted out of this school and be home myself to entertain him."

Sandy answered that hospitality. "I'll be glad to have you spend some Sunday in Dorchester with us."

"Delighted to do so," said Shannon Couturier. He seated himself on the table, upon a heap of Sandy's notebooks.

"I was expelled from school in Charles Town. Mother insisted that Father send me to school at Harvard, but he told her he knew they'd not put up with me."

Expulsion was to a Purbeck synonymous with disgrace. Sandy was staring at him in honest surprise.

"I'd as lief be in Boston—except that I miss the hunting, and the house where I eat doesn't serve wine with the food. The taverns here are just as good and the wrestling matches better. There'll be another tomorrow night. Will you go with me?"

Sandy shook his head, partly in negation and partly to clear it.

"Why not?"

"I've got to study."

Surprise was in Couturier's face and voice. He demanded: "Why?"

"To get my certificate. I want to teach."

"Why on earth do you want to do anything like that?"

79

Instead of irritation, Sandy felt attraction toward this ingenuous and outspoken young man. He heard himself explaining.

"I not only want to teach. I'm engaged to a girl and must marry and support her."

The Southerner leapt from the table and pounded him on the back.

"Now that's a reason a man can understand! My good wishes to you. I'll drink your health and hers."

He sounded as if he meant it. In Dorchester Sandy and Ness had received approval; but enthusiasm was to that as wine is to water. Couturier's attitude made him feel pride in both his betrothal and his betrothed.

"May I ask the young lady's name?"

"Her name is Gentleness Goodman, and she is both gentle and good."

"And fair, I know," said Shannon Couturier.

He put a hand on the breast of his well-cut coat and made Sandy a formal bow.

"It's the loveliest name I ever heard. It sounds like snowdrops in early spring. My congratulations, sir. You are a lucky man."

Sandy felt warm with pleasure. Not usually talkative, he seemed to have caught the trait from his companion.

"She is small and fair-haired. We have known each other all our lives, and we were baptized in the same church."

"I admire blondes," said the dark-haired boy. "Most of the southern girls are brunettes. Blondes are scarce in hot countries. But—God bless them all! Will you go to the tavern with me as my guest in order to drink a toast to your Mistress Gentleness?"

Sandy longed to go, but he shook his head.

80

"I thank you, but I must finish this work."

"That's a pity—but I admire you for it. You Quakers are a hard-working lot."

Sandy recoiled in horror.

"We allow no Quakers here. They are put to death for practicing that heresy."

Couturier gave him a look of surprise.

"I thought they were peaceful folk. With an Irish Romanist mother and a French Huguenot father, I've never been able to make up my mind which was the heretic."

He moved away and sat upon Sandy's trunk. Apparently he had no idea of going out alone but intended to stay and talk and prevent further study.

"It's all mixed up—like names," he said. "My mother named me for an Irish river. Besides that, the English in South Carolina insist upon calling Couturier 'C'traire.' "

That meant nothing to Sandy who had no French. But the intimate details made him desire to unburden himself of his own unhappy secret. It would have to come out in classroom. Better to reveal it first to a friend and ally. He was already certain that his roommate could be called both.

"I wouldn't mind if they'd named me for the Nile or the Neponset. But—but that A stands for something—"

Couturier was on his feet, his face expressing sympathy —but anticipation too.

Sandy stammered: "It—it stands for something out of the alphabet."

"Are you telling me they named you just for the letter A?"

"No," said Sandy despairingly. "It's even worse than

81

that. I'm named for my grandfather. I told you they were all teachers. My father, who was a schoolmaster too, had me baptized *Ampersand*."

Broken only by Saturday nights and Sundays in Dorchester, Sandy's semester was going on its way. He managed to persuade his happy-go-lucky roommate to study enough to keep his place in college. In return he went more than once into Boston with Couturier, to watch a bout of wrestling or of bare-knuckle boxing. He found it pleasant to stop afterward in some tavern where students gathered and drink a pint of ale in good company.

Seeing the swift pace of Couturier's diversions, it crossed Sandy's mind that the boy from South Carolina might be bored by a day in a Puritan village. But Couturier seized upon his invitation with alacrity. He appeared at ease in the Purbecks' simple cottage and ate heartily of their simple fare. He was comradely with Peregrine, admiring of Ness, and attentive to Mrs. Tompson and Mr. Goodman. To Sandy's relief, Rose did not appear during the evening visit or at church next day. Ness said that her absence was due to a spell of indigestion.

Mrs. Tompson added: "Her spells come always on Saturday. They keep her abed while Ness and I do two days' work preparing for the Sabbath, and they excuse her from attendance at church meeting."

82

Couturier had then been talking with Mr. Goodman and Peregrine, and Sandy had been content for his friend to remain unaware of the friction. For his visit turned out to be an unmarred success. Peregrine took to him at once and was on his best behavior. Sandy, grateful for his brother's attention to his friend, reproached himself for his past misgivings and told himself that Peregrine was unselfish and truly noble.

When they returned from their visit next door, the three sat long past midnight in talk. Sandy could only listen while Peregrine questioned Couturier eagerly about the land to which he expected to go. His enthusiasm made the other man explain.

"While there is plenty of gaiety in the seaport of Charles Town and in New London, if your mission goes inland you will be both lonely and quiet."

"The mission will have its community," Sandy put in, "and the life of that community will be modeled upon the life we have always led here in Dorchester."

Peregrine's face fell. His expression was that of a small boy who sees a red apple beyond his reach.

"You're right. Our life will be apart and different from that. But"—and his eyes lit again—"sooner or later I'll get to Charles Town! To think of dancing minuets with girls in brocade gowns—girls with dark ringlets falling to their bare shoulders!"

Sandy exclaimed: "Peregrine! Have you lost your mind?"

Couturier laughed aloud. But he sided with Peregrine.

"You don't have to lose your mind for that. Any man of sound mind would enjoy it. They are lovely girls—as modest and good as your Puritan girls. I think it's

83

merely the difference that attracts your brother. I feel the same way in this colony whenever I see a pretty face peeping out between a demure coif and big white collar."

Sandy said no more, but Peregrine murmured: "To hear harps and violins play, to drink Spanish wine at the governor's ball—I tell you, sooner or later, I'm going to Charles Town!"

The two returned to Cambridge, and as examinations drew near Sandy deprived himself of all diversions and tried to perfect himself in every detail of his subject. It was after twelve o'clock of one night and he was still at work when Couturier came in and threw himself in a chair.

There was laughter in his voice. "I've just seen a girl who knows you."

Couturier's arrival meant study's end. Sandy closed his book and looked up.

"I've met no girls here. Who is she?"

"She's a barmaid—and a handsome one. You never told me, my Puritan friend, that you numbered barmaids among your acquaintances."

Honestly puzzled, Sandy stared.

"I don't. I don't know any—except the cross-eyed one who serves us ale at the Square Sails public house."

"That's not the one I'm talking about. This one has just come to Boston. None of our crowd had seen her before. We saw the wrestling match, and then we started on a round of the pubs. After we had sampled the drinks at all the old places, we tried that new one by the Frog Pond. There was a tall girl with yellow eyes and a yellow bodice that fitted like—"

"Rose," exclaimed Sandy. "Was it Rosa Zuider?"

"She didn't tell me she was a Hollander. I've found the Dutch aren't popular in this colony. Maybe that's why."

"She's New York Dutch—but she married a Dorchester man."

"So she told me. She called him an old goat and said she might have been able to stand him and his daughter, but that his mother called her a witch."

Couturier appeared highly amused, but Sandy was aghast.

"She must have done something to make Goody Tompson accuse her. But how did she get away? How did she escape arrest?"

"She didn't tell me that. But I can tell you she's free as air and serving ale in Boston. She's a good-looking wench, and you should be pleased that she inquired about you."

"How did she know you knew me?"

"Gamaliel Black was so taken with her that he leaned on the bar all evening. In the course of conversation, she asked him if he was a Harvard student and if he knew a man named Purbeck from Dorchester. Gamy crossed the room and told me. So I introduced myself to her and offered to bring you a message. You don't look pleased to get it."

"I'm not."

"Why? Is she something out of your questionable past?"

"Of course not! I neither like nor admire her. She married Ness's father last winter. This means she's quarreled with Ness's grandmother and left him."

The other man sobered at once.

85

"I had no idea of that and I'm sorry to hear it. But I can't blame her for clearing out if she was accused of witchcraft. Although I don't believe in it, I know it's a serious charge up here."

"I don't believe in it either. Yet it's hard to understand how else a woman like her could have made a man like Hosea Goodman marry her."

Shannon Couturier fell on his bed and doubled up with laughter.

"Sandy Purbeck, you're too good to be true!"

Sandy was indignant. "This is no laughing matter."

The other man rose and wiped his eyes with a large, embroidered silk handkerchief.

"I beg your pardon. I've seen many men bewitched. All a woman needs for the spell is a rose in her hair and moonlight. But down South we encourage it. We don't hang them for it."

Sandy was thinking too hard to reply, so Couturier went on in conciliation.

"I must say she doesn't seem to me the kind of woman to get on with Gentleness Goodman."

"She isn't."

"Well, then, maybe this is the best way out."

"Maybe," said Sandy.

There was nothing he could do and he was weary in body and mind. He slept that night, in spite of bad dreams, and got through the next day's classes. When he reached his rooming house in late afternoon Samson Dyer's boy Dogood was in the hall with a letter.

"Master Peregrine sent it—and he says to make all haste."

Sandy tore it open. His brother's scholarly script sprawled wildly over the page.

> *Sandy, come as quick as you can. Ness has disappeared. I looked for her at first in the meadows by the ponds, thinking she might be trying to get to Boston to you. Now I'm going to Calicot's mill. Others are searching too.*
>
> Peregrine
>
> *Postscriptum: It's all my fault. Goody Tompson caught Rose in the orchard with me.*

COUTURIER HAD APPEARED upon the scene while Dogood was untying the horse. Upon learning what the matter was he had, without words, vaulted over the wheel onto the board seat and taken the driving reins from the boy's hands. Between his long, thin fingers their clumsy leather slid with the grace of ribbons, and the cart horse settled into a faster trot than Sandy had known it could do. After giving directions as to the shortest way out of the city, Sandy began to question Dogood.

"What's this about Ness Goodman disappearing? Have any Pequots been seen? Could they have taken her?"

"Could not. She went of her own free will."

"But *why? Why* should she go?"

"For fear of being took for a witch."

"Who dared call her a witch?"

"Nobody," said Dogood.

Sandy seized his shoulder and shook. "If you don't tell me . . ."

" 'Twas the woman with cat's eyes lived at the Goodman house."

"Do you mean she called Ness a witch?"

"No. Goody Tompson called *her* a witch."

"For God's sweet sake!" exclaimed Shannon Couturier, and hit the horse with the end of the lines, causing it to break into a jerking gallop.

Sandy implored: "Are you telling me that Ness ran away because her grandmother called Rose a witch?"

"Am not telling you. Am telling 'twas the tomcat."

Sandy shook him more violently, and Couturier poked him in the ribs with the butt end of the cart whip.

Dogood Dyer spoke slowly, quite calm and unperturbed.

"When Goody Tompson called her a witch, yon yellow-eyed jade screamed and cursed until the whole village heard. She went out of town afoot, for my father refused to drive her. And as she went she shook her fist and cried aloud to all she met that there was witchcraft in Goodman's house but it was not of her making."

"Whom did she accuse?"

"Nobody."

"Boy," said Couturier, "if you don't talk I'll choke it out of you!"

"She accused no human. Have already told you she accused the cat. She said the beast walked on two feet like a man and she had heard it talk with its mistress."

"Ness taught it to rear up and beg. About its talking Rose Zuider lied. She lied shamefully," said Sandy.

88

"She said it could talk and it spied on her and brought tales to the old woman."

"I say she lied. What else did she say?"

"Said no fire could burn it. Said it slept on red-hot coals. Said Mr. Goodman himself told her it could make itself invisible."

"She lied again. It lay on the hearth where the ashes were warm. It's an ash cat."

Couturier lashed the old horse savagely. "What is an ash cat?"

"A mongrel cat—the color of ash—that loves to sleep in warm ashes."

"Well, whatever kind of cat it is, *why* did your girl run away?"

" 'Twas for this reason," said Dogood. "The people all stood in the streets while the woman went out of town, screaming herself like a tomcat. Elder Mather and Elder Pratt heard the noise and came and said 'twas not seemly. Mistress Ness was weeping."

"Where? Where was she?"

"At the Goodman gate she was. She was calling, 'Rose, come back! Do not leave my father! Do not say such cruel things!' "

"Did Rose Zuider answer her?"

"Aye. She turned and called back: 'I have naught against you. 'Tis the cat carries messages between the old witch and the devil.' "

"If she said *old* witch she meant Mistress Tompson."

"Aye. My father and all others who heard her took it so."

"Then what started talk about Ness being a witch?"

" 'Twas at the school next day. Savemore Upsall sits

89

next to me, and he asks Master Purbeck if a cat be witch or familiar. Master says the next pupil who speaks of things such as that will get a dozen blows of the cane for impudence. But in the noon recess Savemore and Jem Atherton begin arguing whether all cats or only black cats serve the devil. The rest of us are but listening when Moll Freely pushes up. Makepeace Phelps gives her a slap and says, 'Get away! You come of Irish Papists, not of the true Church, and you know nothing of this matter.'

"Moll begins bawling then. She bawls, 'I know more than you! 'Tis the gray witch cat that withered my arm when its yellow eyes looked on me.'"

Merciful God, prayed Sandy, do not let this be true! Aloud he said: "The Freely girl is ignorant and vicious. Ness took her cat in a basket to the Freely house to cheer and amuse her while she was abed."

"'Tis what Master Peregrine said. He caned both Savemore and Jemmy, and he made Moll sit on the dunce stool for the rest of the day with her face to the wall and the dunce cap on her head."

"But," said Couturier between his teeth, "I suppose the children talked."

"That they did," said Dogood. He appeared to be wound up now. "And Moll had a foaming fit in the night and screeched that a witch sat on her."

Sandy asked: "Did she say who the witch was?"

"No. She did little more than screech. So, when she could walk again, the elders took her to the Goodman house to confront the cat and the dame. Goody Tompson gave them back as good as they gave her."

"I'm glad she did," said Sandy. "But how do you know?"

90

"My father was called to be one of the witnesses, and he says Goody faced them with hands on her hips. 'My son-in-law's wife is both a witch and something that sounds like a witch,' says she. 'The Freely girl is half-witted from birth and now paralyzed by disease. Call Dr. Blake and he will support my word.' "

"Did they call him?"

"They did—but he had gone miles away to a sickness. So, my father said, the elders talked together, and it sounded to him as if they believed the dame and wished to dismiss the matter. But the Freely girl screeched, 'Witch! Witch! I tell you the witch killed my sister! All year have the children at school told me that a witch had looked on my arm and withered it with an evil eye! All last night she sat on my chest! She will come back, I tell you, and kill me!'

"Then Mistress Tompson said, 'What you need, Moll Freely, is an apple switch on your backside to cure you of lying. But'—and she turned on the elders and stared them right in the face—'if you doubt me, William Pratt or Increase Sumner, call your wives to undress me and examine me. I am an old woman, but I have no mark on my body.' "

"Did they do that?"

"Nay. They still appeared unwilling. They talked together, and then Mr. Sumner told her: 'Dame Tompson, you bear a good name in Dorchester Township. As you know, we are not as quick as some towns to put our decent citizens to the question. Let us think more about this. But, meanwhile, let us examine the cat.'

"With that, my father says, Mistress Ness catches the cat in her arms. She begs, 'He is only a dumb beast. He has done no one harm.'

91

"But, then Moll Freely falls on the floor and screeches louder than she yet has. She beats her head and foams at the mouth and stretches an arm toward Mistress Ness.

"She screeches, 'There stands the witch and her cat that carries her word to the devil! I see the witch mark upon her face—the black witch mark by her mouth!' "

SANDY WAS PRAYING silently, with his head between his hands. He had not stopped for a hat, and the thickening snow was falling on the back of his bent neck.

Witch mark? The small dark mole that set off the whiteness of her skin?

Couturier was cursing aloud as he stood up to lash the horse. Unlike the Puritan, he could not understand the tragic series of events which had led like steps up to this crisis.

Dogood protested: "If you founder the horse my father will punish me!"

Couturier pulled to a stop and pushed him roughly.

"Get out then, fat boy! I'll be responsible. You weigh as much as Sandy or me, although you're only half-grown. Get out and walk the rest of the way so as to lighten the cart."

Having jettisoned Dogood ruthlessly, he drove on toward Dorchester. There was now only the one track running between snow-covered fields where Ness had in summer seen "variable flowers." An occasional low wall was merely a ridge of white, and the field stones were ghostly outcroppings. Sandy raised his head to make sure of directions, and once to ask desperately: "Can't this horse gallop?"

"He can; but a draft horse makes better time kept in a steady trot. Try to calm your soul, my friend. I may not be good at Latin, but with a pair of driving reins I get more speed than most men."

Lights burned in the town hall, where a group of older men kept watch. Hosea Goodman, haggard and wet, had just come in.

"Tileston and Andrews and I have searched every foot of the bay front. No boats are missing and nobody saw Ness."

Sandy seized him. "When did Ness leave home?"

"Sometime last night. Both her grandmother's basket and the cat are gone too. I think she feared for the animal —more than for herself—and has taken it somewhere to hide it."

Elder Mosely spoke. "She was a good girl. All the town knew that."

Couturier saw Sandy's hands clench. "Then, why—" he began, but his voice broke.

Couturier's grip on his arm was hard and Couturier's voice was hard. "You've driven her off—in the night and snow. That's all that matters. Tell us where your searchers have been, so we may know where to go."

"We've searched everywhere," Ness's father said. "The whole village has turned out. Men went in every direction."

Sandy was already halfway to the door. "If she's carrying the cat, she's gone to the water mill."

"Your brother went there and hasn't come back,"

Elisha Benham told him. "So another party started up-river this afternoon."

But Sandy Purbeck and Shannon Couturier were already in the street.

"I once heard Mistress Calicot tell Ness she would take the cat if ever Ness wished to be rid of it. I'm certain she's trying to get it to the mill."

Men's tracks led into the wood and out again to the riverbank, but Sandy and Shannon met no one returning. The Southerner stumbled through drifts in the wake of the other who knew the path, giving vent to occasional oaths which but faintly expressed his feelings. As they came free of the trees he saw that the snow had stopped falling. The skies had cleared and the northern stars blazed with the brilliance of diamonds. Watching over the village which his friend had told him was shaped like a swan, he saw heavenly Cygnus spread in high eternal flight.

Sandy had fallen on his knees to look for tracks. Couturier pulled him to his feet.

"Her father told you she went last night. A lot of snow has fallen since then. Besides, men in heavy boots have been trampling along here."

"I know," said Sandy hopelessly. "I needn't look, be-cause—because I know she came this way."

He staggered, and Couturier caught him again.

"But the ice is not yet set. She couldn't have crossed the river."

"She couldn't," said Sandy, "—but she might have tried."

Just then Couturier came to a sudden stop.

"Listen! Wait! Do you hear—"

Sandy stopped in his tracks. "Was it a voice?"

"It's a kind of howling—not human. It comes from the river."

Sandy started on again in a weary trot. "It may be an animal in the woods, or an Indian on the farther bank."

Couturier's principal fear for the girl had all this time been of Indians. His heart leapt into his throat. But just then a light appeared around the bend ahead. Mr. Calicot, large and kindly, carried a lantern.

" 'Tis you, Master Sandy. I knew you would be here."

Sandy gasped: "Mr. Calicot, how did you get across?"

"Rowed myself—miles farther down, where the river is free of ice."

He gripped Sandy's shoulder and tried to reassure him.

"I've examined the ice above the falls. I don't believe she tried to cross."

"That's where she would have tried. You would have found no trace if—if—"

"Now, now, the lass is born and bred to this country. She knows the river freezes first out from the shore."

Couturier had not known it. He stared at the black Neponset. Were those patches of dirty white snow on the ice? Or were they foam on a death-swift current between and under the ice?

He heard Sandy asking: "Was your boat at the bank?"

"Nay. I moved it weeks ago, so the ice would not smash it. Ness Goodman would have known that well enough."

"Yes," said Sandy.

He spoke low and quietly now—but the friend who loved him recognized complete despair in his voice.

"Yes, she would have known that—and have tried to walk across."

"That we do not know," Mr. Calicot told him. "But it seems more likely to me she would have seen the ice was unsafe and gone farther upriver to cross."

She might have done so, Couturier prayed to himself. But his heart was freezing as cold as the northern river. Its ice was as black as water. If a little blond girl in her terror had tried to cross with a basket . . . if in her terror . . . and in the night . . .

As Sandy moved forward the miller tightened his grasp.

"The searchers have gone on upstream. No need to follow them. They will cross where the ice is fast and then return on the other bank down to the mill. Come with me now and cross in my boat. Belike—between the two parties—we'll find the lass with my wife."

"No," said Sandy. "I will first see the crossing myself."

Since they could not stop him they followed him. Above the falls a sheet of ice like a dark mirror stretched from the shore. As they stepped upon it, it was sound beneath their feet. Toward mid-channel they felt its stress and Calicot stopped.

" 'Tis folly to go farther. Will ye look?"

Couturier looked—and as close as this he could see. The surface of the smooth ice was cracked in spider-web patterns. Not far beyond it dropped suddenly into a saw-tooth border for the pent black current, open and running fast.

The miller took Sandy's arm. "She could not have crossed here, lad."

Sandy did not reply to that. He allowed himself to be drawn along by the two of them, like a child. As they retraced their steps down river, Couturier could see he had given up all hope. But a quarter mile below the falls Couturier heard the sound again. He stopped, bringing the other two to a halt.

"It's the same noise I heard as Sandy and I came up-river. I tell you *something*'s howling—somewhere out there."

Calicot listened. " 'Tis the cry of a wild beast."

Although Shannon Couturier did not know their country, he was plantation bred and taught to track and hunt. He led them farther downstream where jagged ice blocks were piled by the bank. The noise was louder and clearer there.

Sandy said suddenly: "It's a cat!" and he started out on the ice.

The bare willows, relieved of green weight, stood out along the bank. The frozen masses of water made a perilous footing. Sandy was crawling now and Couturier was following him toward the unearthly noise.

Thirty feet from shore and between two blocks they found it: a stout covered basket, bent but still unbroken. It was tight enough to have stayed afloat and taken little water, and the ice instead of submerging it had pushed it upward and wedged it securely. It took all their strength to tear it from that frozen hold. It was crooked and wet and half-flattened, but its cover was still held in place by Goody Tompson's loop and peg.

Couturier relinquished it to Sandy's frantic grasp and staggered ashore behind Sandy and that yelling burden.

Mr. Calicot stepped aside as Sandy opened the cover.

And Couturier saw a huge pale cat leap with an infernal yell from the basket and bound away into the pale, frozen woods.

97

Part Two

VOYAGERS OF FAITH

Below the dock the small skiff was rocking perilously. Its boatman held it with boathooks and ropes against the slippery pile, while Elder Sumner climbed down on ladderlike crosspieces of wood. His feet in their square-toed shoes groped for a purchase; above them long knitted stockings were drenched on his skinny legs. He slipped on the last rung and half fell, half jumped to a thwart.

Several voices called from the wharf: "Are you hurt, Mr. Sumner?"

Huddled under his long cloak, the churchman replaced the tall hat on his head. He looked up, his face pale in the lantern light but set and determined.

"For voyagers of faith, God sets the sails," he told them sternly. "Nevertheless, you'd better beware of that last foothold. It's nailed crooked."

Above on the dock Shannon Couturier was gripping Sandy's shoulder hard.

"Why can't you and those old owls wait for better weather?"

"The brigantine sails with the tide—at midnight."

"She's chartered for your mission and cannot sail without you."

"Good-by, Shannon, and thank you. Thank you for everything."

"I've done nothing. I only wish I could help."

They clasped hands, and Sandy swung down the wharfside and dropped into the boat. From the pier a dock hand pushed them off in the wild harbor.

At once the little craft was caught in the savage rhythm of the gale. It was drawn high upon towering swells and flung back into their valleys. The boatmen labored steadily, shouting to each other in order to give directions above the tumult of noise.

"Lay to sta'board, Tam O'Toole, if you're thinkin' to make the brig *Friendship!*"

"I'm pullin' direct for her mast light, but it's more likely hell we'll be makin'."

Deacon Pratt there added his voice to the uproar, bawling even louder than the Irish oarsmen.

"I will have no blasphemy, fellows—less so in the face of danger!"

Sandy raised his head, trying to shake off the numbness which had dulled him for so many weeks. I am on my way to a new life, he told himself. I am embarking to go south with Mr. Lord's mission. I have lost Ness—and Peregrine too—but I am taking Peregrine's place. I must arouse myself, for I am starting a new life.

Alongside reared a concave shape of water more black than the night. Already it was curving its monstrous claw above them, when they were dragged from its reach by another wave equally high and spun to its moving summit as the torrent crashed behind them.

It seemed to Sandy as if some black and enormous feline batted the skiff from paw to paw in hideous play. Perhaps this was the beginning of death instead of new life for him. Perhaps he was going to drown, as Ness and Peregrine had drowned, struggling and strangling and pushed deeper and deeper by tons of water which thundered above and around him.

He had seen storms on the bay, but never before had he been at the mercy of one in a small boat. The Boston watermen strained at their oars undaunted. Elder Pratt was praying in a strong, firm voice. With every sickening lift from trough to crest, they could see that the riding lights of the brigantine were nearer.

Then something more solid than sea or night was suddenly rushing upon them. Along with the crash and thunder of storm, he heard the screaming hiss of water torn apart and foaming by the bow of a ship. She carried no lights and she gave them no warning. She was upon them all at once—like a witch riding the tempest.

To the shouts of the boatmen were added cries of horror from the passengers in the skiff. The craft running them down was manned although unlanterned; for startled answering calls came down to them from her deck. Had she struck them head on she could have cut their slender boat in half. But at the last moment she veered sharply away, giving their gunwale a glancing blow and dragging her hull along it. Sandy heard the crack of wood and felt the skiff tilt perilously. Then she righted herself with a lurch and rocked crazily in the wake of the larger vessel.

One pair of oars had gone overboard, and had nearly been followed by the man using them. His hand was crushed; all the tholepins to starboard were broken; the skiff was taking water through a plank stove in her side. Several of the older men had been thrown from their seats by the collision and had suffered minor injuries.

Sandy, younger and stronger, found himself unhurt. But he had lost his hat and was wet from head to foot. The icy December wind was a blade that struck through his cloak. He gazed around and no longer saw the lantern in the *Friendship's* mast; so he yelled to the nearest boatman: "Where are we going? And where's the brig?"

"The brig's behind us," the man yelled back. "We're runnin' with the sea."

"Away from her? Can you not row back again?"

"Away from her. And may God help us run to shore! Only the port oars are in use, and the boat is leakin' fast!"

The sea appeared a little less wild, since they lent themselves to its will. The boatmen were using their oars only to steer because, had the skiff turned broadside, it would at once have capsized. Sandy, who knew the harbors of both Boston and Dorchester, realized they were being carried out to sea.

He strained his eyes for seamarks, but blackness enveloped them. The ship which had struck them had vanished completely, either unable or unwilling to follow and help. Aft and starboard the faint lights of Boston water front grew fainter and finally disappeared.

But the storm was abating. They rode more smoothly now. Their boatmen dared pull on the port oars to steer them toward the coast. There was no longer a question of reaching the brigantine. There was only increasing hope that they might reach land instead of being carried out to open sea.

Hours afterward they felt the skiff's bottom bump and grate on sand. Her oarsmen and Sandy Purbeck jumped out in knee-deep surf and dragged her up on a narrow, wind-swept beach.

T HE SMALL BAND of Dorchester men bound for the brigantine *Friendship* had been swept by the storm tide out of Boston harbor and cast up on the long sandspit known as Dorchester Neck. Cold and wet and weary, they made their way ashore. Two days later they boarded the sailing ship which was to carry them south.

Upon that voyage, which lasted two weeks, they discussed the misadventure of their setting out. The unexpected return bore a strange resemblance to the arrival of their first ancestors from Plymouth, England. They quoted to each other the diary of that voyage, set down by Roger Clap and left in manuscript to his family. According to it, the captain of *The Mary and John* had for some reason refused to keep his agreement and set his passengers ashore on the mainland. He had forced them to disembark upon Nantasket Point, a sandspit not unlike the one they later called Dorchester Neck. It was possible, they agreed, that the captain had feared an unknown harbor which might, in his opinion, have submerged sandbars as well as those showing above high tide.

Whatever his reason, their forefathers had overcome

the difficulty and made their way ashore. Now their great-grandsons—worthy descendants—had been confronted with just such an obstacle. Worn and battered and drenched in the freezing wind, they had tramped the miles back to Dorchester, and the next day set out again for Boston port and the ship awaiting them.

From that time on the voyage was uneventful. Fair winds hastened the brigantine, and as she drove south the weather grew steadily warmer. To Sandy's disappointment, the great cape of the Hatteras Indians was hidden by fog while they rounded it. It was the one landmark he had hoped to see, and he and Mr. Lord had come on deck before dawn so as not to miss it.

The young pastor was only a few years older than Sandy, and he was now Sandy's only companion. He sought out the unhappy young man and endeavored to help him. For he knew himself responsible for Sandy's decision to go south with the mission.

Immediately after Mr. Lord had been ordained to the ministry, Sandy had come to him.

"Before you leave you must get a new master for the Dorchester school. I cannot teach children whose malicious talk has resulted in the death of an innocent girl."

The newly made pastor had sighed and shaken his head, but he had not uttered the rebuke for which Sandy was resentfully waiting.

"I cannot blame you; but I do not see what you will do for a livelihood. Would you not be equally unhappy working at the trading post?"

"I shall not be working at the trading post—or anywhere else in this colony. I'm going away—as far away as I can."

"In that case, why not take your brother's place and go with me to South Carolina to teach at the new settlement?"

Sandy had not agreed at once but had thought it over. He recalled that he had at first planned to go with the mission when he believed Ness loved Peregrine. Now, after a complete reversal of those plans, destiny seemed to be pushing him back into the same position.

Again he heard Peregrine saying: "We cannot escape destiny."

He could not yet think of Peregrine. He checked himself whenever his thoughts turned that way. For he could not but realize that his brother had brought matters to a climax by that last meeting with Rose. Peregrine had acknowledged it in his letter; he would now have acknowledged it if able to speak. It had always been Peregrine's way to acknowledge his offenses, ask forgiveness and charm those he had injured into granting it. That had often angered Sandy more than the injury had. But in this same case Peregrine had made his greatest acknowledgment when he—afraid of water—had given his own life trying to rescue Ness.

Troubled, Sandy wondered whether he had misjudged his brother. At the thought he was overcome by un-Puritanic humility. Who was he to have condemned Peregrine for yielding to Rose Goodman's lure when Peregrine had at the last made the supreme sacrifice? Had Peregrine's careless gaiety been a cloak for deep emotion? Was it possible that Peregrine had loved Ness as deeply as he himself had? Peregrine's words came back to him: "What's troubling me is the fear that you merely copied me in making yourself believe you were in love with Ness Goodman."

No other girl had attracted him, so he had no range for perspective. He had admired Ness all his life, and when she chose him he had warmed with the pale fires of pride and protectiveness. Unlike Peregrine, he had not yet felt any flame of passion.

Forbearance White had been his only other experience. The preference she showed for him had troubled and annoyed him. In comparison with her Ness shone like a star, far off and pale.

Walking the wet deck of the brigantine, while the elders huddled in the cabin and Mr. Lord prepared sermons by a ship lantern's light, all this came back to Sandy although he tried to forget. He had lost the two whom he loved best, and there was nobody else he loved. He knew no kinfolk in Dorchester, Dorsetshire. Three generations away from England had completely severed the bond with any Purbecks there. He had friends in Massachusetts, but now his one wish was to escape from them. They represented the structure of law and religion by which both his betrothed and his brother had been destroyed. He was honest enough to admit to himself that he and his forefathers had helped build it along with them and theirs. But he could not live with them, and he would not teach their children—the same children whose taunting tongues had caused Moll Freely to do what she did.

He could now see that, like the tale of the voices calling, every smallest word and deed had built toward tragedy as small stones are piled to build a tomb. Looking back now, he knew that it had started with Minnie Freely's death and the strange disease which had warped

Moll's arm and Moll's mind. Then Hosea Goodman had brought Rosa Zuider home, and Ness's own grandmother had antagonized the woman with the yellow cat-eyes. The cat went all through it. It was marked with the cat's paws. It seemed almost as if the cat had been the witch Rose called it. Rose had hated the cat and laughed when its fur was scorched. Ness had loved it enough to lose her life trying to save it. Without help from a devil-master, must it not have been drowned as she had been? How else could the basket, no matter how stout and tight, have ridden the falls and come safe to rest between two ice blocks? Perhaps the ignorant, ungrateful Freely girl, who played with the cat in her illness and then accused it, had truly recognized it for a familiar of Satan. Perhaps, in order to make mischief, it had led Dame Tompson to the orchard where Rose and Peregrine—

No, he told himself, standing by the brig's rail and watching the dark, formless swells lurch along her side. No; he must not let himself be caught in the black snare which had entangled those whom he loved. Witch-craft was superstition, and he was a teacher—a teacher of youth. He must teach the children who came to the new settlement that it was superstition and could harm them only if they believed in it and allowed it to influence them. He must teach them to discard it and to hold by the great principles upon which their Church was founded: enlightenment of mind, freedom of worship, and truth.

But if there was truth and any justice, why had Ness had to die—little Ness who had never done anyone harm? Why had that evil woman Rose Zuider Goodman escaped punishment and been left to laugh across a public bar in her tight yellow bodice?

Although he tried not to think, such questions seemed to ask themselves while he tramped back and forth on deck in the fog off Hatteras. And their answers, like the fog, enclosed him, blind, hopeless, and smothered.

If Ness in her anxiety to escape had only taken the road to Boston and to him. . . . If she had only come across the fields between the ponds, instead of trying to cross the Neponset. . . . Would death have been waiting on the field road for her, as it had waited upon the river's uncertain ice?

What use to ask? That way had been closed to her by the fog of superstition. Mrs. Calicot, who loved her, had told her about the voices. Had she not done so, Ness might have taken that meadow path leading to him—and perhaps to life.

Had it all been predestined? Had Ness belonged to Peregrine, been intended for him, been obliged to follow him in death if not in life? Or was it only chance—cruel, blind, stupid chance?

He knew that was a question no churchman should ask himself. Besides, all questions about Ness were useless now. More than a week of the voyage had passed; the fog had lifted during the night, and the sun was a luminous shield in a soft pearly sky. Although veiled, it had warmth enough to cause him to remove his cloak from his shoulders and carry it on his arm as he walked toward the bow of the brigantine.

UNTIL THEY REACHED the southern port the voyagers had sighted no land. Now, with low, sandy islands port and starboard, they crossed a bar to an outer harbor. Sailors ran to unlimber the small cannon carried by the *Friendship*. The officer directing gave the signal, and the gunners fired three times.

Sandy had drawn near to watch. He had noticed the gun on deck.

"I've been wondering why you carried it on a coastwise voyage."

"A coastwise voyage is as dangerous as a transatlantic crossing. Pirates are watching these ports of the New World. On the other hand, the ports watch for unidentified craft. There is a signal cannon on that island starboard. This brig is expected, and a friendly salute helps the watchmen to recognize her."

Just then a burst of artillery sounded from the town ahead. Nine times it rang out, and smoke along the water front hid the low skyline which Sandy had just glimpsed. He was startled, but the officer appeared pleased.

"There goes the salvo in return for our salute. Your settlers must be welcome, for they've given you three guns for every gun the brig gave them."

Welcome to the Puritan colonists only began with the guns. As the brig reached inner harbor a small boat rowed out to meet her, and as soon as she dropped anchor a delegation of citizens climbed aboard. They were led by Mr. William Norman, a prominent Independent Churchman, who had long been urging the Dorchester elders to bring the Church south. He claimed those dignitaries and Mr. Lord as his guests, then turned to introduce Sandy to a thin, dark, elderly man.

"Mr. Lenoir will be your host. He belongs to the French colony."

Mr. Lenoir spoke English with a definite accent. His welcome to Sandy was more graceful than the Puritan's response.

"I do not wish to put you to inconvenience. Is there no inn—no hostelry—at which I can stay?"

"There are taverns in the city," said Mr. Lenoir.

"Then, why should I not lodge in one of them?"

The Huguenot spoke gently and without Latin gestures.

"Only because I had not thought them suitable for you."

"Why do you not think them suitable?"

"They are frequented by men who drink and fight. I can at least offer you a peaceful room in my small house."

It was small, but as spotlessly clean as if kept by a Puritan housewife. Madame Lenoir was as plump and bright-eyed as a bird. She showed him to an attic room with small windows and slanting walls.

"You will now rest and arrange *les bagages*. You will be call for the supper."

His baggage was only the traveling box which he had taken to Harvard and a roll of cloak and clothing which he had worn on the ship. He unlocked the trunk and raised its lid, wondering whether to unpack his books. In with them, wrapped in oiled cloth, was the old bell-mouth musket. He lifted it out and frowned as his thoughts went to the Brown Bess.

He had wished to bring the Brown Bess with him to

this wild new land. But in those dark, confused weeks before his departure the gun and several other things had been stolen from his house. He felt sure the thief was a Pequot. They watched for and raided deserted or unprotected homes, as that lone warrior long ago had attacked the Minot house. Doubtless the thief had watched Sandy leave for Cambridge that day, as he had gone to collect his belongings and his Latin certificate. At any rate, when he returned, the Brown Bess and some of his and his brother's warmest clothing had been missing.

So the old bellmouth would have to do for whatever Indian fighting or game hunting came Sandy Purbeck's way. It had always done for him in the colony farther north. The long-barreled, newer gun had been preempted by Peregrine. For that very reason Sandy would have liked to have it. He had loved his brother deeply and his brother had become, in spite of all faults, a hero to him. His brother had died—Sandy reminded himself again —trying to save Ness who had rejected him for Sandy. Ness's body had been found, battered and swept out in the bay. Of Peregrine there was no trace, except his footprints in the woods nearby that tragic crossing. Under a tree whose limbs had sheltered them from the snow, had been found his tracks pointing toward the river. They were cut deep into the half-frozen top soil, mute witnesses of his terrible haste.

As he remembered, Sandy recalled that his brother's name meant an alien. Peregrine had once said that. It was his destiny. In death as in life he would have sought and reached the distant places. His body must have been swept to sea, while Gentleness came home to rest.

In the low-walled attic room Sandy tried not to reawaken such grief. But to have had the Brown Bess would have brought back loved and familiar things: turkey hunts with Peregrine, river thickets, falling snow, the bird they had taken last winter to Goody Tompson and Ness. . . .

His thoughts were interrupted by a tap on the door, and he reached and opened it.

A girl was standing just outside, a girl in a gray homespun dress. Its bodice fitted her like a glove; over its long, full skirt she wore a starched white apron. She was taller than Ness had been but not so tall as Sandy.

He noted that in the seconds she looked up at him from the tangle of thick black hair that fell uncoifed to her shoulders. There was watchfulness in her dark eyes, a smile on her wide red mouth.

"Monsieur," she said, "I am Nicole Lenoir. I come to call you to supper."

SUPPER WAS CARROT soup, followed by a pilau of rice and small shrimp. It was all too highly seasoned for Sandy's taste, although hunger forced him to eat it. Secretly he longed for dumplings and cold venison, boiled turnip root and baked Indian pudding.

Nicole, across the table from him, rose frequently to serve them. She moved with quick and easy grace and did the work neatly and competently. Although in justice he approved that, he did not admire her. Rosa Zuider was dark; therefore he disliked dark women. But she had yellow cat-eyes, while this girl's eyes were smoky brown.

114

Sometimes they remained sad, even when her lips smiled at him. He did not return her smile, and her defects made more impression on him than her graces. He noted that her mouth was too wide, her hands were larger than Ness's had been, and her dark hair was so thick that it appeared tousled.

He was more interested in the questions Mr. Lenoir was asking about the proposed settlement.

"I hear that Landgrave Morton is anxious for your colonists to choose the Edisto."

The name caught Sandy's attention.

"It would please me if they did. The only friend I have in South Carolina lives near New London on a silk plantation."

"You have three friends," said Madame Lenoir, "who sit at the supper with you."

Sandy glanced gratefully at her but found no words to reply.

Mr. Lenoir inquired: "You speak perhaps of Monsieur Couturier?"

Sandy stared back at him in surprise. Shannon had told him New London was a day's journey by horseback or by boat from the seaport.

The Frenchman shrugged. "There is no mystery in my guess. There are few French in the colony, and we keep in touch with each other. Besides"—he paused and looked earnestly at his guest—"sericulture is my business. It is a subject upon which I am anxious to talk with you."

"I had heard that the French emigrés were adept at spinning and weaving silk. I did not know that their work with the industry went beyond that."

"It is they who brought silk culture to this colony. A

wild mulberry abounds in the woods farther inland."

The name took Sandy's thoughts back to the Indian mulberry trees, now bare-boughed in Dorchester's streets and in the surrounding country. The Massachusetts Indians had used the fruit for their food, not to nourish worms which gave it back in the coin of vanity and pride.

"I know little about silk," he said bluntly. "My people consider it a vain and useless stuff, alongside of good flax and wool."

Madame Lenoir threw up her hands.

"It is necessary and right for women to look beautiful for their husbands and lovers, is it not?" she demanded.

To Sandy that was a new idea and a startling one. Before his mind's eye a vision of Puritan women took shape. Smooth-haired and carefully coifed, white-collared and cuffed, decently and shapelessly clad in their long, full gowns, they gazed severely back at him from the vantage of his approval. Any one of them, he was sure, would have felt it immoral to beautify herself for lover or husband. But before he could voice his opinion the Frenchwoman rushed on.

"A woman is wrong and foolish if she does not do all she can to make herself attractive to the man she loves. If she does not, the blame is hers when he finds another attractive. No?"

"My dear," inquired her husband, "were we not speaking of silk?"

"We were. I am. I speak of silk which makes a woman alluring for—"

Mr. Lenoir interrupted: "You speak to a Puritan."

"He is a Puritan. That I know. But he is also a man. And I, being a woman, know men."

116

"Being a man, I know women," her husband told her. His eyes twinkled at Sandy. "I know them well enough to know that we can talk of business better alone and walking in the night by the sea wall."

The winter night was so warm that the man from New England did not even take his cloak. The moon rode high in restless clouds, and the restless harbor was strangely quiet. As they walked southeast the infantry wall stood breast-high on their left. Right and ahead, the low skyline of the city rose, yellow-windowed. Sandy was content to hold silence, and they reached the end of the long sandspit before the Frenchman spoke.

"I have already talked with Mr. William Norman on the subject I wish to discuss with you."

"What is the subject?" Sandy asked him.

"It is silk culture. For that I must take up a tract of land in the country—a tract large enough to support a mulberry orchard."

Sandy listened without replying, for it was his way to be sure before he spoke. The soft, damp wind against his face smelled like that from Dorchester Bay. It was gentler and warmer, but he would have welcomed in its place the freezing sting of far-off northern spray.

"I am not wealthy like Mr. Couturier," Mr. Lenoir was saying. "A plantation is in itself a unit like a city, and it can both support and protect itself. But a small farm—which is all I can hope to own—must be on the outskirts of a settlement—a settlement such as your compatriots plan."

It had not until then occurred to Sandy that others, like this Frenchman, might wish to attach themselves to a Puritan colony. He already liked Mr. Lenoir for his simplicity and directness; but the rule of the Church was that the elders should make decisions upon questions such as this.

"I hold no office as churchman since I am the youngest of the mission. My work will be that of schoolmaster when the children come."

"Mr. Norman told me so; but I wish you to know of my hopes and plans. While in my house you will have a chance to observe the Huguenot way of life. It should not be, in vital things, too different from your own. We, like you, have revolted against the barriers of ambition and greed builded by unscrupulous men between a man and his God. We protest. You seek to purify. But the end we desire is the same. Perhaps you will accompany me upon the coming Sabbath to a service at the French church."

Sandy made no promise. He found it hard to believe that any other religious sect could in any way approximate his own. Madame Lenoir, he thought, was definitely worldly. Her husband appeared serious and anxious to work at his trade.

The daughter resembled neither of them. For a young girl she appeared mature, both in looks and in manners. However, she was nothing to him. Nor was this strange seaport. Its wind had risen as the tide came in. It blew through the small attic windows, ruffling the starched red curtains and bringing a strange restlessness. The same sea wind in Dorchester had been harsher but less disturbing. He was weary in body and mind, and he longed for the solace of sleep.

But sleep refused to come to him in the alien place. On the brigantine, he recalled, he had at least had his own people around him. As he turned and tossed in a strange bed, he still felt himself swayed by the motion of the ship which had brought him so far from home. He was now in Couturier's country, but Couturier was still in Cambridge. Was he going for evening diversion to the tavern by the Frog Pond? The tavern where Rosa Zuider plied her old trade, after doing all the evil she had done in Dorchester.

Cursing her, Sandy rolled over and buried his face in the pillow.

Outside he heard the sea wind, harsh in the palmetto fronds, and the cry of the watch passing below in the street: *"Twelve midnight of the clock—and all's well in Charles Town!"*

A FINE COLD rain was blowing in from the harbor next day. Beyond his attic windows Sandy saw the town's low roofs: a rectangle less than a half mile in width and following the water front for no more than a mile. The red French curtains seemed to warm as well as light the unheated room. Downstairs he found Madame Lenoir and a breakfast of dark bread and cheese.

"My husband has already gone to the warehouse," she told him. "He has schooling, my old one, and he works at accounts for this time until he can start again his silk culture."

She broke off to cry in horror as Sandy raised his drinking cup: "But water is bad for your stomach! I implore you to mix it with wine!"

Sandy shook his head stubbornly and continued to

drink water. Across the table his hostess was peeling vegetables.

"Even in winter they grow," she said. "Our kitchen garden yields all year round. There is no hunger in this land for anyone willing to work."

He asked her: "What does the seaport ship, Madame Lenoir, and with what ports does it trade?"

"Our ships take lumber, pitch, and tar to the West Indian islands, and they bring back to Charles Town sugar and rum. At this season the trappers are bringing bales of hides from the forests. They go to England, and in exchange we get English cloth and all manner of household utensils. But in these last years the plantations of South Carolina have been producing a crop which is our biggest export."

Sandy had heard of rice. "But don't they ship that in autumn?"

"It is shipped in autumn, just as soon as it reaches the seaport in barges. Ah, but you should see it come from the great coastal rivers—out to sea—and then across the harbor to the warehouses. By Noël of the usual year the water-front sheds are empty and the last ship has cleared the bar with the last sack of grain. This year is not a usual year; it is truly a year *formidable*. The crop of rice has been so large that night and day the barges came. For weeks and months, by river and sea, they came with rice and more rice."

"The country must be fertile. That means prosperity."

"That means pirates," said Madame Lenoir. "In some way they know of the rice ships. They lie in wait outside the bar like tigers of the sea."

"How can they know? Don't they come from the West Indies?"

"They hide in the great sounds north of us—Currituck, Albemarle. As for how they know, it is a scandal *effroyable!* There are merchants in this port known to be friends of pirates."

The door opened and Nicole blew in, a milk pail in her hand.

"I'd like a pirate for a friend," she said. "He would give me a Spanish shawl and golden rings for my ears."

"You speak," said her mother sharply, "like a species of imbecile. Set the milk in the kitchen and get your woolen shawl. You must take a basket of *déjeuner* to the warehouse to your father."

The woolen shawl was plum color. It hid the girl's heavy hair and framed her piquant face. She slanted her big dark eyes at the Puritan.

"Do you care for a walk, monsieur, and a glimpse of the town?"

As he hesitated she added, in distinct provocation: "Ah, but it is raining still! Perhaps, on a sunny day—"

"I am well accustomed to rain and cold," he interrupted her sharply. "Your winter seems to me no more than spring."

She made no reply but passed him with downcast lashes as he threw open the door. At once the fine blown rain began to soak into his clothing. The girl at his side was getting wet too, but she walked demurely, in silence. However, he gave her credit for no true demureness. He saw that her nose had a slight but impudent tilt and her wide mouth a mocking curve. Why, he asked himself, should she give him inviting glances and then try to humiliate him by remarks about the rain? It was slackening, but the sea wind blew and he felt the chill through his jacket.

"There is the French church," Nicole said. "We will have evening service today."

She had little accent except for the liquid *l* and the pretty sound of her *r*. Her voice ignored all that had passed and had no trace of teasing. She added politely and formally: "What church do you attend, monsieur?"

He told her shortly: "The Independent."

"Ah, we are all independent—of the churches of Rome and of England."

Sandy was shocked. "But we are not alike."

"Have you ever attended a service in the French Protestant Church?"

"No. How could I? There are none in my colony."

"Then, monsieur, how do you know?"

"I know because I know my own Church. It is different from others."

She shrugged a slim shoulder and dropped the argument.

"Is that so? Here is the wharf where my father works."

The wind was doing its bitter best to blow them from the narrow plank. Below and upon both sides the scummed dock water surged giddily. Sandy felt slightly giddy too. Never before had he known such a girl. Ness had never attempted to stir up trouble; but in any case of importance she had argued to the last. Nicole seemed to enjoy tossing the apple of discord. Then she shrugged it all away and changed the subject. She must be a child of the climate, changing and inconsistent. She was intensely feminine and yet strangely independent. She still carried the small basket with her father's breakfast. He had not offered to take it and did not intend to do so. The last basket he carried had been for Ness to the mill. . . .

Upon the wharfhead was a closed shed. Nicole gestured to its door.

"*Voilà*," she said. "We have arrived, monsieur."

A<small>GAINST HIS BETTER</small> judgment, Sandy went that evening with the family Lenoir to the French Protestant church. Nicole had not mentioned the subject again. She had left him with Monsieur Lenoir in the office on the swaying wharfhead.

"He wishes to see the ship loading, Papa. I have errands to do. He can find his way home."

Little she'd care if I didn't, thought Sandy indignantly. Let her go on her errands. I'd rather be with her father.

Lenoir had taken him up the schooner's gangplank and to her master's cabin.

"Mr. Purbeck arrived yesterday from the colony of Massachusetts Bay."

"I saw the brigantine come in," Captain Gaddis told him. "I know Boston harbor, and I'd prefer to be clearing from there than from here tonight."

Mr. Lenoir asked gravely: "What is the news from the pilot boats?"

"One of them is cruising now in the outer harbor. The other has just brought me word that no sail is in sight."

"So far, so good," said Mr. Lenoir. "Isn't the rain in your favor?"

"Less in my favor than in that of some buccaneer who may be hiding beneath bare poles out there between the follies."

Through the port and between rain gusts Sandy had glimpsed the harbor, shaped by its barrier islands of sand dunes and low trees. He saw them still as he listened to the prayers and hymns in French. The service was simple but otherwise unlike his own; and he could not help feeling that it was inappropriate to worship God in a foreign tongue.

It was gray dawn of the next morning when he came awake with a start. For a half moment he heard no sound, but the air was full of vibration. Then came a drumbeat, sudden and loud. It was taken up farther away—all along the waterfront—in a long roll of alarm.

He swung his feet over the bedside and sat listening. There was warning in those drums. Something was wrong in the seaport. Could it be an Indian raid?

He ran to the door, flung it open and saw Monsieur Lenoir struggling into his coat at the foot of the stairs. In his excitement the Frenchman reverted to his own tongue.

"C'est le tocsin qui sonne! Il faut me dépêcher!"

He disappeared through the street door, leaving Sandy in complete ignorance of his words but more certain than ever that trouble was abroad.

Throwing on his own clothes and snatching his bell-mouth musket, shot bag, and powder horn, he ran downstairs and through the house. Once in the street he saw other men running. Only some carried weapons, but all ran toward the sandspit where he had strolled with Mr. Lenoir the evening of his arrival. On the crude watchtower at the low wall's end stood a sentry yelling: "Schooner, ahoy!"

Sandy saw her then. She loomed through the mist like a low cloud just off Windmill Point. She was under full sail and making what speed she could; but even in retreat she was beautiful and proud. He recognized her at once as the rice ship he had boarded in dock.

Just then the sentry shouted again: " 'Ware to her aft and starboard! Enemy galley, ahoy!"

For minutes the men at the foot of the watchtower saw no more. The schooner drove on toward them, as near as the depth of water along the sandspit permitted. Then she leaned to starboard as a gull leans on the wind. She turned with a rush of white water under her keel, and she swept by as a bird sweeps when pursued by a hawk.

Just as she passed the mist lifted and Sandy looked across the channel in her wake. Off the beach of that island which bounded the harbor north, a longer and lower craft was gliding even more swiftly. Under square sails as sharp as hawk wings, it darted boldly forward in an attempt to cut the schooner off from her berth. It was still beyond range for the small cannon on the mud wall; but Sandy saw militiamen loading and training them.

On came the strange ship, cutting the water like a knife. And suddenly a white flower bloomed across and above her stern. Over the water came a low *boom* which left the air in vibration. Feeling it, Sandy realized that what had awakened him had been the explosion of a cannon. He had been sleeping so soundly that he had not come awake quickly enough to hear the noise consciously. But once awake, he had felt this same ominous vibration. Around him men were cheering and waving their muskets.

"Bravo, Florence O'Sullivan!"

"O'Sullivan's fired upon them with the signal cannon!"

"Cheers for our Assemblyman O'Sullivan!"

O'Sullivan's aim had not been good, but he and the ancient signal gun had done their best. The attempt had the effect of driving the buccaneer farther into mid-channel. A rustle of activity ran down the line of defense. A hundred yards nearer would put the enemy in their range. But the enemy again veered back and toward the cove which lay between the southern end of O'Sullivan's island and the oak-fringed mainland east of Shemee Creek.

A voice from the crowd cried: "They're heading into Rebellion Road!"

Meanwhile the rice schooner was standing upriver and off the guard post at the foot of the Broad Street. Two small pilot boats ran circles around her, and her crew was furling sail. From this point on, she was covered by the guns along the wall. In order to attack her, Sandy realized, the pirate galley would be obliged to place itself within range of those guns.

Matters had come to a deadlock, and militia officers were holding a hurried conference. From men in the crowd Sandy learned that the spot where the pirate had dropped anchor was the only place in the inner harbor which could not be reached by the harbor's defending guns. A tall young man wearing a mason's apron with his trowel still in its pocket explained the situation to the New Englander.

"His Excellency the Governor has ordered that no ship stays in harbor longer than twenty-four hours without written permission from him. More than once, rebellious captains have moved into that road and dropped anchor and defied him. That is why you hear it called Rebellion Road."

Sandy asked the question which had been in his mind ever since Madame Lenoir had spoken of pirates.

"How do the buccaneers know so well to go straight to that protected place?"

The face of the young workman darkened.

"They have knowledge they should not. There are merchants in this town who are friendly to them in return for rare merchandise which they buy untaxed. It will be an ill day for them when honest men catch them betraying their own seaport."

The group of officers had now broken apart and were giving instructions to their militiamen. Some of these remained to serve the cannon, while others started north along the wall. Sandy and his new friend followed the latter up to the wharf where the day before the schooner had lain in dock.

The two small pilot boats were nudging her in. The militia captain called to the deck of the nearer: "Johnny Cock, will you set twenty men ashore past the mouth of the Wando?"

"I will," said the pilot calmly. "What will they be after there?"

"They'll cross the mainland and row the creek to O'Sullivan's island. He's there alone, and it may be those scoundrels in Rebellion Road will send a longboat ashore tonight to murder him and burn his house."

Men stepped forward to volunteer as the pilot boat came alongside. The militia officer was choosing them carefully.

"No man is wanted without a gun. Step back there, Jerry Glynn! Come on, Will Cutler! That makes eleven. . . ."

Women and children had by now seeped into the crowd. Sandy was watching the volunteers too closely to notice them. He was jostled in and out of the line by the press of bodies, and he tried to move free of it. This was neither his home nor his fight. He could afford to look on . . . look on and speculate as to what adventure on the barrier island these young men were heading.

Just then he felt a light touch on his arm. Nicole Lenoir was looking up at him. Framed in tendrils of dark hair curled damply by the mist, her face glowed like a rose under the plum-colored shawl.

"Monsieur," she whispered, "I had to come close to tell you how wonderful you are—how brave—to go out— you, a stranger—in defense of my town!"

For seconds her dark eyes held his. Then he broke the lock and stepped forward into the line and to the edge of the wharf.

The militia officer said: "Fifteen. You've a gun? Very good. Get aboard!"

As THE PILOT boat pushed off from the wharf, Sandy's thoughts were churning like the water under her. Only a minute before he had been a bystander watching a drama from which he was completely detached. Now he was involved in its action—action which threatened to lead to a fight with buccaneers. He gave no thought to personal safety, for he had never lacked courage. But his orderly mind rejected the inconsistency. All his life he had been taught to look before he leapt. Why had he suddenly let a few words of admiration from a girl with dark eyes make him leap aboard a strange boat among strange companions on an errand strange to him?

Could Nicole Lenoir's caprice and the capricious climate of this warm and misty South be having an effect upon his behavior?

No, he told himself firmly. It can be better explained by a subconscious sense of duty. This new land is not yet my home, but it may yet be. I have nothing to do while lingering in the seaport, and I prefer occupation to idleness. Madame Lenoir annoys me with her worldly chatter. I suspect Nicole of being the kind of girl who likes to coquet. But there was no coquetry in her eyes just now at the wharf. . . .

However he felt on the subject, he could not have found a quicker way to make friends with the young men of the seaport. Realizing that he was a stranger, they crowded around him on the short voyage up the Wando, asking questions and offering welcome. The tall mason with whom he had talked by the sea wall was there. He had left apron and trowel and carried a long gun. Sandy eyed it wistfully, thinking of the Brown Bess.

In less than an hour the party had disembarked in thick woods on the east bank of Wando River.

"Its Indian name is Hobcaw," said Saxon Toll, the

mason. "Shipyards are springing up around here, because of the oak trees for timber."

Upon that eight-mile tramp Sandy saw them on every side: huge of trunk and low of bough, dark-leaved, symmetrical. He compared them to monstrous green fountains springing from a soil which bordered on marsh and must have in it the sea as well as the land. From the depths of their billowing branches the gray moss flung, as soiled foam flings from ocean waves.

But all talk was of the pirates and of the business ahead. Those of the party who knew the path led them swiftly to the creek which separated O'Sullivan's island from the mainland. There at a trapper's cabin they borrowed a canoe and made the crossing by repeated trips. Toll pointed downstream.

"The buccaneers' anchorage is less than two miles away. The land's curve hides them from us, as we are hidden from them."

Assemblyman Florence O'Sullivan lived in a small house not far from the lower end of the island. A ladder led to its roof, and from that lookout Sandy saw outer harbor and white water on the bar. Turning his gaze cityward, he saw the low skyline of Charles Town, its small houses huddled along the upper river. Between them and the island rode the low black ship: watching, as a falcon waits, for its chance to strike.

He climbed down again and went to inspect the signal gun. It was mounted between two blocks and trained upon the channel.

O'Sullivan said with pride: "It's as good a gun as the raiders have. If only they'd take the nearer channel out to the bar!"

130

Sandy looked off at the long curve of the island's end below them.

"Couldn't we get it on a sled and drag it down there—within range of the ship?"

The big Irishman shook his head. "Not through deep sand and marsh. All we can do is to wait for night. Now that they can't seize the rice schooner, they'll certainly move out on the turn of tide after dark."

"You expect them to send a party ashore?"

"They'll never leave without doing so. Freebooters are vengeful scoundrels. This gun alerted the town, and they know *she's* able to defend herself and her wharves. But they owe me a visit in return for what I did, and they don't know that I have re-enforcements. That's why I asked you lads to go one by one to the rooftop. Seeing only one man up there, they'll take it for me watching them."

The men from Charles Town appeared to agree with O'Sullivan about this. Sunset came before six o'clock, and the tide would turn three hours later. As soon as it was completely dark Florence O'Sullivan led them down a sandy path between sweet myrtles and tamarisks. It came out on the island's back beach, overlooking black mud and the slow salt creek.

"They'll sneak in along here and come ashore on a shell bank. They'll never chance the front beach, because of my cannon." He sighed with regret. "Ah, for the one grand moment I was thinking the ball would punch a hole in her cursed black hull! But, knowing tide was against her, I'd miscalculated her speed."

He dispersed them along the waterway at all possible points of landing. These were places where oyster shells had built small natural causeways; for a man who stepped in the creek mud would at once sink to his knees.

Sandy found himself standing under a tall water cedar. Every time he moved, its fronds tickled his ears and the back of his neck. He knew Toll to be stationed a hundred feet harborward. Signal at sight of the longboat was to be the mew of a seagull. The men who had been sent to O'Sullivan's rescue were young and high of spirit. They felt themselves a match for the crew of any longboat, and they wished not only to repulse the raiding party but to strike a blow at the tigers of the high seas who waited outside their young port and destroyed their merchant shipping.

The ocean breeze was as soft and as salty as it had been when he strolled two nights before on the long white point with Monsieur Lenoir. Even danger, Sandy thought, walked softly in this southern land. It had not the stark reality of a Pequot raid in the North. Its winter was as seductive as spring. Under the low southern stars he saw the salt creek running smoothly to its flood.

Was Nicole watching the harbor from one of the city wharves? Were her great dark eyes troubled at danger to her town? Was she even remembering that he—her guest and a stranger—had gone out with her compatriots in her town's defense?

Above him a seagull floated, ghostly, returning from sea to seek the lonely rookery which was its roost by night.

From just beyond it came its catlike mew.

For seconds he thought the seabird had cried as it drifted over. Then he realized suddenly that Saxon Toll was giving the signal agreed upon.

132

So he cried out softly and mewingly as the white shape moved up creek. And the faint high note was taken up in the wake of the gull alongshore.

Parting the ferny tamarisk boughs, Sandy peered through an interstice.

A long rowing boat, night-colored and shadow-swift, was gliding upstream behind O'Sullivan's island.

THE LOW, DARK boat came swiftly and almost silently on, while Sandy watched it through the water cedar's foliage. His eyes were by now accustomed to the darkness, and he counted twelve heads above its gunwale. Wrapped in dark headkerchiefs, they had the sinister suggestion of hooded birds of prey. Their long oars dipped cleanly without a splash as they swung toward the bank and alongside an uneven mound of oyster shells.

Each second of waiting seemed an hour long. Was he, he asked himself, really facing pirates? The privateers, who were less evil, had terrorized his New England coast. He had heard tales of buccaneers. His comrades had talked on the pilot boat and Florence O'Sullivan had expressed his opinion. They were the outlaws of the sea and they gave no quarter. Nor did they expect it. They would fight to the death, since they knew that capture meant hanging by the neck on the sandspit at Charles Town.

It was hard to wait; but the single militiaman who had been sent in charge of the volunteers had ordered them to hold their fire until the enemy was ashore. He had explained that when fired upon they would probably rush back to their boat and, in crowding into it, offer enough delay to be a good target for a second round of fire. His reasoning had been sound but had not gone far enough. He was facing men who had far more experience in warfare than he had and who knew the danger of retreat under fire.

A short, broad man just then leapt from the longboat with its painter in his hand. While he held its gunwale steady his fellows disembarked. They appeared unhurried and easy, speaking low together. They expected no ambush. They had been sent to slaughter a lone man who had warned the city and so prevented their capture of the rice ship. It was a pleasant errand, for they would loot his house before burning it to the ground.

The first man ashore had by now moored the boat to a low branch. They were moving together up the bank when Sandy heard his commander cry: "Ready, lads! *Fire!*"

Almost before the guns roared out, Sandy saw the buccaneers throw themselves flat in the coarse marsh grass and vines. Curses and screams bore witness that some of them were wounded. But some, he was sure, were unhurt. What would these do? And what should he do? Remain hidden or advance upon them?

His doubt was resolved as he saw a young man of his party step rashly out into the path. A pistol cracked from beside the creek, and the boy cried out and fell.

The militia officer shouted aloud: "Stay in hiding! Men with guns that scatter shot, fire into the enemy! Men using a single ball, wait for a single target!"

The old bellmouth, thought Sandy, was coming into

134

its own. He had lost all indifference. The battle was now his own. His mouth twisted with a savage pleasure as he rested the trumpet-shaped barrel on the limb across which he was looking and aimed into the pale grass which swayed in the starlight.

Half a dozen other muskets of the same type as his were also pouring their scattering shot into it. He had pictured pirates as stoics, but now they cried out like other men—like the boy they had just shot down in the myrtle path. One of them attempted to rise and escape from the trap. As he raised head and shoulders a long-barreled gun cracked, and he fell back without a sound.

Squatting under the tamarisk to ram his third charge in the old gun, Sandy was thinking fast and clearly. Although the militiaman's strategy had not worked as expected and the pirates had not rushed their boat, the plan was working well for the defenders. The enemy did not dare rise from the tall grass which concealed them. They had no means of knowing the number of their opponents. What would they do next? What would he himself do if caught in the same position?

As he rose to his feet to fire again his question was answered. Strong arms grasped his legs, jerked them from under him and threw him with violence to the ground. He dropped his musket in order to defend himself with his hands. Touch told him the man was larger than he. He loosed Sandy's legs and clawed like a wild beast for his throat.

Fighting for his life on a strange shore under a semi-tropical tree, the Puritan's mind flashed back to the wrestling he had done in sport on the bank of the Neponset. He had not known, when he had thrown Peregrine or Nahum Wales, that he had been practicing for a match to the death with a pirate on a Carolina island. He needed now every trick he had learned, every ounce of strength that clean, hard life had given him.

He arched his body suddenly, butted for the other man's face, and managed for the second to free himself.

He saw they had rolled out from under the tree. Starlight was all around them, misty and vague—too soft a setting for the work being done. And all around them were other men fighting hand to hand.

A yell went up. "The boat! Don't let them get away!"

Scattered shots followed the cry. In spite of himself Sandy was distracted. For a split second his eyes turned toward the creek—then they returned to his foe.

The man had risen to one knee and his hand was at his belt. Starlight glinted on steel, and the knife whistled as it flew.

Sandy flung himself to one side—but a half second too late. As he moved a pain like a burn streaked through the flesh of his upper left arm.

THE RED FRENCH curtains fluttered in the breeze from the harbor, and Sandy, waking early, blinked at them as he remembered.

Only a few days before, he had been returned to the Lenoir house with Saxon Toll supporting him on one side and the militia officer on the other. He had not asked or wished their support. He had tried to push them away.

But they persisted, firm in their conviction that he—a foreigner—had risked death in their cause.

Madame Lenoir had cried out at sight of the blood on his clothes and the bloody sling. Nicole had only stood and stared, her dark eyes large. The sight of her provoked him. She had caused him to volunteer as surely as if she had dared him. That rankled in his mind, and he was coldly polite to her when she brought him food or a message.

His arm was extremely painful, and it had caused a fever. A physician had called once and then left him to Madame Lenoir. She dressed it with cooling herbs, and he suspected that the drafts she gave him made him sleep. But he had no use for soft living, and he was anxious to be downstairs and about. Mr. Lord and Mr. Norman had called to inquire, and Saxon Toll had visited him and given him all the news.

Three dead pirates were buried in the beach growth where they had died. Five had made their escape in the longboat back to the ship. Four had been captured and brought to Charles Town where they lay in chains at the guard post dungeon. The black ship had that same night made her way out of the harbor, taking the middle channel and carrying no lights. O'Sullivan and others had watched for her departure and hoped to speed it with a ball from the cannon. But she had moved like a dark ghost out of Rebellion Road and toward the bar, keeping beyond gun range of both city and beach.

Sandy asked: "Were any of our men killed besides the boy who stepped out in the open?"

"He wasn't killed, but he's badly hurt. Next to him, you've the worst wound. Leftenant Maury was wise in posting us as he did. We outnumbered them from the first, and before we came hand to hand we had reduced their numbers even more."

"My wound is my own fault," Sandy confessed gloomily.

"How so? You wrestled successfully with a desperate man. I was trying to get to you, but I saw you had the best of him."

"I wrestled successfully with him—then took my eye off him long enough to let him draw a knife. My father, who taught me to wrestle and box, taught me that the first law of fighting is to watch your opponent ceaselessly."

Shame for that fault was tormenting him. Had he not made that mistake, he would, he felt sure, have bested the pirate and made him prisoner.

But Toll was saying cheerfully: "Don't bother about that. I hit him with my gun butt as he let the knife fly. I could have shot him, but I preferred saving him to be tried and hanged."

Sandy's glance moved across the room to his old musket.

"I'm glad you brought it in for me. It's the only gun I have. We had a Brown Bess—my brother and I—but an Indian stole it from the house in Dorchester."

"There's a merchant here who carries guns. I'll show you his shop on the Bay Street. You may pick up a used one there, just as good as new."

"Has the rice schooner cleared yet?"

"Not yet. The pilots, Cock and Bradley and Burningham, report unidentified craft waiting beyond the bar. Two snows, already laden, are waiting in harbor too."

"You're a British colony. Why doesn't your king give you protection? Aren't these merchantmen bound for England?"

"We're a British colony, but not a Crown colony. The king granted South Carolina to eight of his favorite gentlemen. They are our Lords Proprietors."

"What do they do for you?" the New Englander demanded, with the practical viewpoint of his race.

"Little except take the revenue from our trade and give their proud names to our landmarks. But the country is so rich that any man worth his salt should be able to make a good living."

"You know the woods around here?"

"I've hunted them, and the follies which border the harbor mouth. They are full of game, and the soil is rich as cream. If you like shooting, we'll go after a deer when your arm heals."

Sandy glanced down at the bandaged left shoulder. As he moved impatiently he winced with pain. Talk of hunting brought Peregrine back. Where was the Pequot robber who had the Brown Bess? As he thought of it he could see the peregrine falcon, carved with spread wings into its stock. . . .

Saxon Toll had risen to leave. He said: "You'll get a summons."

Sandy's thoughts had been far away—with a long-barreled gun, in a white winter. . . . He frowned as he came back to the present in a small, warm room.

"Summons? Summons for what?"

"You'll be summoned to witness in the Court of Vice Admiralty. They're already convening to try the four scoundrels we captured."

So he, Sandy, would be again and even further involved in affairs of a land which he had not yet accepted as his own. He had the wish to stand aloof until he had made his decision. It might be he would go away—farther north to Virginia. Thought of the trial awakened mixed emotions and brought back some of the excitement of battle. The expedition to O'Sullivan's island had given him a feeling of comradeship which had warmed his heart more than anything else since Ness Goodman's death. He liked Saxon Toll and Mr. Lenoir. Nicole was another matter. He was not yet ready for friendship with any girl—less so a girl different from all other girls he had known.

Toll was looking around the room. "You're lucky to be quartered here."

"Why so?"

"Mr. and Mrs. Lenoir are fine people, and as for that girl Nicole—"

He was trying not to laugh as he glanced from the corner of his eye to the open door and the staircase.

Although he knew he had not the slightest interest in her, Sandy pursued the subject: "And Nicole?"

Toll raised his voice: "She's undependable—scatterbrained and frivolous. She won't milk the cow or sew or bake bread or bring supper to an injured man."

Sandy was just. He said: "You're wrong. She may be frivolous, but she helps with everything about the house. I tell you—"

She stood in the door, her eyes blazing.

"So I'm frivolous, am I? Saxon Toll, how dare you tell Monsieur Purbeck such untruths about me? I have a mind to take back the hot bread and haw jelly that I— a frivolous girl—was bringing to you both!"

TOLL HAD SEIZED from her hands the flat basket covered with a red napkin.

"Don't take it back from a poor bachelor who'll have to sup at a tavern on stale bread and cheese!"

"Explain then to Monsieur Purbeck that what you said was not true."

"He knows I was joking. I saw you coming up the stair and wanted to tease you."

Sandy had not known. And he had not the light banter with which to fence as these two did.

Toll was asking: "Besides, why should I explain to him?"

"Because I value his good opinion. He is a *jeune homme très sérieux*—not a philandering fellow who visits all the taverns in town and makes love to every girl with whom he exchanges the time of day."

Sandy had no idea what she had called him in French, but her comparison told that it was complimentary. She was putting a plate in his hands, and the bread smelled even more delicious than the loaves Goody Tompson had once sent him and Peregrine. The jelly was clear and firm and tart. Saxon Toll was wolfing his share. Nicole set down the basket and went to sit on a low bench under the window. Her almost-black hair was loose and fell to her shoulders. Framed in its darkness, her face was piquant and elfin.

"And now, Mr. Toll, will you tell me all about the battle—and what Mr. Purbeck did—and how he was wounded?"

"*Mister* Toll?" he reproached her. "My *friends* call me Saxon."

"Saxon," she said slowly, and the lovely word was even

141

lovelier with her faint accent. "Yes, I will call you Saxon
—if you do as I ask."

He sighed in exaggerated regret.

"So I must tell you of the bravery of another man,
when I was hoping to tell you of my own bravery."

Listening, Sandy was confused by his own contradic-
tion of thought. All this was frivolous to the point of
unseemliness. He had never spoken so to a girl, or heard
another man speak so. Yet through the disapproval of
his judgment, a sharp blade of envy was lancing him.
Why could he not laugh and joke as Toll was doing?
Such talk might be light-minded, but what harm did it
do? Toll had proven himself, both as a friend and a
fighting man. At the moment he was generously enlarg-
ing upon Sandy's part in the battle. Agonized with embarrassment, Sandy broke in.

"I did nothing. I deserve my wound. For I stupidly
took my eyes off a man who was trying to kill me."

"You outwrestled him," said Toll, "although he was
heavier than you are. Only his knife gave him the
advantage."

Nicole looked from one to the other.

"Whose story shall I believe?"

Sandy flushed. She was making fun of him. He had
been a fool to let himself think for a moment that she
really wished to hear of his part in the fight. He felt
suddenly depressed and disillusioned, and he no longer
envied the small talk he overheard. His arm had begun
to throb, and he wished they would go and leave him to
the twilight in the little red-curtained room. He should
never have consented to be the guest of people of different blood and different faith. Why had he gone to church

with them when never before had he been inside any other church than his own?

But the girl still lingered when Toll had said good-by. She stood with hands clasped in her apron and coaxing in her voice.

"On the street all my friends ask me about the young man in the house. They may laugh at the others, but they admire *you*."

"Laugh at the others? Do they dare laugh at the elders and the pastor?"

"It is because of their strange hats and their big white collars and cuffs. And more than all, it is because they frown at others and do not laugh."

Sandy's Puritanism was aroused and militant.

"The men at whom some empty heads are laughing, are men of education and intellect. They are too important and serious to waste time in laughter."

Her wide gaze was fixed on him in amazement and distress.

"One does not waste time in laughter, monsieur. Laughter is a physic to heal the hurt of hearts. My father and mother taught me that at a time I barely remember . . . a time when we heard no laughter . . . and terror was all around us. . . ."

He looked back at her, wondering what she was talking about. Her voice had caught on the last words, and now she changed the subject.

"I have asked Papa to take me with him to the Court of Vice Admiralty. I shall be there to hear you give evidence."

He did not wish to be rude to her, but his Puritan conscience was torturing him with the reminder that he was accepting praise under false pretenses. He had joined the fighting party not from any love of the land they defended but because of this girl's false assumption that he was volunteering. Once she spoke, his pride had not allowed him to explain that he had no idea of going out in battle against pirates. It was all her fault, and he vented his anger upon her now.

"I did no more than my duty, and I don't want to talk about it."

It was her turn to flush, and there were sparks in her eyes.

"Then I shall not ask you again," she told him shortly.

As she spoke she moved forward and relieved him of the empty plate. The gesture was no more than routine and meant she was going to leave him in peace. But the emptiness of the departing plate reminded Sandy of his obligation and angered him even more. So he accused her of his own fault.

"There is no need to get angry. It is only that we are different."

"If so, that is your own fault—your own Puritan hardness and narrowness."

"I do not consider my people either hard or narrow. It is merely a difference."

"A difference in what?" she demanded.

"In everything: opinion, manners, creed, dress, climate, food."

Madame Lenoir came through the door. "Who is speaking of food?" she inquired. "Did you not like the supper I sent you?"

"It was more than acceptable. I ate it all," Sandy told her.

"But he doesn't like it," Nicole cried. "He doesn't like our food, or climate or dress or manners or opinions."

"*Chut!* What are you talking about? The man is ill and unreasonable. I tell you not to annoy him."

"I am not ill," Sandy persisted, "and your daughter is quoting me incorrectly. I did not say I disliked the things she mentioned. I merely said that in all of them we were different."

Madame Lenoir hushed him again. "*Chut!* You are foolish young people. As for differences, they are of no consequence."

"Are you speaking, madame, of religious creeds?"

"I speak of creeds and all things else. They are the same, I tell you. For example, you find French food too highly spiced for your taste. Do not try to deny it. I observe you cough and sneeze."

"I ask your pardon, madame. It is just that I am not accustomed—"

"Is that not what I am saying? It is merely a matter of custom. The food we eat is the same, and so is the God we worship. It is only that we—the French—no matter how earnest we are, must have laughter in our lives and spices in our food."

He stared at her without reply. Nicole had said much the same thing. Foolishly, he argued against her spate of words.

"Spices disagree with me. I have never been accustomed—"

"So! It is custom only. We agree about that."

He did not agree, but he could find no reply. And he did not need one, for she was rushing on.

"I will now take my daughter away, so that she may

145

not annoy you. Yet I tell you—I who speak—that I would not have a daughter who was not capable of annoying young men. It is the spice in her—just as it is in the food."

For SOME DAYS after that Sandy had no glimpse of Nicole. He endured Madame's visits with a politeness engendered by gratitude; and he truly enjoyed his talks with Monsieur Lenoir. The Huguenot had never again mentioned the subject of taking up land with the Puritans. But in Sandy's mind were now both a hope that he might do so and a determination to help him toward that end.

Conversation still centered around harbor shipping and pirates, for trade was the lifeblood of the young port. Sandy rejoiced when his host told him that the waiting vessels had at last gone out.

"Besides the rice schooner, two snows and a bark were ready to put to sea. They waited until this morning in order to be joined by a brig which came in yesterday from New York. She was glad to pick up cargo and make the run with them. And she reported the bar clear of enemy craft."

"She was fortunate not to be taken by the pirates."

"They've evidently given up their deathwatch on Charles Town. They dare not remain too long in one place. Or they may have had word of richer cargoes to be looted at some other port."

"What did the ship from New York bring?"

"A mixed cargo: mostly cloth and furniture and

kitchen goods. Also she brought two passengers, personable young men who are thinking of making their home here."

In the name of His Majesty King Charles the Second, Sandy received a summons as a Crown witness next day. He walked to the Court of Vice Admiralty with Monsieur Lenoir, and Madame and Nicole walked behind them. His one glance at the girl had assured him she was excited by anticipation of a spectacle. Her eyes were bright and her cheeks glowed, and as he walked in silence he heard her chatting gaily with her mother in French. He did not admire her attitude; for he was aware of the gravity of the proceedings afoot. A seaport's shipping had been threatened, men's lives had been risked in battle and men's lives were going to be taken in retribution. According to his summons, the peace and dignity of the whole British realm had been endangered.

Once inside the courtroom, he was assigned by a bailiff to the long row of benches where were arrayed his companions of the island expedition. Several wore bandages upon heads or hands, and Sandy's arm was still in a sling. They rose as Judge Moreton entered, formidable in his robes of office and his huge wig.

Before he seated himself the bailiff thumped the floor with his staff and the clerk of court intoned slowly and solemnly: *"In the Name of God, Amen!"*

At the words the four filthy wretches in the dock cowered like servants of Satan confronted by the cross. Sandy looked away from them, stirred by an emotion which he would not own as pity. His eyes came to rest on Nicole, and he saw she was leaning forward, her glance upon them and her lips parted in fascination.

Captain Gaddis of the rice schooner had been obliged to leave but had written his deposition. It was read droningly by the clerk. Hearing it, Sandy saw again the schooner beat back to safety. Only by the courage and quickness of her crew had she been put about and saved from capture. Had she sailed farther into the trap, the men who saved her—good men and brave men, risking their lives in their duty—would now be dead and the cargo in the hands of sea robbers. He looked again at the bearded, ragged prisoners, and he frowned without any twinge of compassion.

One after another the witnesses for the prosecution followed: Captain Cock, whose pilot boat had taken the schooner to the bar; his fellow pilots, John Burningham and William Bradley; Florence O'Sullivan, who had watched the schooner pass and seen her come about in mad haste and drive back into the harbor. Even before he sighted the vulture craft in pursuit, he had realized her extremity and descended his ladder and fired his signal gun. He identified the prisoners, which neither Gaddis nor the pilots were able to do.

The lawyer appointed for defense attempted to challenge him. "All was night and confusion. Men's lives are at stake. Can you swear?"

"What would I be doing but swearing? I shot that scoundrel myself—the one with rings in his ears and the green kerchief on his head. And didn't we march the four to my house and look them over by lantern light? I'd know their ugly faces anywhere from here to—"

The judge frowned blackly at him, and he left his sentence unfinished and came down from the stand as the militia officer was called. One by one the young men of his party followed him, each one tying the now almost-visible rope tighter around the necks of the villains cringing in dock.

Sandy refused to identify the man who had wounded him, and both prosecutor and judge took his refusal as an affront. The latter leaned and glared at him, but he stared back stubbornly.

"You wrestled for minutes with a man and allowed him to stab you with a knife, yet now you cannot depose that this is the man?"

"Your Honor, we wrestled at night under a tree with thick branches. I did not go afterward to Mr. O'Sullivan's house and see the prisoners by lantern light. Somebody bandaged my arm and took me away at once in a boat."

But Saxon Toll was willing to swear. "I saw him wound Purbeck, and as he did I hit him over the head. He was still unconscious in the same place when—after bandaging Purbeck—I went back and tied him and took him to O'Sullivan's house. I saw him there. The wound in his head is from my gunstock. I recognize him—and his fellows too."

There was only one end to be reached, and the pirates saw it coming. No longer were they bold buccaneers, careless of other men's lives. With their own lives at stake, courage abandoned them. Even before Judge Moreton asked if they had anything to say, they shivered against each other and whimpered aloud. As he reached and put on his black cap, one howled like an animal.

Sick of it all, Sandy was glad to get into the open air and take the first walk he had been allowed in a week. With Toll and several other young men, he strolled north across Governor's Bridge and into the country.

When he returned to the Lenoir cottage Madame was putting a hot supper on the table and only three places were set. He hesitated, wondering if she wished him to eat upstairs.

"Be seated," she told him and her husband. "The girl has wept herself sick and she will eat no supper."

Sandy was startled. The girl had appeared in good health and good spirits, so much so that he had thought her callous.

He inquired: "Has she been taken ill?"

Madame shrugged. "It is no more than a *crise de nerfs*. What will you? A young girl is delicate and brutality offends her. The poor child has wept her eyes out with compassion ever since she heard Judge Moreton sentence the pirates to hang."

I N SPITE OF exasperation over Nicole Lenoir's inconsistency, the desire to help her father remained in Sandy's mind. He wrote a long letter to Couturier, saying that he stayed with the French family and that Mr. Lenoir was, like Mr. Couturier, a sericulturist. He set down in writing his determination to do what he could to secure for his host a farm in or near the proposed settlement. And when Pastor Lord called on him shortly after the trial, Sandy dared broach the subject.

"Will men outside the mission be permitted to take up land in the mission grant?"

Mr. Lord looked searchingly at him.

"That question has already come up. Mr. Norman

favors it. So do I—provided the proposed settler meets qualifications demanded by us of the mission."

"Would those qualifications bar men of another faith?"

"In the opinion of most of the elders, they would. In my opinion decision would depend upon *what* their faith was."

"Would the whole mission vote upon that, or the elders only?"

"Suppose," suggested Mr. Lord, "that before we go any further you tell me of whom you are thinking as a settler in our midst."

"Of Mr. Lenoir. He wishes to secure enough land to plant a mulberry orchard and raise silk."

The pastor said slowly: "I did not know he was a silk culturist, but I have heard only good of him. The mission is indebted to him for all he has done for you. Mr. Norman tells me the French Huguenots are industrious and honest and make good citizens."

Sandy was encouraged. He spoke eagerly. "I can vouch for the Christian life in their home. As for their form of worship—"

The look on the face of his minister stopped him short. It was grave, and so was his voice.

"It is about that I came to see you, Sandy Purbeck. We have heard that without consulting the elders you attended a religious meeting other than your own. The elders wish to question you on the subject."

At the time he went to the French church Sandy had felt compunction. Now a stubborn anger rose in his heart and mind. In silence he walked back to the Norman house with Mr. Lord. Mr. William Norman admitted them and shook his hand cordially.

"I have not seen you, except in court, since the mission disembarked. But I know you to be in good hands. Mr. Lenoir is one of the most highly respected men of the town."

That augured well from the mission's sponsor. But in the room to which Mr. Norman led him Elders Pratt and Sumner sat stiff and uncompromising. As Sandy stood before them, there flashed into his mind the ludicrous vision of a pair of thin sticks of legs kicking wildly before their owner fell into the skiff. Then, along with the picture, he heard the calm and unfrightened voice of the other churchman praying in time of their peril.

As the memory came and went, Mr. Norman was offering a comfortable chair. "Sit down, Mr. Purbeck," he said, and drew his own chair alongside.

Sandy sat, as stiff as his judges, holding his high-crowned hat upon his knees. Exactly a year before, he and Peregrine had faced a similar situation. Peregrine was not with him now to find the easy way out; and Sandy was in no mood to offer excuses.

Mr. Sumner cleared his throat. "Ampersand Purbeck, when we chose you for teacher of our children in a new land, we did so in the belief that you would hold faith with conscience."

Sandy bit his tongue in order to keep from asking, "With whose conscience?" His temper was always aroused when he was called Ampersand. In Dorchester no boy of his own age had dared utter the word after he had thrashed Warham Wales for doing it. But he could not thrash the elders. He gripped the hard brim of his hat, as if seeking to keep a grip on his anger.

"I have kept faith with my own conscience, Mr. Sumner. Can you ask any man to do more than that?"

Mr. Norman started: "That is what—"

But Mr. Pratt broke in.

"Dare you say you keep faith with the Independent Church when you attend a service in and consort with the congregation of an alien church—a church founded and maintained by the worldly and dissolute French?"

"The French Protestants, Mr. Pratt, are neither worldly nor dissolute."

He stumbled as he recalled Madame Lenoir's views about silk and the allurement of women. But he felt that in spite of her chatter she was honest and good, and he rushed on in his defense.

"The French Protestants, like ourselves, rebelled at empty ritual and power given dissolute men to use in the name of God."

"No other church is like ours. You must have seen that when you attended a foreign service. And, in the first place, you should not have attended."

"I attended in courtesy. Mr. Lenoir is my host, and I owe him something."

"Nothing to compare with what he and the whole colony owe us for bringing them the Independent Church."

Goaded too far, Sandy replied: "According to English colonists and the colony records, it was here before we came."

Mr. Sumner shot out of his chair like a marionette pulled by strings. Mr. Pratt folded both hands over the head of his cane and spoke grimly.

"Can you, as a schoolmaster, substantiate that statement, young Purbeck?"

Mr. Norman intervened. "It is true that Church of Englanders call all dissenting groups Independent."

"That," said Sandy, "is what I mean. I do not agree."

Mr. Pratt's voice was sharp and sarcastic. "For that concession, at least, I am grateful."

Sandy rose to his feet, looking from one to the other of the three. Elder Pratt's expression was grim, Elder Sumner's outraged; but Mr. Norman's face wore a look of distress and sympathy.

"All I can say, Elders, is that you must use your discretion in regard to keeping me as schoolmaster or getting another teacher for your children."

As he paused for breath, Mr. Norman exclaimed: "I implore you not to be hasty!"

"I am in no haste," said Sandy. "I shall await the decision."

"Their decision will be, I am sure, to ask you to keep the position. I have tried to explain to them that they are no longer in the Massachusetts Bay Colony."

"And I have explained to you, Mr. Norman," said Elder Pratt, "that our mission is bringing the true faith and way of life from that colony to a wild and godless land."

Sandy's hand was upon the door. He repeated: "I shall await your decision."

Then he said good-by and went out into the street.

THROUGH MUDDY, RUTTED lanes leading from Bay Street down to the docks, Sandy walked aimlessly for hours. But his thoughts were not aimless. The longer he reflected on the interview he had just concluded

with the churchmen, the more loudly his Puritan stead-
fastness told him to hold his own. No matter the cost,
he could not and would not go against his conscience.
He knew that if the same situation should arise again,
he would do and say the same.

Hunger reminded him of the midday meal. Mr.
Lenoir's sane quietness would be a help, but he could
not talk with an outsider about his own people. Besides,
it was Mr. Lenoir's innocent invitation which had caused
the trouble.

Innocent? Yes! He still swore to himself that he had
done nothing wrong. Looking back on the French service, his objections to it faded. It had been simple, like
his own, and free of bigotry. Bigotry? Could that word
which Puritans used against Roman Catholics and Church
of Englanders be applicable to Puritans themselves? No.
He must call a halt to any such thoughts. He would stop
thinking about it and go to dinner. Madame's incessant
chatter was, after all, harmless; and since the trial he had
seen Nicole only at meals. As he walked rapidly back
along the cobblestones, he felt himself hastening to a
refuge.

The winter days ran like bright wine, and his arm
healed rapidly. But the winter days came and went without any word from the elders. Mr. Lenoir informed him
that they had gone to New London to look over the land
of the Edisto.

"Mr. William Norman told me they would visit Landgrave Moreton. Both he and Governor Blake are anxious
for your mission to choose that site."

"Do you approve it?"

"For some reasons. It would help me to be within reach

of Monsieur Couturier and to get advice from him and his son. The young Couturier is said to be as good a sericulturist as his father."

The praise of Shannon pleased Sandy. "I've had no word of him. I hope he's getting along well at Harvard."

The waiting seemed long—and longer because he felt himself under a cloud. He consulted Mr. Lenoir about applying for work at the wharves.

"I am qualified as a clerk. And I am not willing to visit you longer without recompensing you."

"It is known in Charles Town that you will soon be leaving with the mission to settle inland. A man who is going to make his home here would be preferred to you. If you wish to recompense us, there is a spade in the garden. My daughter is working overtime at spring planting."

To his own surprise he enjoyed working in the green southern garden. The sun shone and the hours flew and Nicole laughed and sang at her easier share of the task. Toll arrived one afternoon and declared himself green with envy.

"As green as those leaves of lettuce. Purbeck, I'll swap you my trowel for your spade."

Sandy had no intention of making the trade. But neither did he intend to flatter and tease the girl as Toll continued to do. She was hard-working and she made a pleasant companion. She did not coquet with him as she did with the other man. He told himself he was glad of that. He was finding much good in her. But he still felt that she was silly and inconsistent to go to a public trial with anticipation of pleasure and then weep when she heard the pirates sentenced to hang.

156

That night drums beat again, this time through the city streets, and men ran from their houses to discover the reason. As they neared the public watchhouse, Sandy and Mr. Lenoir heard the news from others.

"The four buccaneers have made their escape from the dungeon!"

"The door is open and the man on guard gone with them!"

"That man should never have been on guard. Nobody knows where he came from, and he looks like a Spaniard."

"The prisoners probably killed him and threw him in the river. This is the work of men higher up—of merchants in our port who find it to their advantage to deal with the pirates."

Drums beat and the watchman yelled that every house in town must be searched. Militiamen did the task but found no trace of the fugitives. Toll gave them the details when he came by next day.

"The militia is searching the islands now. There are hide-outs for outlaws on these follies which border the harbor."

"Why are you not searching with them?" Nicole demanded pertly.

"Because I served my turn last time, you heartless wench! Do you wish to send me into danger?"

Sandy said: "Captain Coming stopped by and took my name today. I told him I did not yet know where I would settle, but that I expected to make my home in South Carolina."

Nicole was looking at him without words and without laughter. Toll nodded.

"The Assembly is passing an act to regulate the militia

and make it more efficient. The name of every man between sixteen and sixty is to be sent to the governor. It's a good thing. We should have organized defense against both pirates and Spaniards."

Nicole asked: "Do you think the pirates who escaped are really hiding on one of the island follies?"

"I don't know, but I think it would be well if Purbeck and I went across the river to investigate. I've been planning to take him on a hunt for game. Shall we bring you back doves or quail or snipe?"

"Take me with you! I love to ride in a boat, and I'd like to see you shoot."

Sandy could not help saying: "And you'd weep when we shot the birds."

She turned on him, her eyes flashing with anger. Then they changed to a look of reproach—misted with tears— and she turned her back and went into the house.

Sandy, wretched, called after her: "I apologize! I'm sorry!"

"Don't be," said Toll; "for she probably isn't by now. She changes from sunshine to storm, just like the Charles Town weather. Will next Saturday suit you for the hunt over the river?"

Sandy cleaned the bellmouth, wishing as he did so that he had a gun like Toll's. Toll had guided him to the gunsmith on Vendue Range, but the man had only new ones which he could not afford. He promised to notify Sandy as soon as he got his hands on a used one. Longing again for his father's Brown Bess, Sandy sat rubbing with buckskin on metal. He heard voices downstairs—growing louder—approaching—

As he went to his door and opened it a young man

leapt up the steps and seized Sandy in a bear hug and beat him on the back.

"So you're not only in my colony but living with my own people! Mr. Lenoir told me on the wharf—just now —as my ship was docked!"

Sandy put both hands on the other's thin shoulders and gazed, unable to believe his eyes. All he could say was: "Shannon! Shannon, I'm glad!"

"MY LUGGAGE HAS been taken to The Cup and the Cobblestone. It's a bad tavern but the best in town. You're going there with me now, to stay as long as I stay."

At the tavern in its crooked lane they talked for most of the night. Shannon recalled Mr. Lenoir as one of his father's friends.

"You'll get a good citizen if he settles among you. Silk culture is still an experiment in this colony, but if any man can succeed with it Mr. Lenoir will."

"He is completely absorbed in it. In the kitchen garden with the vegetables, he has rows of mulberry slips planted. I've been working there with his daughter."

"I'll wager you found it pleasant work—with his daughter. I saw her this evening for the first time, when I called at the house."

Sandy said stiffly: "I find any work for Mr. Lenoir pleasant. I am indebted to him."

Couturier laughed at him. "From what Madame Lenoir

159

told me, a number of people feel indebted to you. Has your arm healed completely?"

"It has," said Sandy crossly. "And I don't see how Madame could give you all that gossip in the minute before you ran upstairs."

"Madame Lenoir," Couturier told him, "is capable of giving the history of the New World in less time than it takes a man to run upstairs."

"Well, you've heard all about me. Are you on vacation or have you left Harvard?"

"Neither. I was booted out, as I told you I would be."

"What did you do? And why did you do it? If I were only able, I'd like nothing better than to go back to Cambridge and study for years."

"Well, I wouldn't. They're an ungrateful, narrow-minded crowd. I'm glad to get home again and see a girl like Nicole Lenoir and throw a leg across a horse and drink a cup of wine."

He held out the bottle to Sandy. "It's only a light Madeira."

The Puritan shook his head. "Go on telling me."

"Very well, then. Now that I'm back I'll have the country life I love. And if Monsieur Lenoir settles with you and raises silkworms, it will be a fine excuse for me to visit you—and see his daughter."

As Sandy stared at him, he added: "All sericulturists inspect each other's orchards and *magnaneries*, exchange silk seed and help each other."

"I asked you about Harvard. What did you do, Shannon, to get yourself expelled?"

"After you left I missed you—and I just couldn't get

that hussy of a barmaid out of my mind. She was the cause of my first offense."

"Do you mean Rosa Zuider?"

"I mean the cat-eyed slut who made the trouble in Dorchester. My one desire was to see her at the tail of a cart being whipped through the town. Having been raised on the very silly tradition that a gentleman doesn't beat a woman, I couldn't bring myself to take steps while I was sober. But one Saturday night when that barrier was down, I found myself telling the crowd that I knew a witch who had done terrible deeds. The next thing I knew we were down by the Frog Pond fighting the city patrol, then in the guardhouse and charged with half-drowning a barmaid."

Sandy wasted no sympathy upon Rosa Zuider. Besides, he knew that what Shannon had done had been done upon Ness's account.

"You say that was 'the first offense'? Were you not expelled at once?"

"Except for two things I would have been. It happened that the boys with me were sons of Boston councilmen and powerful families. Then the woman's reputation deprived her of all sympathy. She was ordered out of town, although not at the tail of a cart, and I was given solemn warning never again to disturb Puritan peace."

"A ducking stool is not for a witch but for a scolding wife. A witch is tried by ordeal: thrown into the water, in order to see whether she sinks or floats."

"We were in no condition to observe such fine distinctions. We just kept on ducking her and she kept on yelling until the soldiers arrived and arrested us."

"She deserved it," said Sandy. "I pretend no pity for her. But what did you do after that to disturb the peace?"

Couturier's tone was injured. "I acted according to Scripture and tried to help the poor."

"They could not expel you for helping the poor."

"But they did—for helping the widowed and fatherless. News came of two soldiers killed in *la petite guerre* on the border, and we heard that their families were destitute in Boston. So I suggested we get up a horse race and donate the proceeds to the widows and orphans."

"The proceeds?" asked Sandy.

"Yes—all the money won. Our committee went through the dormitories and persuaded students who could afford to bet to bet as heavily as they could in the good cause. They understood they were doing a thing both sporting and charitable. For if they lost they lost; while, if they won, Gideon Hill was to collect the winnings and turn them over to Widow Terry and Widow Cod."

"Was the race run?"

"You bet it was—on a holiday morning along the bank of the Charles. Two students from Virginia rode, and a chap from New York and I."

"Shannon, didn't you know that a Puritan college would certainly expel you for either horse racing or betting?"

"I suppose I should have known, but I really thought we were doing good. There was a board of inquiry, and Giddy Hill and I told them the truth. We wouldn't lie, and they turned our own words against us. They charged us with corrupting sons of godly fathers by enticing them with snares of the devil. But I'm glad to say that before we left Cambridge, Giddy and I collected nearly a hundred pounds and turned it over to the orphaned Cods and Terrys."

Sandy sat in silence, frowning slightly and thinking hard. He disapproved of both horse racing and betting. Yet, widows and orphans had received help from those evils. Was there a curse on such money? This careless and prodigal land to which he had come was different from New England. Here he found it harder to see life all in black and white. . . .

Even with Shannon, he did not care to spend the night at the tavern. The attic room at the Lenoirs' had become home to him. But Shannon had brought Ness back to him, along with the memories of New England. As he walked through the streets in the late hours, trying to avoid the watch, he was thinking that after all she might have been happy in Charles Town. But he was going inland—into a wilder country. And if the elders' verdict went against him, he would have no occupation and be in search of work. Suddenly he regretted his hasty words to them. They were his own people and he wished to live among them. If only Ness might be with him too. . . .

He opened and closed the Lenoir door quietly. And Ness's small ghost went with him up the stair of an alien house.

THEY WERE THREE instead of two for the Saturday hunt, since Shannon Couturier was included. Saxon Toll had a piragua in the creek which formed the southern boundary of the town.

"She's too light for open water, so we'll make for the inlet between Windmill and Cummings points."

A red-gold winter sun, looking as large as a cart wheel, came out of the ocean before them as they crossed the harbor. Toll seemed tireless, although the other two offered to paddle.

"Tide's with us until we get into the creek."

In the creek white heron fed in the draining mud upon small, luckless fiddler crabs which came out as the water receded. Upon every side was the marsh, shaded from dull gold to young green. Long, thin flights of pelican were etched on the pink-and-blue morning sky. From a wide salt lagoon between islands, hundreds of ducks rose with a whistle of wings. Couturier snatched at his gun, but it was wrapped against the dampness and he was too late for a shot. Sandy achieved one, but by the time he did the swift quarry was out of reach of a bellmouth.

They came ashore on the back beach of a wooded island which reminded Sandy of his landing at O'Sullivan's. It was a true folly, a tangle of trees and shrubs and vines and other foliage. Thickets of yaupon glittered with clotted berries which looked to be made of polished crimson glass. He could smell the sweet myrtle, crushed as they broke through it, and he recognized the smaller gray berries from which Madame Lenoir and Nicole molded candles. He saw everywhere feathery fronds of tamarisk, like those which had given him shelter when he waited in ambush. Vines of smilax, wild grape, chainey briar, jessamine, and honeysuckle twined themselves around his neck and tried to trip his feet. Toll answered their questions.

"This is the first island south of the harbor mouth, as

O'Sullivan's is the first island north. Nobody lives here, so it's even wilder. Pirates are known to come ashore upon it."

They encountered no pirates, and they came out at last in pineland upon a higher ridge of sand. Here great coveys of fat quail went up before them with a whirring sound which amounted to a roar. By midday each of the three had as many birds as he was able to carry. Couturier called a halt.

"Let's not be greedy. We'll sink your piragua if we have to take back any more."

They broke their way through more jungle out to the ocean beach. Down to the high-water mark its sand was whiter than any other beach Sandy had seen, and it was strewn with shells of all sizes and shapes: exquisitely intricate conches, fluted fans of dark purple and mauve which broke from their own weight, round sea biscuits from the size of a shilling to that of a saucer, fragile butterfly wings of pearl or pale pastels.

Standing upon a sand dune, Sandy looked out upon it. Beyond the beach was ocean, changing from sapphire blue to dark and deep green laced by long lines of foam.

Couturier said: "Look while you may. There's only ocean between you and Spain."

The words carried a sinister and omnipresent threat.

"Have the Dons ever made a landing here?"

"No," said Couturier. "Why should they? The island is deserted. When they come their objective is murder and plunder. Just about ten years ago they raided the country around my home. They never reached Silk Swamp, my father's plantation; but they killed a kinsman of Governor Moreton and stole his silver and his slaves."

Spaniards were upon Sandy's mind as they walked up the beach, built a driftwood fire and cooked a dozen of their birds. He had been amazed at their abundance.

"Are there deer on the island?"

"A small, stunted species," said Couturier, who appeared to know the country as well as Toll did. "At some time they swam the inlet to escape some danger, and years of inbreeding have caused them to deteriorate."

"A man could live here and get his food from the woods and the sea."

"Men do," said Toll. "This island was searched for the escaped buccaneers. If we walk farther north along the beach we can look across the harbor mouth and see O'Sullivan's watchtower."

Tall sand dunes marched north with them, first line of defense against the sea. Beyond them lay a valley of sand, with coarse low growth of grass and vines. Still beyond that, the jungle rose in a green rampart which appeared impenetrable to one who did not know its paths. Where the beach made a sharp curve to the left they looked across a wide salt creek upon what Toll informed them was known as Middle Bay Island. Behind the dunes was a sun-warmed hollow of sand, and all three were sleepy from their early rising.

Sandy, choosing his couch not far from the other two, suddenly caught sight of something fifty feet farther. He walked on through the deep sand and stood staring down at it. It was the remains of a campfire, sheltered by the dunes from the wind. Ashes mingled with sand and shells, pieces of half-burned wood lay around. Nearby was a forked stick cut to serve as a gun rest. Upending it, he saw it was made by a man of just his height.

For seconds he held it upright, and his eyes began to burn as he recalled the gun rests he and Peregrine had cut. Then he flung it from him and called his companions.

"Somebody's been camping here! It may be a trace of the pirates!"

Discovery of the dead fire on the island folly gave new life to the hunt for the four pirates. But Sandy had no part in that. Although his name had been set down on the rolls of the colony militia, subject to his remaining in South Carolina, he had not yet been called for duty or even assigned to a company.

In the week that followed, Couturier left for his plantation and Mr. Lord and the elders returned from the Edisto. The pastor found Sandy watering mulberry slips in the garden back of the Lenoir house.

"Our decision has been made. We will not go to New London. Our settlement will be made upon the Ashley River near Mr. Norman's estate."

Couturier's parting words had been in hope of having Sandy near him, and Sandy had cherished the same hope. His face reflected his disappointment.

"There are reasons," said Mr. Lord. "We will here be closer to Charles Town, yet be without reach of its ungodliness. Lord Ashley's river will afford us a highroad for trade with the seaport."

It was the river, after all, which had brought about the decision—a different river from the Frome or the Neponset, but a river to run by their homes and bear their boats upon errands.

Mr. Lord continued: "Mr. Norman has from the very first advised that we settle somewhere on the Ashley. The place he showed us is a bluff and has its advantages. His friend Mr. Stevens can at once secure us a tract of eighteen hundred acres."

Mr. Norman appeared to be the power behind proceedings. A silver lining to the cloud of Sandy's disappointment was the thought that Mr. Norman would exert that power in favor of permitting Mr. Lenoir to join them. Then he remembered that he himself was not sure of participation. His face darkened.

"Why are you telling me? I have not yet been notified as to whether or not I go with the mission as schoolmaster."

The minister looked his distress. "Surely you did not think. . . . There was never a question, except in your own mind."

Sandy struck while the iron was hot. "I must tell you that I favor allowing worthy settlers of other Protestant sects to settle among us at the spot you have chosen."

Mr. Lord refused to commit himself. "The subject has come up. It can be decided later." He looked beyond Sandy. "Good morning, Mistress Nicole. Do you work in the garden as well as in the house?"

Sandy turned to see her standing behind him. She wore wooden sabots and held a rake over her shoulder. He wondered how long she had stood there and how much she had heard. He felt that in justice he must answer the pastor.

"She works all day at indoor and outdoor tasks. You

168

will find the French Huguenots, when you know them, as sober and industrious as our own people."

Mr. Lord looked surprised and slightly offended. "Some may be as industrious, but hardly as sober. Hold yourself ready to leave early this next Sabbath for Mr. Norman's country place. He has invited me to preach in his house and the mission to attend."

As he departed Nicole laughed and tilted her already tip-tilted nose.

"Sober? Does he ever laugh—that old sober owl?"

"You need not laugh and call him names. He has the wisdom of the owl."

"That is a silly saying. I don't think the owl is wise. It is a stupid, clumsy bird which blunders around in the dark. There are people who blunder around that same way in the dark, and do not even see what is before their eyes."

"You are getting your metaphors mixed. Owls can see in the dark."

She attacked a plot of ground with the rake. "Do not use long words—like a schoolmaster."

"I *am* a schoolmaster," he told her, provoked. "That is my reason for coming south with the mission."

For minutes she did not answer. Her sleeves were rolled high on her slender, rounded arms. They were not white like the skin of other girls he had known. The sun had burned them to a pale brown, with a faint tinge of rose. Her thick hair fell forward and hid her face as she worked. Even in the long, full dress and the clumsy shoes, her every movement was supple and graceful. Suddenly she threw down the rake and turned and faced him.

"Do you mind when I tease you?"

"Yes," he said truthfully.

Her face sobered. "Then I ask your pardon. It is no more than I do to your friend Monsieur Couturier and to Saxon and other young men. But I shall try not to do it to you; for you—you are different."

He frowned at her. "How am I different?"

"I saw from the first that you were *un jeune homme très sérieux*. And besides—"

She moved a step toward him and shook the tangle of dark hair back from her face. "—Besides, I am grateful to you."

"Grateful for what?" he asked her.

She came still nearer, and her face glowed like a rose from her exercise. She stood close, with it tilted up and her big eyes fixed on his.

"I am grateful because you are trying to help my father. I heard you speak to the pastor as I came up behind you. I am grateful and wish to thank you—with all my heart, Sandy."

ALWAYS A RIVER, Sandy thought, as on that winter Sabbath he listened to Mr. Lord's sermon on the Ashley's bank. With a dull heartache he remembered the same man's sermon fourteen months gone by. Peregrine had then been there, holding the Brown Bess upright although he yawned; and Ness, her sweet face serious, had been in the congregation.

The year had dulled his heartache. He had taken up

life again, and he looked forward to making a new start in it. He had discovered a world beyond that of his Puritan birthplace, and he had intelligence to judge before condemning other men's ways. Stubbornly, he still compared all other girls to Ness. She never had teased as Nicole did; yet Nicole had promised to try—

He jerked his thoughts back to the sermon. The service, although in midwinter, was being held under the tent of a great live oak. Mr. Norman had invited them to make his country house their place of meeting, but the landowners of the neighborhood had attended in numbers too large to get inside. They weclomed the newcomers warmly, and invited them into their homes as guests for whatever time it would take to build the proposed village.

This first Independent service on the Ashley River was followed by the sacrament of the Lord's Supper, and then by a business meeting to elect the new deacons.

Events followed each other swiftly after that. The very next day Mr. Norman took the New Englanders to overlook and approve the chosen site.

Sandy found it wild and thickly wooded, but Mr. Norman assured him that it would be correspondingly fertile. A low bluff on the river afforded both an outlook against attack and a conspicuous location for the trading post. Sandy saw the town in his mind's eye. He pictured streets and dwellings and a small white meetinghouse. There would be little farms to supply fresh vegetables and grain, and a mill to grind by horsepower since there was no waterfall. Even in winter grass sprang green along the creekside, and with a little clearing those acres would serve as a common.

Although he would for personal reasons still have preferred the Edisto, he could see that this place had natural resources. As he looked at the straight-soaring long-leaf pines, he recalled that Shannon had said there was no lack of timber. There were tough black gums and swamp maples, enormous oaks and the native cedars whose wood resisted decay. Looking, he imagined them transformed into walls and floors and roofs.

Creeks and river, Mr. Norman said, were jumping with fish and the woods full of game. There ranged the same wild turkeys he had hunted with Peregrine. Deer were abundant, and also rabbits, squirrels, opossums, and raccoons. In the broomgrass and pine were the same quail he had just been shooting on the barrier island.

It was a land of plenty, a softer land than his own. Its winter was drawn in sepia rather than white and black. Yet his heart cried out for snow underfoot instead of the brown pine needles. When he gazed at the masses of evergreen which walled him on every side, his eyes stung for the dark jut of field stones on rocky hillsides and the pattern of naked boughs darkly delicate on gray sky.

He would not go back to that again, but he could go back to the seaport and the Huguenot family who had befriended him. He refused invitations of landowners nearby and returned to Charles Town for the short time intervening between choice of location and start of building. Other men were asking to join the settlement, and he felt he could tell Mr. Lenoir that his chances were good.

While he described it Nicole gazed at him across the table, and even the voluble Madame held her peace.

"I saw red mulberry trees growing wild, not far from the river."

The thin face of the Huguenot was alight with anticipation.

"If I have the choice, I shall choose land which does not lie on the river. Have you any idea of what size the lots will be?"

"Someone—I forget who—mentioned fifty acres."

"Fifty acres is quite enough to afford a generous orchard. My wife, my daughter and I are in your debt, monsieur."

Saxon Toll's arrival just then saved Sandy embarrassment.

"A secondhand gun was brought in while you were out of town. It's in good shape, and little over half price. I've argued the gunsmith into keeping it for your approval. Let's get down to Vendue Range before he closes his shop."

It seemed to Sandy a good omen. He would build his own house in the new town and have to kill game for his own table. With Toll he hurried through the twilit streets. As they entered the gunshop the smith turned to a tall cabinet.

"I got it at a bargain. The fellow seemed desperate. And I'm selling it for small profit."

Sandy took it in both hands. He knew it at once, but he moved nearer the door and gazed at it in the half-light. He could not speak, and the gunsmith thought his silence was faultfinding.

"It's a bargain," the smith said sharply. "I can sell it elsewhere. Saxon Toll asked me to keep it for you. He said he was sure—"

Sandy turned to face him. "I'll take it," was all he could say, while his fingers followed the pattern of the falcon carved in its stock.

Part Three

DORCHESTER THE THIRD

THE YOUNG SCHOOLMASTER lay full length upon the loamy, leaf-matted ground, with his Latin text propped against the root of a swamp cedar. Below him the river moved slowly around its curve under the bluff. Tide was full in the winter-brown marsh, and its movement was west and away from the sea. Although it had deepened and narrowed at this place—narrowed so that he could throw across it one of the stone arrowheads he found every day in the forest—the river did not hurry as New England rivers did. It moved upstream with a languorous glide, seeming to pause for obstacles like the bend of the farther bank or the uprooted cypress which clutched with thin arms to delay it. Over and through those waterlogged limbs it coiled with sinuous ease, leaving small arrowed ripples as only token of effort. It gave no sign of the strength below its surface of opaque glass, or the pull of hidden currents under that half-submerged tree. He knew, because he had dived at the spot a few days before when little Praise God Daken had fallen from the bluff. The current had carried both him and the child under the cypress trunk, twisting and tearing with a fury which surprised him and which had almost wrenched the child from his grasp.

Could he, he questioned bitterly, have saved another victim from another river, had he been in Dorchester instead of away at Cambridge? She had weighed hardly more than the child, and he was himself a powerful swimmer.

He put the thought away from him. It went compliantly, with the gentle compliance of her who inspired it. It was hard to picture her in this alien country, so different from the landscape of their New England birthplace. Her image seemed to pale against its vividness. She could not have met its hardships as Nicole Lenoir was doing.

Nicole and her mother had just arrived from Charles Town. Mr. Lenoir had come as soon as notified he might take up land, and Sandy Purbeck and Mr. O'Kelly and Willy had helped him to build his house and silk shed and transplant his mulberry trees. His forty-five acres were woodland, beyond the common, where Dorchester Creek went into Rose Creek swamp.

Sandy had thanked his stars for the opportunity to make return for the months spent in Charles Town. He and Mr. Norman had stood side by side in meeting to insist upon admitting the Huguenot. There was land enough for outsiders. Besides the Booshoo tract, an even larger adjoining tract had been secured from Mr. Rose and added to the township.

They had called it Dorchester for its parent villages: English Dorchester, on the Frome, and Dorchester, Massachusetts, on the Neponset. That was the name beloved,

178

and Dorchester on the Ashley was a Puritan town in a southern wilderness. Its building had gone forward with a Puritan orderliness which was alien to the almost savage beauty surrounding it. It sat, as demure and tidy as a coifed New England housewife, in its landscape of primeval forest and jungle and swamp.

But in spite of different locations there had always been a river, Sandy was thinking as he watched the Ashley's tide. He had drawn a lot fronting upon it, on the street called River Range, when the settlers had drawn their numbers from a hat. This street followed the Ashley northwest, from the parade ground near the creek mouth to Mr. Norman's property upstream by Stevens Bridge. Along it were twenty-six lots of fifty acres each. Back of them ran the Road Range, paralleling the River Range; and fronting on this second street were twenty-six lots of forty-five acres each.

The rest of the town had been laid off with the same New England precision. Upon the highest point of the bluff, commanding the river bend, Sandy Purbeck and other men had worked to throw up earthworks and ring them with palisades. The tribes of the Cusabo fishing confederacy had so far appeared friendly and eager to trade. But memory of the Pequots was still with the men from Massachusetts Bay. In case of attack they could place their women and children within the shelter and fire in defense from loopholes between the tall stakes.

Alongside of this crude fort, twenty acres had been cleared for a public square and parade ground. Twenty more, when cut free of brush, made a big tree-shaded park. Along the southeast boundary formed by Dorchester Creek, one hundred and fifteen small quarter-acre lots were subdivided for market stalls of the trading post. Already, bearded trappers were mooring their piraguas on cypress limbs and bringing bales up the river-bank. Occasionally a red man or squaw slipped from the woods like a shadow, anxious to exchange beads and baskets and other artifacts for the beef they loved better than any game.

Mr. O'Kelly was owner of the largest herd on the commons. With the aid of his oldest son, twelve-year-old Willy, he fed, milked, butchered and sold the meat of his cattle. His property, like that of the orchardist Lenoir, lay outside the actual town, beyond the commons and mill land.

Thinking about it, Sandy glanced up the bluff's slope to his own small house. It was box-shaped and not yet painted, but it was his home. When he cleared the acres around it, he would plant fruit and corn. Tied to a cypress root at the foot of the bank was the piragua Willy O'Kelly had helped him to make. For days their fire had smoldered in the half-log, hollowing it.

The house was his home and the town was his, and the dark, strange river too. It was moving upstream and past him with a luster like that of black glass. He had at first disliked it; but now its movements intrigued him: its drowsy tides and its life of fauna and flora which were new to him. He and Willy O'Kelly had paddled the dug-out upstream and under Stevens Bridge, between narrow-ing banks that trailed wild smilax and sultry-colored, trumpet-shaped bignonia. They had at last emerged upon a wide, shallow lake at the Percival plantation which was called The Ponds. They had journeyed downstream too, through marshes white-flowered with heron. That strange half-sea, half-land of the marsh kept time by the clock of the tides. When they were at full it disappeared, except for blade tips of green. When they withdrew, its mud sucked and plopped and from it came shy denizens: fiddler crabs and turtles, alligators and bull frogs, families of raccoons on the hunt for oysters.

It had surprised Sandy to learn that here—twenty miles from the ocean as the white heron flew, but almost thirty miles if you followed its winding channel—the river was subject to the tides, as they were subject to the moon. When the moon came out of the sea they foamed into the harbor and around the peninsula known as Oyster Point. How many hours later, he wondered now as he watched it, did that urge flow and check in that narrowing channel where it passed the Puritan village of Dorchester?

Into his thoughts obtruded the voice of Willy O'Kelly, bawling: "Schoolmaster! Master Purbeck! Are ye here?"

Without rising, Sandy called back: "Here—by the river."

The small, valiant Irishman came in sight around a corner of the house. He held a dirty fold of paper in his hand.

" 'Tis a letter brought by a trader come upstream from the seaport."

The letter was from Saxon Toll, whose enthusiasm outran his orthography. He told Sandy of daily work, of drilling with the militia, of a new acquaintance recently come to Charles Town.

His name is Hawke and he tells he's a clark,
but he's browne as a Injun from life in the sunne.
He is wishful to gette a gunne and has the golde
in his pocket, but he wod not goe as you did to
the gunsmith with mee.

Sandy was reading aloud, while Willy O'Kelly commented.

" 'Tis well ye got the Brown Bess when ye did, or he would have had it."

The boy had seen the gun in his house and had heard the tale of Sandy finding it in Charles Town. Sandy had told no more than that, for he was still troubled and puzzled. It must be, he assured himself, that it had been stolen by a Pequot who sold or traded it to a white man sailing south. Men adventuring into strange colonies usually provided themselves with guns. It must be that the adventurer had done that, and had been obliged to pawn it upon arrival. Sandy would have liked to know the truth of the matter; but even not knowing it, he was glad for his father's gun. And whatever he thought about it, he could not and would not think that anyone of the mission band was a thief.

He dropped his eyes again to the page and began to read aloud:

I'm coming to Dorchester when I can. I noe—

Willy was listening with both ears, but Sandy read the rest to himself. For Saxon Toll had written:

Nikkol likes you the best, but I don't yette give
up hope.

182

THE CHILDREN CAME early next morning by twos and threes into the school. First to arrive was Deacon White's daughter, and she was followed by six O'Kellys and two families of Sumner. These alone filled the small room; for Deacon Increase had taken his baptismal name in all seriousness. The other benches were crowded by young Normans and Stevens and Osgoods and Ways and Clarkes. As Sandy Purbeck rose from his chair to face them, he thanked providence that nimble Praise God and other urchins were still too young to attend.

Even these were far too many for one master, since they varied in age from seven to seventeen. Mr. Lord, in addition to his duties as pastor, was accustomed to supervise and to hold the classes in Latin and Sacred History; but the minister had been called away from the village this day.

The extra work his absence entailed could have come at no worse time for Sandy. Since the afternoon before he had been seized with depression, and he felt out of tune with a new land and new duties. Toll's letter had for some reason upset him. Surely a Pequot had stolen the gun. It was out of the question to suspect his fellow churchmen. And he had looked forward to Toll's visit. He had written and asked Toll to be his guest in the newly built house. But he had not dreamed that Toll really cared for Nicole Lenoir. The young mason had always teased her—treated her more in the fashion of a younger sister—and he had once spoken with undisguised longing of a girl in England who might yet come to him.

A whisper ran like a little breeze along the hard pine benches, and the schoolmaster frowned and tapped with his cane on his desk. Although it was midwinter the window behind him was open, and the warm, resinous scent of the pines came through it into the room. But he refused to enjoy it. His heart went back to New England with a sudden deep homesickness. The landscape there would be as chastely pale as Ness had been: white snow piled softly high with deep blue shadows in angles, and clean naked boughs, as uncompromising as geometric figures, drawn in black ink across a low, cloud-gray sky. . . .

Thankful White was standing up, with wrath on her face.

"Master Purbeck, Willy O'Kelly pulled my cap awry."

Sandy wondered wearily why she should make an issue of a prank which, once called to the master's notice, must be punished. But he called Willy O'Kelly to his desk and gave him a half-dozen sharp blows of the cane.

"Now go sit in the dunce corner with the dunce cap on your head."

The little Irishman grinned defiantly back, although he rubbed the seat of his trousers and a tear trickled down his snub, freckled nose.

"I took me lickin' for pullin' the hair of the lass, but I haven't acted the dunce, Master Purbeck."

Sandy would have liked to reply: Oh, yes, you did! You acted the dunce when you pulled her thin ginger-colored hair, instead of pulling the thick black curls of Joanna Stevens, who would only have stuck out her tongue at you instead of reporting you to me. But he realized with self-reproach that such was alien thought induced by an alien country and a warm piney breeze on the back of his neck. So he restrained himself and asked with perfect logic: "Did you really get enough pleasure from molesting Thankful to balance the caning I just gave you?"

"I did not," answered the Irish boy, his eyes on Thankful's prim mouth.

"Then you committed a stupidity, as well as an offense against the order of the school."

"I'm thinkin' I did," said O'Kelly; and he retired, still grinning, to the tall stool in the far corner.

Having worked off his irritation—and a little ashamed of himself—Sandy carried on the lessons for the day. When he dismissed school he locked the door and pocketed the key. Although the local Indians had so far made no hostile gesture, they picked up and carried away any object which caught their fancy.

Schoolmaster Purbeck passed his own house and walked on toward the trading post. Mr. Lenoir was expecting a batch of silk seed from France. Possibly it had come upriver with Saxon Toll's letter. To tell them of the letter would be a good excuse to go into the little house which he had helped build and which Madame and Nicole had already made homelike. Not that he needed an excuse. He was always welcomed there. Even though Nicole was coquetting with Toll and most probably going to marry him, Sandy was a family friend and could still visit and talk with her father.

The sky above was a cloudless blue, and against it swayed slowly the tall pine crests. The wind which moved in them made a sound like distant surf. Sandy's mind went back to the island where he had hunted with Toll and Couturier. He saw again the ashes of the campfire which must have been made by the pirate fugitives.

He passed the smithy, and the red glow of iron on the anvil brought him back to Dorchester-on-the-Ashley. Leaving the trading post on his right, he took the path through the commons. O'Kelly's cows gazed placidly upon him as they chewed, and he continued past the sprawling O'Kelly house. Only a hundred yards beyond, the Lenoir cottage faced the creek called Dorchester by the New Englanders and by the Indians Booshoo. The orchard lay behind it, on higher and drier land.

Sandy was walking the path between orderly rows of young mulberry trees when a slim figure in a green skirt flashed between them and cut him off. She threw her head back, and her black mane of hair tossed and her black eyes blazed at him.

"You beast," she cried, "how dare you whip Willy O'Kelly when he was only defending *you* from what that hateful girl said?"

S ANDY COUNTERED SHARPLY: "What did Willy tell you?"

"Nothing. He's no talebearer. I haven't even seen him since—since you beat him cruelly."

"I didn't beat him cruelly. And, if he didn't tell you, how do you know?"

"Thankful says you did. She was highly pleased."

So it had been Thankful. He might have known that

186

Willy would never have complained. Loyal Willy suffered in silence. But Nicole did not; her Latin temper flamed.

"She told me—at the trading post. I met her there a half hour ago. I was so angry I nearly threw the butter I carried right in her face."

That would have been calamity, Sandy realized, even in the midst of his own puzzled indignation. No quarrel between the two girls could have equaled the outrage of Madame Lenoir had ten pounds of freshly made butter at sixpence a pound been wasted.

"Willy pulled Thankful's hair and caused confusion in class. I had to punish him. I am the schoolmaster and responsible for order."

"You're the schoolmaster," she mimicked; "but you can't see—or rather hear—what goes on under your nose."

"Nothing else went on, that I saw or heard. What are you talking about?"

"About that girl. The reason Willy pulled her hair was that she was whispering gossip about you."

Sandy frowned at her, hardly believing his ears.

"What gossip could Thankful White whisper about me?"

Nicole tossed her head again, and her eyes shot sparks.

"You can ask Willy that. I'm not going to tell you."

She turned on her heel and started away—and then turned back again.

"And while you're asking, I hope you'll be just enough to beg his pardon for what you did to him."

He watched her green skirt disappear between the

sweet myrtles that hedged the house, but he did not follow her. He turned back to the O'Kellys' and found Willy cutting wood.

It was the village custom to lend a hand each to the other. So the schoolmaster doffed his jacket and picked up a second ax. The boy had greeted him cheerfully and gladly. For nearly an hour they chopped and split in a silence broken only by Willy's blackbird whistling. When the task was done and the logs piled higher than Sandy's head, he replaced the ax in the shed and dusted his hands together.

"Willy, I've heard more of what happened in class today. I'd like to talk with you about it."

Willy glanced toward the unrailed piazza of his house, where two of his small sisters played with a yellow dog.

"I got a bench down by the creek. I made it my own self. A man's got to get away from the womenfolks sometimes."

Sandy's heart responded to that, as he followed along the wet path. The boy had taken his licking and let the matter drop. Except for Thankful and Nicole it would have ended there, sparing Sandy damp shoes and a nagging worry of mind.

The bench was half of a split cypress log, fastened with rawhide thongs upon two cypress uprights. Whenever O'Kelly shot a deer he cured and used the hide. With eight mouths to feed, he was not accustomed to buy expensive hand-turned nails from the blacksmith.

The two had just seated themselves when the yellow dog loped up, showing its sharp white teeth in a grin of joy at finding its master.

Willy stooped as if to pick up a nonexistent stone.

"So ye've turned informer, have ye?" he accused his pet. "Ye'll lead the gurrls to me hidin' place, ye yellow traitor!"

At the awful accusation the animal turned tail and disappeared in the bushes more swiftly than it had come. Willy turned to Sandy.

"He'll not be comin' back. What was it ye were after askin' me, Master Purbeck?"

Sandy found himself stammering. It was difficult to explain. His dignity as a teacher did not allow him to ask a child who was his pupil to repeat gossip. Best, he decided, to blurt it right out.

"Nicole Lenoir says I was wrong to whip you this morning for pulling Thankful's hair because, Nicole says, Thankful said something about me."

"Something she'll not be sayin' again, lest I jerk her bald-headed," said Willy.

Sandy looked his astonishment. "But what have I done? What could she say?"

Willy was scowling at his bare, muddy feet, which he had stuck out straight before him.

"Ye've done nothin' ye should not do. Sure—as me father often says—every man has a right to his little affairs with the women."

"Affairs with women?" There was horror in Sandy's voice. "Do you understand what a dreadful thing you're saying, Willy?"

" 'Tis not what I'm sayin' but what Thankful said— and what caused me to jerk her hair."

"Did she really accuse me of—of having affairs?"

"She said if ye knew what was well for you you'd stop your dallyin' with a French hussy who'd no right in a Puritan settlement."

Sandy went icy with anger. "Was she talking about Nicole?"

"Who else?" inquired Willy. "They're the only French in the township." He added: "As we're the only Irish. May God help us!"

Sandy was too preoccupied with his own affairs to sympathize. He was wondering just what Thankful had said to Nicole. If her words had been the same that Willy had just repeated, he did not wonder that Nicole was angry. He not only valued his friendship with the Lenoir family, he was happier with them than with any other family in town. In spite of Nicole's teasing and the letter Saxon had written, he knew that Nicole looked upon him—Sandy—as only a friend. He had learned more about her during his long stay in her home. He had learned that her laughter was a challenge to hardship and hurt, and that laughing she accomplished harder tasks than did many women who worked with sour faces. He was not in love with her, or any other girl; but his friendship for her was deep enough to make him dread losing it.

What had the wretched ginger-haired little gossip said to her? Were others in Dorchester town criticizing him for his innocent visits to the Lenoirs?

He spoke resentfully. "I'm doing no dallying. I'm all alone—a bachelor. I need my friends—and I have a right to them."

Willy asked eagerly: "Do ye mean ye're not betrothed to be married?"

"Certainly not. What gave you that idea?"

" 'Twas Thankful said you were—in the class today."

"Thankful said I was betrothed?"

"Her words were that you were goin' to marry a Puritan lass in the Bay Colony."

Sandy choked with anger and pain. Could even the village gossips be cruel enough to refer to Ness and drag her into their scandals? Could they not let her rest in peace and let him try to forget?

But at least he would tell Willy. Willy was his friend and ally. He spoke slowly because of the catch in his throat.

"I was going to marry a Puritan lass. I loved her and I was betrothed to her. But she—she died—I mean she was killed, Willy. That is the reason I left home and came here with the mission."

The blue eyes in the upturned face darkened with sympathy.

"I'm sorry—for her and for you, Master Purbeck. And of one thing ye may be sure. I'll destroy Thankful entirely if she speaks the name of the lass."

"Don't do that, Willy," he implored. "I don't want to punish you."

Recalling Nicole's parting advice, he groped for words to ask pardon.

"I know you're my true friend, Willy. I thank you for taking my part. And I thank you for her—the girl. Her name was Gentleness Goodman."

The blue eyes went wider, and anger brightened them.

"That was not the name Thankful spoke. I might have known she was lyin'. She boasted you'd marry her cousin, who would come soon from the north. She said her cousin was comin' to live here at her home, and she said her cousin's name was Forbearance White."

A<small>FTER THAT CONVERSATION</small> with Willy on the bench, Sandy tried to dismiss the matter from his mind. Being a teacher, he had observed the attachment of younger girls to older ones. It was natural, he told himself, that Thankful—who had followed her cousin Forbearance foot to foot in Massachusetts—should admire the older girl and imagine romance for her. Gossip, however, was neither natural nor seemly. So, without calling names, he administered a sharp rebuke in class, threatening to send up to trial by the elders any pupil who offended again.

His principal fear was for Nicole Lenoir, the innocent sufferer. But Willy O'Kelly said: "Just you lave her to me."

Sandy did so; and when he next went to the Lenoir house, Nicole met him with welcome and a smile. She was gay and friendly again, with the Latin changefulness which he could not understand but which wove a spell for him. During the visit she mentioned that Willy had told her his schoolmaster was plagued by mendacious pupils. Anxious to avoid that subject, he said he had recently heard from Toll.

"I too had a letter from Saxon," she said, "and a letter from Mr. Hawke."

"This man Hawke I do not like," interpolated Madame Lenoir. "He writes my daughter but asks her to show the letter to no one. It is a mother's duty to read her daughter's letters from young men. Yet, when I read this one, there is no secret message in it."

Nicole's cheeks flamed scarlet and she tossed her dark hair back.

"Did I not tell you there was none? I told you you need not read it."

"And why was there none?" asked Madame, her hands upon her hips. "It is only nature for young men to confide love secrets to young girls. To me it seems there is something wrong with any young man who does not."

Sandy changed the subject again, for he himself had no love secrets with girls.

"I didn't meet Hawke, but Toll spoke of him in my letter."

"He came to Charles Town," Nicole volunteered, "before Maman and I left. He is a most agreeable young man. He said he was anxious to meet my papa."

Madame's voice was tart and her eyes were snapping.

"He was anxious to get the position your papa was vacating."

"But, Maman," Nicole pleaded, "Papa had vacated it. Will you blame a young man for trying to better himself and rise higher in the world?"

"He shall not rise in my husband's shoes," her mother answered her. "There are other positions. Why must he seize upon this one the moment my husband departs?"

"Saxon had told him that Papa was leaving. Mr. Hawke has education, and he loves ships and wishes to work at the wharves."

She must like him, Sandy thought, to plead his cause

so earnestly. But it was evident that Madame did not like him.

"Work?" she exclaimed scornfully. "I tell you I know human nature, and this young man is one of those who wants no honest work."

There was work aplenty in Dorchester, for the new town was growing. Midday at the trading post was a chorus of voices and of ringing metal from the blacksmith shop nearby. Traders who rode in left their nags to be shod while they bargained at the market stalls. While the farrier worked on draft animals from farms and coach and riding horses sent from plantations, the smith made or mended wheels, plowshares, axes, saws, and barrels for muskets.

Below the bluff waited in moored clusters the dugouts in which both white men and red men had brought hides, rare shells, game, oysters, and inferior pearls. In exchange they took away cloth of good Yankee weaving, meal and flour, stout leather shoes and other things made in the village. Through the open school door which he faced while he taught, Sandy often saw a Cusabo man or woman leading away along the road a cow or steer obtained by bartering.

Farther along that same road at the opposite end of the settlement stood the little White Meeting House, patterned after its parent churches in Massachusetts. Centering its four-sided peaked roof was the small tower for its drummer, and for a sentry to keep watch during service. Here was no need for watching, or for the guard service which Sandy and Peregrine had done in New England. But the church was the same, with lofty pulpit and high seats for deacons and elders in the front ranks of the congregation. Customs too were the same in regard to services. Upon the Sabbath Day and on Friday afternoons these took place in the meetinghouse. On Tuesday evenings men and women met in some private house for prayer. Upon Saturday afternoon the children and young people went to the church for religious instruction. Sabbath began at sundown of Saturday, as it had begun in other Dorchesters. Until sundown of Sunday, no man worked and no woman cooked or heated food.

But all six other days of the week were days of industry. In addition to their professions or trades, most men of the young town planted small farms. Their lots were generous enough to grow fruit, vegetables, and corn, and the soil was as fertile as Mr. Norman had promised. Apples did not thrive as they did in New England. Their fruit remained stunted and sour. But thrifty housewives learned to use in their place the native crabapples, persimmons, muscadine grapes, and small black cherries for preserving. They knew that in early summer they would be able to pick blackberries from vine and bush, huckleberries, blueberries, and a small wild strawberry. Haws of several varieties promised to ripen in autumn. Men transplanted to their orchards the Chickasaw plum which grew in thickets by roads and fields. At the post they were eager to trade for young peach and fig trees brought by the Indians.

At town meetings new problems arose each month for the councilors. Mr. Prior had applied for a license to open a tavern. He was a man of good repute, and a tavern would offer food and lodging for benighted travelers riding through the village. The idea was approved by tradesmen, but some of the stricter churchmen objected.

The whole life of the settlement, Sandy could see, was showing a similar clash of ideals and ideas. The older men and most of the women held to strict Puritanism. Even in small matters which did not suit climate or landscape, they insisted upon doing as they had done in New England. The younger men and the children were glad to fraternize with neighboring settlers who were Church of Englanders or who belonged to other Independent sects.

The Lenoirs and the O'Kellys were broad-minded enough to incur censure from the conservatives. Sandy, a friend of both families, attempted to defend them and thereby brought down on his own head the wrath of the elders. Matters came to a climax one day when two young Englishmen who worked at Saint Giles rode the long miles over Stevens Bridge to pay him a visit. They introduced themselves as friends of Shannon Couturier, and Sandy was pleased at the attention.

But Mr. Samuel Sumner, who lived on the River Range close by the parade ground, had rapped that night on Sandy's door. After inquiring who the strangers were and whence they came, he had shaken his head.

"My brother the deacon smelt wine on their breath when they asked him the way to your house. He told me too that their riding coats were gaudy and they wore lace at their throats and wrists."

A year before Sandy would have agreed unreservedly. Even now he frowned as he recalled ruffles and velvet coats of plum and maroon. He might have kept silent before the rebuke, but Mr. Sumner went on.

"Something should be done to stop the French girl wearing a green skirt. It is unwomanly. I am glad I voted against their settling here."

196

"And I am glad I voted for them," Sandy told him heatedly. "Mr. Lenoir has brought a fine industry to the township. As for his daughter, she's more womanly than any other girl I know. She works from dawn until dark helping her father and mother."

· Mr. Samuel Sumner had been both surprised and displeased at this defiance from the young schoolmaster. As he walked the short way home he was wondering whether the Reverend Joseph Lord had been wise in his choice of Ampersand Purbeck as an instructor of youth. He told himself that young Purbeck had changed. He no longer resembled the clerk who had worked in a trading post up north in the Bay Colony. He was now tanned by the sun almost to the shade of his light-brown hair, his broad shoulders had broadened, and he held himself so straight that he seemed to have grown inches taller.

SPRING CAME WITH a mist of dogwood in the lighter green of the forest. The slender limbs of the Judas trees were encrusted with rose-colored jewels. By creeks and pools, wild iris flickered like thin blue flame. Through miles of swamp where Sandy walked or canoed with Willy, atamasca lilies opened alabaster chalices upon a million fragile, naked stems.

But when the young mulberries leaf-budded, Willy was hired by Mr. Lenoir to help with their gathering every afternoon. For the same degree of spring temperature which uncurled the mulberry leaves was hatching the silk seed spread in trays on the shelves of the *magnanerie*.

Sandy, to whom sericulture was a new and interesting experience, went as often as he could to volunteer his assistance. It was needed; for in the long, shallow trays, tiny worms were emerging from their specklike eggs. At first they resembled bits of black thread no more than· a sixteenth of an inch in length. But as if anticipating their brief life span, they started at once the orgy of feeding which caused them to grow almost visibly and to mature in only forty-two days.

Upon that first afternoon Sandy overtook Willy rolling a wheelbarrow load of freshly cut mulberry leaves along the orchard path to the shed. Nicole was busy there, spreading yards of coarse netting over the hatching trays. While Willy went back for another load, Sandy helped the girl chop the leaves finely and scatter them over the netting.

"They will eat without ceasing for six days," Nicole informed him; "then they will fall asleep and lie dormant for twenty-four hours."

"Did you learn all this about them in France?"

"No, I was only a baby then."

Her eyes clouded, as they had done once before when she spoke of her childhood. Then she lifted her head and flung her hair back like a battle flag.

"Papa taught me—gave me books to read—so I could help him with them. He will take care of them at night and I shall do so in the day."

"You mean they eat all night long?"

"Night and day for six weeks—stopping only to sleep on the sixth, twelfth, eighteenth, and twenty-sixth days. If they all hatch together now, they will all sleep at the same time. If they hatch at different times they will sleep on different days, and the ones awake are likely to smother some of the sleepers."

As he watched, Sandy thought it rather sad that each cocoon should be for its spinner a shroud and for some human being so many yards of raw silk.

Nicole saw his expression and laughed.

"Do not blame them for gobbling their food. They do their share of work in the world, and they do it swiftly. At every feeding they will eat more and more, because they are growing so fast. If you come tomorrow you'll see how much larger they are."

When he arrived the next day, Sandy saw that what Nicole had predicted was true. They had almost doubled their size overnight, and Willy O'Kelly was bringing his wheelbarrow loads of leaves at a run now.

"Papa and I gather the leaves in the morning," Nicole told him. "But Papa must sleep in the afternoon in order to stay up all night."

"I'm going to help Willy gather. But I wanted your father to read this letter I've just received from Shannon Couturier. He's coming—to stay with me, and to give his help and advice to Mr. Lenoir."

She cried out: "How good of him! Papa wrote to ask him questions. There is some difference, you see, between the silk culture in France and in Carolina."

Sandy went on to the orchard, thinking about Couturier. He was glad of any excuse that brought his friend to him. And—to his own surprise—he realized he was enjoying his small part in sericulture. For the rest of the afternoon he helped Willy gather and carry the leaves, stopping at the *magnanerie* to give a hand with the feeding. Not until darkness had fallen and Mr. Lenoir came out did he start on the mile-long walk back to his house.

And as he walked he was wondering whether Nicole Lenoir preferred the stranger Hawke to honest Saxon Toll. As for Saxon's words about her liking him—Sandy —best, he knew them to be only Saxon's nonsense. If Saxon really loved her, he hoped the mason would get her. Any man who got her for wife would be a fortunate man. Even to a task as difficult and unpleasant as the raising of silkworms she brought laughter and cheer. . . .

It came over him suddenly that he no longer mistrusted laughter. The French girl and the small Irish boy laughed together as they worked—and he, a grown man and a Puritan, was glad to work and to laugh with them. Nicole had said in Charles Town that laughter could heal hurt hearts. He wondered where she had learned that, young as she was. But wherever she learned it and whomsoever she married, he knew as he walked through the southern night that laughter was her gift to him.

He set a foot on his low doorstep and pushed open his unlocked door. And as he did so he froze where he stood.

Someone, he sensed, was in the room which he was entering. Sound or vibration told him that he was not alone.

Could Shannon Couturier have already arrived, upon the heels of his letter? He had not noticed the letter's date, and carriage of mail was uncertain in this new land. It would be like Shannon to play a trick on him.

But not a trick of this kind. This would be unlike Shannon. Some prescience of trouble told him it was not Shannon Couturier.

He stepped in and reached for the candle which stood

200

on a table close by, struck light and touched the wick and raised it above his head.

From the shadows a figure moved toward him: a man with a thin, hard face burned brown as an Indian's and looking ten years older than—than when last—

Sandy could neither move nor speak. He felt his heart thud and his throat contract. But the other man laughed, low and amusedly.

"Don't you really know me?" he asked, voice bitter in spite of his laughter. "Or does this mean that you intend to disown your prodigal brother?"

Sandy managed to ask hoarsely: "Peregrine—is it really you?"

Again he heard that low laugh, half sneering and half amused.

"It's I—though not so solid of flesh as I used to be. I've already helped myself to bread and cheese. I was starving."

"You know you're welcome. But how—"

There was real anger in the voice that interrupted.

"Don't start questioning and preaching at me! I'm still hungry for hot food. I've eaten nothing but wild fruit all the way up this dark river. And when I got here I was afraid to build a fire and cook, for fear some prying friend might see the smoke and come in."

"I left the house early, and from school I went directly —somewhere else. But, Peregrine, I have the right to ask you: *What of Ness?*"

The thin face twisted in agony beneath its stubble of beard. Peregrine Purbeck sank into a chair. Then he raised his head, and his voice was again defiant.

"What could I do? You know I can't swim."

Sandy spoke slowly. "I know you're afraid of water."

"I am. I don't deny it. But I got there too late. I saw her starting out from the bank and I shouted, but she ran faster."

Sandy told himself: She would have, because she would have thought someone was trying to take the cat and torture or kill it. He managed to ask: "Then you saw—saw her break through the ice?"

"Yes, I did. But I swear to you that I was too far to help her. I ran—but I couldn't get there in time. It was bright starlight. I saw her trying to cross—and I heard the ice cracking—and then—and then—she wasn't there any more."

With a sound like a sob he dropped his face in his hands. Sandy set the candle down and went toward him. As Peregrine looked up, his brother saw more closely the change in his features. They were ravaged and gaunt and hard, and his expression was bitter.

"Understand—I'm not blaming you for not going in when you couldn't swim. But why didn't you come back and tell me? Why did you let me think all this time you had died trying to save her?"

"Because I wanted to be what you thought me: a hero. Because I wasn't willing to say: I let your girl drown because I'm a coward—because I was afraid to dive in a frozen river."

"You've just said that you were too far—you got there too late—and couldn't."

202

"That's true! I swear it on all I ever held holy! But I couldn't face you. I wanted you—and the others—to—to think—"

That, Sandy told himself, has been the trouble all along. It will always be the trouble for those who wish others to think them more than they really are.

It was hard for him to reason clearly. His grief for Ness had all returned. But he tried to be fair and to ask himself whose fault lay at the root of Peregrine's transgressions. Might it not be the fault of those who encouraged egotism by flattering ready speech and charm such as Peregrine possessed? Might they not by doing so force weakness to pretend strength?

Peregrine cried: "For God's sake give me hot food! I'm starving!"

In the kitchen Sandy turned suddenly from his cooking.

"Why did you come to South Carolina if you're hiding from Dorchester people?"

"I came to Charles Town months ago. I've wanted to live there ever since your friend Couturier told me of it."

"If you got there months ago, I must have still been in the seaport."

"You were—and so were the others of Mr. Lord's mission. That's why I had to clear out."

His voice grew resentful again.

"From what I heard when the mission was planned, its members were going to settle inland—to break new ground and live in the wilderness. But when I came ashore in Charles Town and talked with a Frenchman who worked at the wharf, I found out that all of you were staying in Charles Town."

"Only until we found a site upon which to settle. I was a guest at Mr. Lenoir's house. It must have been he you saw at the wharf. Mr. Lenoir spoke of two young men. . . ."

"Did he? He also spoke of you—said you were staying with him. Until then I had not guessed you had left Massachusetts."

Sandy had not until then realized that Peregrine could not have known. Fleeing from recognition, he had arrived at Charles Town to find not only the mission but his own brother there. What could he have done? Peregrine answered the thought.

"There was another chap with me. He had no more desire to be recognized than I had. So all we could do was sell our few possessions and cross to some damned sea island and hide out until the mission left Charles Town."

Sandy thought of a dead fire on a beach. A light was breaking upon his mind as he set the cooked food on table. Peregrine looked at the ham and fried eggs and the familiar mush.

"So they eat samp here too? Well, I'm glad to get anything."

"They call it hominy here," Sandy told him shortly.

He watched his brother wolf the food.

"How did you get here?"

"Upriver in a kind of canoe called piragua. The fellow who came with me dropped off at Lord Ashley's warehouses."

"At Saint Giles? Does he work there?"

"No—not exactly. But in his work he needs to know when the merchantmen for East India are clearing."

"You came the rest of the way alone?"

"Yes, and the tides betrayed me. In this crooked, narrow channel they do not ebb and flow at the same hours they do in harbor."

"I know," said Sandy. "More than once they've left me high on a mudbank."

"That's what happened to me. I'd tied up for a short nap. When I woke I was fast aground."

And afraid to get out and drag your boat into the water, thought Sandy. His heart still beat hard and his mind was confused. He was grateful, he told himself, that Peregrine was alive. But Peregrine alive disposed of Peregrine bravely dead—and brought back all the agony which time had somewhat dulled.

Peregrine rose to his feet and yawned, well fed and full of assurance.

"I hope you've a good, soft bed for me. I'm bone-weary, dear brother."

"I've a bed for you. It's all ready for Shannon Couturier, who may get here any day."

Something like a spark of alarm flickered in the hazel eyes.

"He mustn't see me, or know I've been here. I must leave before daybreak."

Sandy asked the question he had wished from the first to ask.

"Peregrine, why did you come?"

Peregrine laughed tauntingly and lifted his eyes to where the Brown Bess rested between the prongs of two stag frontlets nailed on the wall.

"To get my gun, little brother—the gun you snatched under my nose when I had to pawn it upon my arrival in Charles Town."

205

Such anger swept over Sandy that his nails dug deep in his palms. Then he unclenched his fists slowly, and he tried to speak calmly.

"You'll never get it. It's mine. You sold it—our father's musket—and I bought it. And I'm going to keep it."

Peregrine shrugged his shoulders. "I feared you might feel that way."

"You should have known—and saved yourself a journey, if that's the only reason you came."

"I wanted to see you, of course. And there's a girl I know who's living here. But I hardly expected to see her, since I'm keeping out of sight. That is, unless she happened to come to your house."

"Girls don't come to my house. Who is this girl?"

"Her name's Nicole Lenoir, and I knew that you knew her."

He added quickly: "But she mustn't find out I'm your brother."

Sandy was so taken aback he could hardly ask his questions.

"Nicole Lenoir? How did you meet her? And who does she think you are?"

"I was introduced to her—correctly, I assure you—by our mutual friend, Saxon Toll. He's recruiting for the militia, and he nabbed me and took my name."

"How, then, can he and Nicole help knowing you are a Purbeck?"

Peregrine smiled. "I did not sign as Purbeck."

"Do you mean you joined the militia under a false name?"

206

"I didn't join; I was impressed. And as a matter of fact, the name I gave wasn't false."

"Then what was it?"

Sandy's eyes followed his brother's glance to the Brown Bess hung on the wall. As he stared at the falcon carved in its stock, the truth came suddenly to him.

"You're Hawke—the man who can clerk—who got the position Mr. Lenoir used to have?"

"Why not? I'm a good clerk. And a peregrine falcon's a hawk, isn't it?"

Sandy knew it to be true, but he knew it was an evasion—the kind of evasion Peregrine had practiced all his life. Also, he disliked the idea of using a false name, although his brother's reason for doing so seemed innocent. . . .

He said slowly: "I heard of Hawke from Saxon and the Lenoirs; but I didn't—I couldn't—guess it was you."

"How else did you imagine the Brown Bess got to Charles Town?"

"I thought some white man had traded it from the Pequot who stole it."

He stopped suddenly.

"Peregrine—you took it from our house then?"

"Certainly I took it. It was mine—and so was a share of clothing to keep me from freezing."

Sandy was staring wordlessly. Peregrine's voice rose in anger.

"I knew you'd get all the rest, which was more than your share. I had a right to what I took. It was only part of my half."

"It was yours. If you'd come openly, I'd have given it to you."

"I wasn't appearing openly. You know why I couldn't. You know the sentence I'd have got if I'd been taken and tried and the old Tompson hag had witnessed against me."

It was best, Sandy realized, that there had been no trial. Punishment would have been severe; so many people would have been involved; Ness's name would have been brought in, her memory desecrated. . . .

"How did you get away?" he asked. "And how did you manage to live?"

"There were some trappers passing through on their way down from the northeast. They were bound for trading posts in the Connecticut valley. I worked there for a while; and there I met a fellow who was trying to make his way to New York."

"Overland? In winter? It would have been shorter and safer to return to Boston and go by sea."

"This fellow had reasons, as I had, for not being seen in the Bay Colony. Traders go overland if their parties are large enough to be safe from the Indians. We found such a party, and they were glad for two more men with guns."

"How long did you stay in New York?"

"Only as long as I had to. I recalled what your Huguenot friend had told me about Charles Town. I knew I'd be safe in the South—and in a warmer climate."

The cold had been bitter even in their small house in Dorchester. His brother must have suffered. Sandy felt his heart soften.

"I'm glad you've a good position in the seaport. I'll be able to see you, since I go down river sometimes."

"Be careful when you do that you don't give me away.

As for the position, I shan't slave all my life as a clerk. There are quicker and easier ways for a man to get rich there."

"I suppose there are," Sandy agreed.

He was thinking a little wistfully that Peregrine would push forward and grasp opportunities for success. Mrs. Lenoir had spoken of the rice industry. Its exports were the life of the new colony. Shipyards, he had heard, were building along the rivers, where the great live oaks he had seen could be cut and transmuted into beams and strakes. Even the produce from inland—hides and tar and silk and indigo—would have to go out by the wharves and on the sailing ships.

"I suppose there are ways to rise in your work, and I hope you prosper," he said.

"To rise in my work?" asked Peregrine.

For seconds he looked really puzzled, then he threw back his head and laughed.

"I see what you mean, and I didn't mean that—although it's my work that'll give me the chance. But I've just a few hours to sleep."

He moved toward the door, then turned.

"Have I what I came to get: your promise to keep my secret?"

"You have. I'm no more anxious for people to know than you are. It would stir up old sadness, and embarrass us both."

"I thought you'd see it that way. You'll not even tell Couturier—or Toll—or Nicole Lenoir?"

Sandy flushed, and his hands again clenched themselves.

"Not if you keep away from Nicole. If you go near

her, I'll not only tell, I'll give you such a thrashing you'll wish you'd never seen her."

Peregrine appeared amused rather than resentful.

"Toll said she liked you."

"She doesn't like me. That is, she likes me only as a friend. But she's too good for you. She's a wonderful girl. I'll not let you amuse yourself, while you're masquerading, by pretending to make love to her."

"How do you know I'm pretending? I might be in love with her. I had pleasant visits with her, after you and her father had left."

"You're in love with nobody but yourself. And you wouldn't have had those visits with her if I'd been there."

Peregrine whistled softly.

"I thought the southern climate was supposed to soften a man. It's hardened you—and matured you—and I like you the better for it."

"It isn't the climate," said Sandy. "That's your bed in the corner. Good night. And keep away from Nicole."

Peregrine laughed. "You overestimate me. But I must live up to my name. A peregrine falcon, you know, swoops down upon its prey."

His eyes went to the Brown Bess and his hand to his pocket.

"I'll pay you double what you paid the gunsmith."

Sandy exclaimed at sight of the opened purse: "That's Spanish gold! Where did you get it?"

"Not for my weekly wages at the wharf, brother Sandy. Are you naïve enough to think that Spanish doubloons are not changing hands every day in Charles Town?"

Sandy had seen a few of them. "I suppose they do. Some were found on the pirates captured while I was there."

It made him think of the sea island.

"We found their dead campfire—Saxon Toll and Couturier and I—hunting on the folly."

"I know you did. I was watching you from a yaupon thicket. But no pirate made that fire. I made it myself."

"So that's the island where you camped! I never guessed. . . ."

"Not even when you picked up the forked limb I cut for a gun rest? I saw you measuring it against your shoulder. You and I are the same height. We always used the same gun rest when we hunted together."

Nostalgia swept over Sandy for the old times when an older brother had taught him woodcraft. But Peregrine was now hunting in far and perilous places. Yet perhaps he—Sandy—even now could help his brother. . . .

Then the thought struck him and he cried: "But you didn't have the Brown Bess! You'd sold it in Charles Town. Why did you cut a rest?"

"I had it when I first arrived—and first went to the folly."

"When you first went? Then you mean—"

Peregrine said impatiently: "I made some money on a deal when I first arrived. And I kept going back and forth to Charles Town. But there were lean times between work, and in one of those I had to sell the gun."

His eyes fell before Sandy's and he added crossly: "What does the time matter? I'm so tired I don't know what I'm saying. Good night!"

SPRING BROUGHT NO apple blossoms to the banks of the Ashley. The shadbush and yellow jessamine followed in bright processional the dogwood and Judas and the wild swamp lilies.

Something about the shadbush—dainty and delicate—always carried Sandy's thoughts back to Ness. It stood shyly but breath-takingly white, just as a Puritan maid might stand in tangled alien woods. It seemed to him to deserve a name of more beauty and romance. But old trappers told him how that name had been won. According to them, it never failed to burst into bloom just when the shad began to come upriver from sea. As soon as they saw its first flower, Indians and white men got their nets and lines, certain that the great fish were running in the Ashley.

Nothing about the jessamine was prim or shy. It wove from tree to tree arcades of cloth-of-gold. It was the guidon of southern spring, blowing in brilliant tendriled grace. It laced the boughs of the cypresses above Sandy's moored canoe, and every lightest breeze launched on the river tide below a fleet of tiny gilded petals.

Madame Lenoir had made a skirt of the same golden hue for Nicole. It was her best; she wore the old green when she worked at the silk shed. Sandy and Couturier, invited to supper, found her in a white blouse and the jessamine skirt. Sandy admired silently, but Shannon Couturier spoke aloud.

"Someday you'll be wearing your own silk. You must be sure to have it dyed gold—gold for the princess who'll grace it."

She shook her dark head and her voice was wistful. "Silk is for the rich only. I would like to wear it, but I must help my father harvest and sell every yard."

Shannon Couturier was helping too, in a way Sandy could not, for he had with his father reared and harvested since his childhood. Every day, while Sandy set off for school, he went to the Lenoir *magnanerie* to give them advice and assistance. Sandy found him still there in the afternoon. Before his eyes the strange crop was running its cycle. The silkworms had now passed their twelfth day, the second day of their sleep. Except for belated brothers who crawled over them in frantic haste for food, they lay as if in a trance. Their skins were discolored and splitting, to allow for shedding when they awoke, and except he was told to the contrary Sandy would have thought them dead.

Couturier, however, examined them with a sericulturist's eye. He pronounced their color healthy and their size satisfactory. He discarded only a few, injured by their trampling comrades. He congratulated Mr. Lenoir.

"You'll have a fine crop, I believe. I wish I could stay here longer and see you through the eighteenth-day sleep period."

As they walked home Sandy asked him: "Why can't you stay?"

"I'm on a week's leave from my militia company. I got a lieutenant's commission when I came home last winter."

"What's the militia doing? Is there Indian trouble?"

"No. If there was you'd be called too, with the companies inland. We're having trouble along the coast, trouble with the buccaneers."

"Have they made an attack, or tried to land any-where?"

"No; but they've sent threats and demands into Charles Town and Port Royal. And the supplies they're demanding are getting out to them. A lot of drugs recently disappeared from a water-front warehouse."

"How could that occur? They couldn't sail in and take the supplies."

"They couldn't—but they have friends ashore. It seems incredible, but there are men in the colony vile enough to do these services for pirates."

Sandy recalled the escape of the prisoners from Charles Town. It could not have been effected without the connivance of someone outside. In fact the sentry's body, with his head beaten in, had finally washed up on a river beach. Someone had released the four villains, and someone had hidden and fed them after release. But they had not had a penny in their tattered clothing to pay. He reminded Couturier of that.

"That mattered nothing," the Carolinian told him. "The captain and crew of their ship would have paid handsomely for their return. And the reason for that is no love or brotherhood. The captain and each man of the crew knew that he might in turn be the next one captured and so was making sure that his mates would ransom him."

"Wouldn't the citizens helping them be severely punished if they were caught?"

"They'd be hanged—as they should be. Several have been already. But greed for gold makes other adventurers take the chance."

They sat together on Sandy's low steps on this last

afternoon of his friend's visit. And they smoked together the long clay pipes, one of which Couturier had brought to Sandy.

"The Cusabos make them," he said, "and the smoke keeps away the mosquitoes."

"I'm sorry you're going," said Sandy. "I'll be lonely without you."

The sun had set, and with twilight came a little breeze from the woods. It was more a stir of air than a breeze, as millions and millions of tiny leaves sighed with relief at the coming night and cooled with evaporation. No matter how hot had been the day, Sandy noticed, this surcease came always with the forest twilight.

And with it came the wood thrushes, calling like bells in the dusk.

Shannon Couturier blew smoke, threw back his head and listened.

"Had you noticed? The hermit thrush has a note like the voice of Nicole Lenoir."

"I hadn't noticed, but—but her voice is sweet."

"Sweet as a thrush," the Huguenot said.

He waited a moment, then added: "You've no need to be lonely with a girl like her nearby."

AFTER COUTURIER'S DEPARTURE Sandy was still needed to cope with the amazingly swift growth of the silkworms. They ate more and more as they came to their full size. But the stripped mulberry trees continued putting out leaves, and Willy and Sandy continued to wheel them in barrowloads.

Upon the eighteenth and twenty-sixth days, the now full-grown caterpillars again lay in sleep as deep as death. Awakening from each of these twenty-four-hour rest periods, they struggled free of their outgrown skins and began to feed again.

When the six weeks' cycle came to an end, the silk-worms ready to weave cocoons raised themselves on the lower part of their body and swayed to and fro. Nicole, who had been warned by Couturier they would do so when they were ready to spin, shrieked in excitement.

"Stay with them, Sandy!" she begged. "Will you watch them while I go call Papa? He told me to call him when they began to do this."

When she returned with her father, Sandy went out with Mr. Lenoir to cut branches of oak for the cocoon nests. These branches were about eighteen inches in length, with smaller lateral twigs growing from that stem. Mr. Lenoir fastened them upright on the shed's shelves. Anxious to spin, the swaying worms at once found them and crawled upward, seeking location for their cocoons. From now on the watch had to be constant, for they frequently chose the same place and tangled their skeins. When that occurred Nicole seemed the only one able to separate them without breaking a fragile thread.

When Sandy came back the next afternoon, the oak twigs seemed overnight to have blossomed with spectral flowers. In the first stages of spinning he could see a worm within its still semitransparent casket moving to a ceaseless rhythm, while building that coffin thicker and thicker. The wheelbarrow loads of mulberry leaves which had for weeks been rolling from orchard to rearing shed were, by some alchemy impossible to man, being transmuted into the silk man coveted.

He knew that for most of the spinners the cocoon would be a coffin. Only the few selected for parents of next year's crop would be permitted to emerge alive. These—carefully chosen for size, shape, color, and other excellence—would be left to cut their way out, leaving in the cocoon a hole which destroyed its value. Of these the females would, after mating, be enclosed in small bags and there left to lay their eggs and die. At this stage the male moths were quickly killed.

Meanwhile, the crop of commercial cocoons was being gathered with care from the oak twigs by Nicole's clever and gently moving hands. Side by side she laid them in the perforated trays prepared by her father over hot-water containers. Mr. Lenoir had already built his fires beneath, and through the trays he drove steam long enough to suffocate the chrysalis in each cocoon without damaging the silk of its container.

As Sandy walked homeward in the late afternoon, he felt a pang of regret that he would no longer be needed at the Lenoir orchard. He realized that for the last six weeks he had looked forward all morning, during the arduous routine of teaching and keeping order, to an afternoon filled with work and interest and friendship. He would miss the brightness of a green skirt at the shed and of a jessamine-yellow one when he was asked to the house. He had been so completely immersed for the short, busy time of the silk culture that he had wasted no time in worry about Thankful's mischievous gossip or about the sudden reappearance of Peregrine.

He had heard no more of either affair. He could only

surmise that Peregrine still worked at the harbor wharf, and that the companion who had come south with him transacted whatever business he had at Lord Ashley's warehouses.

Dorchester was slowing its pace as the spring passed and the summer came. Even the stubborn endurance of the Puritan code was not proof against South Carolina heat. Some of the colonists from the north already regretted their pilgrimage and spoke of ways and means to return to their former home. Of these the Daken family were most anxious to leave. Trouble had pursued them from their first arrival. Mrs. Daken was too frail for a frontier life. The children fell in the river or wandered off in the forest, or developed painful sores from an insect which old settlers called a "chigger." Mr. Daken was offering to trade his house and lot for smaller property in Massachusetts. He was waiting eagerly for the next shipload of Puritans, hoping to sell to or exchange with one of them.

For, upon the other hand, others were still coming; and the majority at Dorchester-on-the-Ashley were full of enthusiasm at the success of their mission. The little White Meeting House was the only church within reach, and consequently it had a large congregation. Mr. Pratt had sailed back to Boston and brought his wife and children south on the return trip, along with several other families. Sandy knew that even now another shipload was on its way from New England.

His thoughts again turned northward as he pictured it. . . .

The ice would by now have melted from the ponds and the Neponset. The turning wheel of the water mill would be throwing silver spray. Was Calicot still tending it? Was his rowboat tied by the weir? Had the first windflower opened yet in the pale green woods?

It was a landscape of pastels, compared to this vivid south. His thoughts of it were tender, as were his thoughts of Ness. Would he do better to go back—as the Dakens were going?

And as he thought it came to him in sudden revelation that, tender as his feelings were, he did not wish to go back. The hardships he had experienced in this new colony had helped turn his mind outward and keep him from brooding upon past tragedy. He had cared for Ness and expected to spend his life with her; but no man could or should spend his life with a ghost. In this land of hardship he would build himself a new life—a life of reality. He had already laid its foundations, not only by raising a house but by making new friends. He would secure it even more by putting a fence around his lot—a stout rail fence to keep out his neighbors' cows—and setting an orchard of wild plums, crabapples, and black cherries. For a shilling a week, Willy O'Kelly would help to cut and plant the palings. Perhaps, when he gathered his fruit, Mrs. Lenoir and Nicole would make jellies and jams of it on share. His bachelor housekeeping afforded little more than bread and cheese and potatoes and meat. The idea of sweets made him hungry, and it would be an excuse to work again with Nicole. . . .

Before going into his small house he walked his property line, with an eye to what he planned to do. After dark had fallen he worked with pencil and paper by the light of a candle late into the night. These southern colonial houses had wide piazzas. There was no reason why he could not build one with his own hands—with his own hands and the help of Willy's hands—onto the front and overlooking the river. And he would plant jessamine vines at its foundation—vines which would blossom in spring with enchanting fragrance and with the color of Nicole Lenoir's skirt. . . .

His plans and his figuring engrossed him so long that he fell asleep in his chair while the candle guttered and died in its myrtle wax.

SANDY WAS AWAKENED next morning by the first drumbeat rolling along the river from the White Meeting House. Astounded not to find himself in bed, he looked around the dining room—at the table littered with dead candle and scribbled pages. As realization came he jerked himself to his feet, stiff from sleeping in a chair, and hurried to his bedroom to throw on his Sunday clothes. To be late to divine service was a serious offense, and more so if committed by one who was expected to set an example to youth.

In the few minutes he took to dress he was calculating how long it would take him to reach lot number nine, upon which the church stood. It was nearly two miles from the lower end of the village, but he had little more than half that distance to go. Jerking his arms through the sleeves of his lighter-weight jacket and slapping his hat on his head, he started out as fast as dignity permitted. He knew that it would cause gossip if the schoolmaster were to be seen running on the Sabbath Day.

He was a hundred yards from his objective when Willy O'Kelly overtook him. The boy was traveling so fast that his bare feet paddled dust from the road, but he was troubled less for himself than for the object of his admiration.

"When a man stays out late by night," Willy commented breathlessly, "he will oversleep the next day."

"How do you know I overslept?" Sandy asked him.

"By the whiskers on your face and by the way ye're trottin'."

Even more embarrassed by that, Sandy felt impelled to explain.

"I did oversleep. But I wasn't out late last night. I was in my house, making plans and writing."

Willy's tone was suspicious. "I could have sworn 'twas yourself goin' to the Lenoir house after I was in me bed."

"It wasn't. I left there in late afternoon and didn't go back. And if you were in bed, how do you know someone went there?"

"Ye know the big brush pile me father an' me left out there to dry for the burnin'?"

"Yes—on the path between your house and Mr. Lenoir's."

"I was just settlin' to sleep when somebody fell fair into it. Whoever he was he was comin' fast, for he hit it with a crash."

"I know the brush pile. I would have gone around it."

But he was wondering who it could have been.

"How do you know this man went on and into the Lenoir house?"

"For the reason I saw him meself when I jumped up and ran to the window. He was gettin' out of the brush pile then, and I just got a sight of his back. The night was dark as Cromwell's heart, but I watched him move

221

like a shadow on and up to Mr. Lenoir's door. Mr. Lenoir opened it, with a candle in his hand. But I never yet saw the other's face, for his back was still to me."

He added: " 'Twas something about the way he moved made me think 'twas yourself."

Who could it have been? Sandy asked himself. So far as he knew, none of the few young men in Dorchester was accustomed to visit Nicole. Whoever he was, it served him right that he fell in the brush pile. And it was possible, of course, that he had business with Mr. Lenoir.

But now, a short way ahead of them, Sandy saw the last group of men entering the church door. From the small square drummer's tower on its roof came the final crescendo of Faithful Wainwright's drum.

Willy O'Kelly raised a hand, half in threat and half in obscene gesture.

"Do ye not wait for the two of us," he yelled to his friend on the churchtop, "I'll lick the daylight out of ye soon as the Sabbath is over!"

Master Purbeck, however, was doing no waiting. The road was clear before him, and he sprinted for the closing door. With Willy O'Kelly at his side he barely made it, under the disapproving glare of the two elders on duty.

Service in that first White Meeting House on the Ashley was as reminiscent of services in New England as was the small wooden structure of its parent church. It stood about a quarter mile down river from Stevens Bridge, and in it the Reverend Joseph Lord preached as fervently as he had lectured in Dorchester, Massachusetts. Behind the elders who faced him from raised front pews, sat a congregation including Lenoirs and O'Kellys.

Sandy could see the three Huguenots seated halfway up the aisle. Being French, they were dressed for public appearance in well-cut but unrelieved black. Nicole's hair, drawn into her bonnet, fell behind it down her back and was no less dark than her clothes. He made up his mind to speak to them and wish them good day after service. He could not ask the question, but they might volunteer who was the visitor Willy O'Kelly had seen.

So, when the worshipers were dismissed, he stood waiting outside.

Nearby, the southern river ran as softly as Spenser's Thames. Above its shallows the May flies danced their brief, ecstatic day. Blue jays screamed, and cardinals flashed their crimson wings through the gray moss. A mockingbird sang on the drum tower which the Wainwright boy had quitted.

As the Lenoirs came down the steps Sandy moved toward them. And just then he felt a hand on his shoulder.

Deacon White faced him when he turned.

"I wish to speak to you, Purbeck."

Sandy's eyes were on the Lenoirs. Nicole gave him a swift glance and a smile. But the deacon drew him aside, and Thankful went with them. Her ginger-colored hair was braided so tightly that it stretched and narrowed her small eyes. Her hands were clasped around a large prayer book.

"It is your turn," said Deacon White, "to meet and welcome this shipload of our people now on their way."

Thought of a trip to Charles Town was not unwelcome to Sandy. He would see Saxon Toll—and Peregrine. He knew that Mr. White was in charge of a committee for welcoming and bringing the new settlers upriver. But, meanwhile, Nicole was moving away with her father and mother.

The deacon gave him instructions in long and tiresome detail. The mockingbird sang louder, as if to drown people's voices. Thankful continued to watch him between slitted green eyes.

When the old man finally released him, the Lenoirs were out of sight and the dusty Broad Path was empty.

SCHOOL WAS JUST now disbanding for the summer, so Sandy knew himself free to make the journey. For the next few days he busied himself with preparations. Then, as he sat alone in his house after nightfall, a knock sounded upon the door he had closed against mosquitoes. Outside stood Willy O'Kelly, with him the yellow dog which grinned as widely as he did.

"From the highroad I seen a light in your kitchen an' knowed ye was home."

"*Saw* a light and *knew* I was home."

But he was glad to see the boy.

"Come in Willy, and bring Hero—with all his fleas."

" 'Tis not the fleas I'm a-fearin'," said Willy O'Kelly. He stooped as he spoke and with a hand crushed from the animal's back a mass of mosquitoes, then propelled it into the house and slammed the door.

" 'Tis nature for a dog to have fleas," he instructed his teacher; "but 'tis not right for him to serve as horse for the schemin' skeeters. They wait outside the door, and then they ride into the house upon his back. But these plottin' divils have had their last ride!"

224

He wiped his fingers on the seat of his breeches, sat in a hide-bottom homemade chair and told Sandy all the news.

"The Dakens are sailin' from Charles Town upon the ship ye will meet."

Sandy was surprised. "I knew they had arranged to go, but I didn't know they were going so soon."

" 'Twas not arranged for a cooter to bite the finger off Praise God—him yellin' his head off too, and his mother swearin' she would leave the wilderness on the next ship come in."

Sandy visioned some strange new form of animal life. "What is a *cooter*, Willy?"

" 'Tis but the name Elder Pratt's slave calls a terrapin. You know how the beast hides in his shell?"

"I know."

"Praise God was pokin' this one to make him stick out his head or his tail, not knowin' which end was which. 'Twas the head he stuck out, and took Praise God by the finger. The way Praise God and his mother roared, ye must have heard them a mile down River Range."

He paused and looked inquiry, but Sandy shook his head.

"All the village comes runnin', and the black woman Sheba says the crayture will not turn loose till the sun sets or the thunder rolls."

"Surely that cannot be true. What time of day was it?"

" 'Twas early this mornin' and no cloud in the sky. Elder Pratt and Pastor Lord say such talk is witchcraft, but Missis Daken, she roars: 'Get Faithful Wainwright and his drum! 'Twill take more brains than a terrapin has to tell his noise from thunder.' "

"Did they really get young Wainwright?"

"He comes a-runnin', an' he beats loud as he can by the ear of the beast."

"Did that make it let go?"

" 'Tis a thing will never be known; for all the time Mr. Daken is pullin' on the terrapin whilst Missis Daken is pullin' on Praise God. Me father tells them 'twill do more good to beat on the terrapin than to beat on the drum. Just then Missis Daken an' Praise God falls over backward, leavin' the crayture with the end of Praise God's finger still in his beak."

"No wonder the Dakens wish to leave. Everything seems to happen to them."

" 'Tis nothin' alongside that which befell me father."

Sandy was interested. "What befell him, Willy?"

"A fortnight gone by he lost a cow. But he says no word about it and he lays a trap for the thief. He sets me to hide on the common each night from dark until midnight. At midnight he slips in the thicket an' sends me home to bed. Last night he sees a Injun swimmin' down Dorchester Creek."

"Was it a Cusabo?"

"One Injun," said Willy, "is same as another to me. This one crawls up the bank and goes with no noise where the herd is asleep. He looks them over careful, while me father looks over him. When he has picked the one he will take, he throws a stick at it. 'Tis a young heifer, an' she gets up without a bellow out of her. Me father keeps on watchin' while the Injun drives her down to the creek. 'Tis low tide, an' the red divil knows that when the river runs in 'twill destroy all footprints of himself and the beast. What he does not know is that

226

me father is close behind him and about to destroy *him*."

"Your father caught him?"

"Cotched—caught him, he did—before he could reach Mr. Eagle's land. Me father took him from behind and held him down in the water."

Sandy knew the strength of the powerful Irishman.

"When he has half drowned him, he pulls him up on the bank and gives him the beatin' of his life in order to revive him."

Sandy shook his head. The Cusabos were gentle but proud. Such incidents were like flint struck around gunpowder.

"If your father had waited, the law would have punished the thief."

" 'Tis not in me father's nature to wait. Himself does the punishin'. When he lets go of the Injun he slips like an eel in the forest. But this mornin' at daybreak me da is awakened by a thump on the door. He gets up and opens it—and a arrow is stuck in the wood."

Sandy said worriedly: "That's a threat of revenge."

"Me da is knowin' it well enough. He says, 'To hell with the heathen!' An' he leaves the arrow a-stickin' there for all to see. Will ye come by in the mornin' an' look at it, Master Purbeck?"

Sandy agreed to do so; but he did not share Willy's pride in his father's victory. As he looked at the arrow next morning—driven deep into a panel of pine—he reflected that this was the first serious breach between an Indian and a Dorchester man. It was done and could not be remedied, but he regretted it. So did Mr. Daken, whom he found at the meat stall.

"I'm grateful to be leaving! Indians—terrapin—"

"O'Kelly beat the Indian, and your boy poked the terrapin."

"It's a man-eating beast, and I thank God to be going. We're to use the long canoe on the voyage down river. We'll need it to carry ten people and luggage."

Sandy knew that the long canoe—a cypress dugout twenty-four feet long—could carry sixteen and that at least four men were needed to paddle. It was difficult to guide at narrow turns of the river.

"Your family and I make only six. You and I could paddle a smaller boat."

Mr. Daken shook his head.

"There will be ten of us. Young Bacon and the Stevens lad are going to help us paddle. And Mrs. Lenoir and her daughter are going to visit in Charles Town."

S ANDY'S SPIRITS ROSE as he heard. It is no more than my duty, he told himself, to go at once to the Lenoirs and offer my services.

Bound on that pleasant duty, he passed Willy's brush pile and walked the orchard path to the Huguenot house. Mrs. Lenoir received him.

"Nicole is making the butter. She is a dutiful child to Monsieur Lenoir and me. Be seated, monsieur the school-master, for I wish to talk to you."

Sandy smiled as he thought to himself that her wording was accurate. Mrs. Lenoir talked *to* rather than *with* her friends. Before he could even inquire, she explained the trip to Charles Town.

"In France my husband was learning to dye his own

silk thread. It is his hope to do that here; for there are advantages in thread dyeing rather than piece dyeing."

Sandy managed to put in: "I thought silk was always piece dyed."

"By no means. Monsieur intends to thread dye his. For that purpose he has kept back one tenth of his crop of cocoons, and Nicole has already unreeled them on spindles."

Sandy recalled Nicole's hands moving deftly among the fairy spinners. Her strong, slender fingers had been sure and gentle. He would have liked to watch her unwinding the gleaming gossamer of the cocoons.

"Before we left the seaport this matter of dyeing was mentioned in the presence of a young man who came to the house. He is not a young man whom I like—*pas un jeune homme sérieux*—but he remembered what was said. Only a few nights ago he came to tell my husband that a ship had brought a supply of new silk dyes to Charles Town."

The man who fell in the brush pile! Sandy told himself. That explanation brought him a sense of relief. The man Willy saw had come on business with a message to Mr. Lenoir. He had not been a friend of Nicole's—a friend close enough to be admitted by her father at a late hour of the night.

"My husband desires to go at once," Madame was continuing; "but he refuses to leave two women alone in the wilderness. Since the cow must be milked and the orchard worked the three of us cannot go. By good fortune, Nicole knows as much of the dyes as Monsieur does. She cannot, of course, go without a chaperone. So she and I will make the voyage—under your protection."

"I'll do all I can," Sandy promised, "to make it as comfortable as such a trip can be made for you and your daughter."

"I thank you, monsieur. For I ask your protection not only upon the voyage but while in the seaport. But—"

As Sandy tried to speak his surprise, she raised a hand.

"Of that I shall tell you presently. What I must tell you now is a thing you have a right to know. You are now too close a friend to the family Lenoir to be kept ignorant of the fact that Nicole is *not* our daughter."

He could only stare in amazement. The devotion of the three Lenoirs to each other was a thing he had admired. Nicole resembled neither of them. Monsieur was small and spare, Madame short and plump, and they both had blue eyes and brown hair. The girl was medium tall and gypsy dark.

"We had no children," Madame said. "It was a grief to us both. With other Huguenots, we escaped from France to Holland. But there were some who did not escape, and Nicole's parents were among those. They were shot down by Royalist troops when almost at the border."

Horror was in Sandy's heart and in his voice.

"Was Nicole with them? How old was she—old enough to know—?"

"She was five years old. She saw it all—and she realized."

"How did she get to you? I've been told that Huguenot children too young to be killed were placed in convents."

"They are, and she would have been—except for a kindly guardsman. There are kind hearts, monsieur, in every religion and every land. This Royalist guardsman took her from the arms of her dead father and handed her across the barrier to my husband. 'I have a small one of her age,' he said; 'and I know that this one will die if sent back to Paris through the ice and snow.' "

"I didn't guess," said Sandy. "She—Nicole—who loves laughter—"

"Ah! But the reason she loves laughter is that she has bought it dearly, monsieur. Do we not treasure those things for which we have paid in pain and blood? When my husband took her from the hands of the guardsman, her little cloak was wet with the blood of her murdered father to whom she had been clinging. We had to teach her to laugh again—*la pauvre petite!*"

Sandy was silent, seeing the girl in a completely different light. He had thought her frivolous and gay, compared to his stern upbringing. Now he saw that laughter had been her weapon against remembered pain. There was nothing she could do—the five-year-old, the poor little one—except cease repining for what could not be helped and try to repay the foster parents who had welcomed her. How gallantly she had done that was now brought home to him.

Madame said: "I feel that you, our friend, should know it, monsieur. My husband and I could not love her more had she been born our daughter. Her welfare— and her future—are close to my heart. It is why I ask your protection for her in Charles Town and on the journey."

"I'll do anything I can," Sandy told her—and meant it. "But why should you—and she—need protection in Charles Town?"

"Because," said Madame, "there is in Charles Town a man whom I dislike and distrust. He brought my husband a message last week only in order to see Nicole. I, as her mother, must choose for her, when she marries, a man to protect her. This man seeks her out not to protect but destroy her. She is young and does not see it, but I see clearly that this man's nature as well as his name is *Hawke*."

T HE PRACTICAL FRENCHWOMAN had put into words Sandy's own estimate of his brother. Now he knew that Peregrine had no more idea of keeping away from Nicole than he had had of keeping away from Rosa Zuider. By that first breach of faith he had destroyed not his guilty partner but an innocent girl. Sandy, as he reminded himself, swore silently that—by any means in his power—he would keep Peregrine from hurting Nicole.

No longer should Peregrine work on his sympathy and brotherly affection. Never again would he trust his brother. In spite of the tragedy in New England, that visit from Peregrine had softened Sandy's heart and made him believe that Peregrine had learned a lesson from it and was trying to do the best he could. Although Willy had said that the way the man moved reminded him of his schoolmaster, Sandy had not guessed that Peregrine would dare return and betray him so soon.

He sat with clenched fists, so angry that he almost burst out with the story and gave away the secret which he too wished to keep. What would Madame Lenoir think of him if she learned that Hawke, of whom she disapproved, was Sandy's brother and Sandy was hiding that fact?

More than ever, he wanted now to keep the friendship of the Lenoirs. They had been his first friends in the new colony. He had liked Mr. Lenoir at once but about the women had reserved his judgment. He had thought Madame a chatterbox and Nicole inclined to light-minded laughter. Now he knew her laughter was a shield against sorrow. She had suffered even more, and at a far earlier age, than he had suffered. It brought a feeling of fellowship to his regard for her. He had subconsciously, he now realized, fought against that growing regard, feeling that he was replacing Ness with a frivolous French girl. Now he knew that, unless she had strength of mind and heart, Nicole could not have risen above the terror Madame described.

Nicole had not come in from the butter pantry, and he had not met her again until they embarked in the long canoe before dawn two days later.

In the gray light he could see her seated up in the bow with an arm around Praise God Daken. The little boy twisted like an eel, leaning over the gunwale to dip his hands in the water; but her reactions were as quick as his and she kept him from falling overboard.

Until noon the four men drove the dugout downstream, resting their paddles briefly to drift with the outgoing tide. They were well below Lord Ashley's barony when they made the midday stop for dinner. A small promontory on the left bank invited, and the dugout was moored to a stout limb of live oak leaning from it.

While Mrs. Daken attended to her unruly children,

Mrs. Lenoir and Nicole spread a cloth on the ground and laid out the food from baskets. The women had baked for days and it was plentiful. Well fed, Sandy rose and waited until Nicole had repacked what remained. Then he approached her, shy but determined to make his amends.

"I've found a path, and I want a short walk after sitting so long. Will you come with me, Nicole?"

She smiled and nodded. The path led up and along the bank, twisting its way around trees and breaking directly through low brush. Sandy walked ahead, holding boughs aside for the girl. When they had gone a hundred yards from the others he turned to face her.

"Your mother—Mrs. Lenoir—told me about you, and I want—"

"It is no secret," she broke in quickly. "And I love Monsieur and Madame like a real father and mother."

His tongue was not facile with compliments, but he felt he owed her the truth.

"I—I didn't know, Nicole—and I ask your pardon."

"For what do I owe you pardon?" she demanded.

There was color in her cheeks, and she had removed the kerchief that bound her hair for the voyage. Its darkness framed her face, and to Sandy's eyes her face was as lovely as a red rose. He stepped toward her and took her hand.

"Because I thought you frivolous. I ask your pardon, and I now know better, Nicole."

She pulled her hand away.

"Then you *should* ask it! How dare you think that of me?"

234

His earnestness was so great that he took her coquetry for rebuff.

"Nicole," he pleaded, "how could I know? You teased both me and Saxon Toll. Then your mother told me about Per—I mean about the man called Hawke."

"I did no more than tease the three of you. What harm is there in a little teasing?"

He stammered: "I—I don't know. But it made me feel you cared for one of them."

"I am affianced to no one. So I hurt no one by teasing."

"Yes, you do," Sandy told her. "You hurt me, Nicole."

It was her turn to stammer. Her cheeks flushed a deeper red.

"How—how can I? What do you mean, Sandy?"

"I mean I care—I—I love you, Nicole. But I was afraid to tell you so. I thought you found me dull—and you loved somebody else."

She was looking at him with her dark eyes soft. "But now—you are not afraid?"

"No, I'm no longer afraid. I've learned to understand. I've learned that you are strong and good—and that you've suffered as I have."

Her eyes asked him, and he told her briefly of Ness. Compassion saddened her mobile face and her voice was tender.

"It is my turn to ask pardon for thinking you stern and gloomy when you first came to my father's house."

"But you understand now?" he begged. "And you feel that the sorrow we have both experienced draws us closer together?"

She nodded slowly and gravely.

"I now know you had a reason. And—"

She paused and her eyes grew anxious and her voice was anxious too when she spoke.

"I think I understand now of whom that horrid red-haired girl named Thankful was speaking."

"It must have been Ness," he told her, forgetting all else in his relief and his hope. "There was no other girl than Ness until I found you, Nicole."

This time he moved even nearer, and he caught both of her hands.

"Can you care anything for me? Will you marry me, Nicole?"

She did not draw away, and she whispered: "I—I— But I can marry only the man my father and mother approve."

He thought even more highly of her for upholding the French convention. Also, it flashed into his mind that he was her father's friend and that her mother trusted him enough to ask his protection from another man.

So he was happy and confident as he drew her close and bent his head. But before he could touch her lips, an expression of such terror flashed over her face that he drew away.

She was staring over his shoulder at something behind him. As he wheeled he saw, no more than ten feet away, four Cusabo Indians in full war regalia.

Tₕₑ FOUR BROWN figures stood utterly still. Motionless and expressionless, they gazed at the white man.

With his right arm already around her, Sandy drew

Nicole close to his side, and he felt her trembling as he did so.

He had no gun. The one musket brought by the party had, he recalled, been left in the moored dugout. There was a hunting knife in his belt, but he dared not touch it. He knew that any sudden or threatening movement was likely to precipitate trouble. If Nicole screamed . . . or tried to run. . . .

The Indians wore the Cusabo dress: a loincloth padded with gray moss, a gray feather stuck through a black topknot. They were painted with yellow and black and carried war hatchets with tassels of the same colors. They were four to one white man, and there might be fifty more hiding in the woods from which they had come.

Sandy knew that such an encounter with Pequots would have meant massacre. He had heard that the Cusabos were not warlike. Curiosity, he hoped, might be their motivation. Or they might have something they wished to trade. But for trading they came singly, or often brought their squaws. In any event, he knew, he must not show alarm. So he looked back at them and tried to speak slowly and calmly.

"Why do you come? What do you want?"

No change of expression crossed any one of the four faces. But there was threat in the voice that replied.

"Come find white man beat my brother—try drown my brother Booshoo Creek."

Sandy had feared that O'Kelly's temper would bring trouble upon them. It was evident that the Cusabos did not wish to attack Dorchester but were demanding some reparation.

"I am not the white man who beat your brother."

The small black eyes observed him for a full sixty

237

seconds, during which he felt Nicole shivering more violently and felt his own skin beginning to crawl.

"Brother say white man big—not young. You young—not big—but you white man."

It was no more than natural that they should hold all white men responsible, Sandy felt. O'Kelly must of course be shielded from bodily harm, but he should be made to pay to keep the township from trouble. However, Sandy's most immediate urge was to get the girl and himself safe from this dilemma. She was acting bravely and sensibly, but he knew she was terrified.

"I'm a white man, but I've never hurt one of your people. I'm sorry that O'—that a white man from my village hurt your brother. But your brother stole his cow."

"Brother no steal cow. Brother go for buy cow. White man beat him so bad he maybe die."

Sandy was horrified. He could only hope that the account of the beating was as far from truth as was the account of the cow.

The speaker suggested: "White man beat my brother maybe try go way in canoe and not pay my brother."

He took a step forward. "Me go look."

Sandy thought fast. It might be the best solution. None of the men in the party were old or very large. If he objected to the interview, the Indians would conclude that he was trying to hide the guilty man. The mention of pay had brought an immense relief to his mind. It was better that O'Kelly be made by the town councilmen to pay than that the town should be in danger of revenge. But Sandy dreaded bringing the war party without warning on his friends. Mrs. Daken would certainly scream and shriek, and Praise God was capable of attacking them singlehanded.

He raised a hand, and the warrior stopped.

"Let the girl—the woman—go and tell them you come only to talk, so the other women will not be afraid. I will stay here with you, and we will follow her at once."

The guttural voice was again threatening.

"They not try go off in canoe without pay."

Sandy loosed his arm from around Nicole.

"Tell them to be calm and talk sensibly. Tell them that, unless they do—"

She clutched him desperately.

"Sandy—I can't! I won't leave you—alone—with *them!*"

He gripped her shoulders and held her off, speaking sternly.

"You can do what will help the others—and help me. *Go!*"

Nicole looked up into his face; then pulled herself free and went. She did not run, he was glad to observe. She walked swiftly, but with dignity and without looking back.

As she disappeared he folded his arms and fixed his gaze on the eagle feather in the Indian spokesman's hair. No more than two minutes afterward the man grunted: "We go now."

There was no use, Sandy knew, to protest. So he turned and preceded them, as slowly as he dared, along the path Nicole had taken.

She had reached the others and given her message. As he caught sight of them he saw they were self-possessed but alert. Young Bacon and young Stevens had waded into the river and stood each with a hand on the gunwale of the boat, ready to snatch up the musket if it came to a fight. Mrs. Daken was leaning against a tree trunk, her baby in her arms and speechless terror on her face. Her unengaged arm encircled another child. Her husband stood beside her, gripping her shoulder with one hand and with the other restraining Praise God. Nicole was close by her mother. Her eyes, huge and dark in her pale face, met Sandy's eyes with joy at his reappearance. Madame Lenoir sat on a tree root and continued unconcernedly to nibble a chicken wing.

"*Voilà*," she said to Sandy, indicating the basket of food. "If we give them something to eat we show our friendliness. Good cooking softens the hearts of men— no matter what their color."

Whether or not the Indians understood her words, their eyes resembling small black stones had fastened upon the food. Sandy recalled their passion for the white man's viands, and he blessed the quick-witted Frenchwoman. As he lifted the basket and turned with it, the nearest Cusabo almost snatched it from him. All four then squatted around it, tearing at chicken and beef bones with their teeth and fingers, pushing whole biscuits into their mouths, lapping like dogs at almost-empty pie pans.

There would be no afternoon meal for the voyagers, Sandy reflected. The Daken youngsters would probably howl with hunger. But it was better that they arrive unharmed and howling than that the whole party be murdered on the way.

He watched the Cusabo spokesman explore the gutted basket and then rise to his feet and look carefully around.

His gaze passed Mr. Daken and the women and children and fixed itself on the two youths knee-deep by the canoe. Sandy spoke quickly.

"They are young boys. You can see they are not old and not big."

The Cusabos were gentle Indians, and these four were softened by food. The man agreed in a tone more kindly than that in which he had last spoken.

"They young boy. They not big. They not beat my brother. Man beat my brother still in your village."

Sandy kept silence. He had made up his mind not to give O'Kelly away unless it came to the point of saving innocent lives.

The Cusabo asked: "You go back village?"

"Yes. I go Charles Town now, then go back Booshoo."

"You make man beat my brother give me cow for pay?"

"I'll tell him what you say. And I'll tell the chiefs of the village to make him give you the cow."

"I watch when you go back. Then I come for cow. I wait on land between Booshoo Creek and Eagle Creek. You drive cow cross Booshoo Creek an' leave um."

"It's not my cow," said Sandy. "I'll tell the man."

The harsh voice rose to a threatening growl.

"You tell man he no give cow for pay, I bring plenty men. Plenty men take all his cow—burn his house down for pay."

Sandy bit his lips in order not to answer that with a counterthreat of the white man's militia. His most immediate duty was to get his party safe to Charles Town without angering four armed warriors. He folded his arms

241

again, and again stared back into the Cusabo's strangely opaque eyes.

But the Cusabo had said his say. With magnificent anticlimax, he turned and led his three comrades back into the forest.

THE WIDE WESTERN marshes of Lord Ashley's river were afire with sunset as the dugout neared Albemarle Point. There, upon Old Town Creek, had been the city's first settlement. Ten years later it had been removed to the east side of Oyster Point peninsula, from which location it now faced the harbor bar.

Madame Lenoir recalled it and tried to chat of the seaport's history and other cheerful topics. But Mrs. Daken wept and the baby wailed; Praise God, at sight of a porpoise, tried to leap overboard to catch it; and all talk kept returning to the Cusabo encounter.

Mr. Daken and Mrs. Lenoir had praised Sandy warmly enough to make him uncomfortable. He had looked at Nicole, sitting now on a nearer thwart, and her eyes had met his reassuringly.

"She did most," he told them. "She saw the Indians appear suddenly from the woods—a sight startling enough to terrify anyone. But she was calm and courageous and went alone to warn you. If she had not done so, I could not have parleyed them."

She shook her head and smiled at him, with a look in her eyes that a more conceited man might have read as adoration.

"He reassured me," she told them. "I saw, by the way

he faced the savages and spoke to them, that he was un-afraid and would protect us all."

"Monsieur O'Kelly," decreed Madame Lenoir, "must be made to yield the cow in reparation. Otherwise, *les sauvages* may attack Dorchester."

Sandy felt the same upon that subject. But another subject was driving all other thoughts from his heart. Nicole's dark hair was blowing around her face, and whenever he caught her glance she flushed and her eyes grew starry.

The Cusabos had interrupted his first words of love to her and prevented her full reply. But memory of what she had said was making his heart pound. Had she not cared and not wanted him to carry on his suit, she would not, he told himself, have practically suggested that he speak to her parents. For she knew as well as he did that her parents were partial to him.

He looked at her: lovely yet practical, earnest and yet gay, feminine to her finger tips but always doing her share. Her slender, sunburned arms were graceful and at the same time strong enough to hold Praise God from disaster.

Sandy was no impressionable youth like Dick Stevens or Michael Bacon. His Puritan standards demanded more than a mere pretty face. He wanted a wife who would be a true helpmate—a wife to whom he could give respect as well as love.

He wondered humbly how such great good fortune had come his way. He had not the ready gallantries or the teasing boldness which, he had observed, most girls seem to like. Saxon Toll had—and so had Peregrine. He had feared them both as rivals, he now realized. But now his heart told him that he need fear neither. Nicole, under her laughter, was steadfast—as steadfast as he. Her eyes, whenever they met his, were telling him what he had hoped to hear from her lips when the Cusabos' appearance had interrupted.

Violent rocking of the boat brought him back from his dreams and caused him to look around. They were nearing the eastern extremity of White Point. Around its end the two rivers met and mingled their tides to form Charles Town harbor. He had learned before leaving the seaport that the water was treacherous here. His arms were sore from the long day's pull and the boat lunged like a living thing. Mrs. Daken whimpered with fright and the baby cried louder. Nicole smiled at Sandy and tightened her grip on Praise God.

As they made the hazardous turn to port, Sandy could see a sentry on the east bastion of the low curtain wall. The man raised an arm in salute. As they drew abreast of him, he pointed to the nearest landing place—a small wharf on the creek which formed the city's southeast boundary. Sandy was so weary that he felt relief at not having to work the boat a quarter mile farther upstream.

Swinging in toward the wharf, he saw a small group of citizens waiting upon it. And then he saw Saxon Toll running the length of its narrow planks, shouting a welcome to them as he came.

He helped Sandy and Mr. Daken get the women and children up the crude ladder, while Stevens and Bacon held the dugout against it. Then he grasped and wrung Sandy's hand.

"I spied you coming around the point and recognized you as you drew nearer. You and the Lenoirs must come to my house for the time you are staying."

Nicole tossed her head at him. "Your house? You have

only a garret room, and you eat bread and cheese at a tavern."

He laughed so heartily that Sandy wondered jealously if the sight of her had caused such high spirits.

"I have a house now—a delightful surprise to match the happy surprise of your arrival. It is only right that you, my best friends, shall be my first guests in it."

Mrs. Lenoir was shaking her head, and Sandy just then was obliged to turn aside to assist the distracted Mr. Daken. Glancing back at the group of three, he saw Saxon Toll stooping his tall head to whisper to the two women.

The intimacy of that gesture rekindled his jealousy. It came back to him that Toll had known them long before he did. Toll had warned him that he had not yet given up hope. Toll had no way of knowing that his friend Sandy Purbeck had any claim on Nicole or any wish to claim her.

And in truth he had no claim—nothing more than a tone of her voice and a look in her eyes. To be sure, she had told him he might ask her parents, but he had as yet been allowed no chance to do that. Could Nicole have been only teasing him? Had Saxon, in joy at seeing her, blurted out his proposal to her mother? If so it was certain that Mrs. Lenoir approved him. For under no other circumstances would she have agreed for her daughter and herself to visit a bachelor.

With sore muscles and a sorer heart, Sandy helped Mr. Daken get his family and his luggage together and, with a wharfman for carrier and guide, start for the hostel where he planned to stay. Then, turning back to his own friends, he saw plainly that they shared some secret from which he was excluded. Mrs. Lenoir was beaming and no longer shaking her head, Nicole's eyes were dancing. Toll slapped him on the back.

"Mrs. Lenoir has consented, and you cannot refuse. Have you no room for romance in your cold Puritan heart?"

Sandy's heart was just then anything but cold, and the word romance struck it like a dagger. So Nicole had betrayed him! She was only a French coquette! All this time she had cared for Toll and had only been playing with Sandy to pass the time.

Toll had already taken her arm and started off ahead, carrying most of the luggage under his free arm. There was nothing for Sandy to do except pick up the last bundle and escort Mrs. Lenoir after them. He walked glumly, through mud and over cobblestones, hearing the two in front chatter like magpies. At the door of a small house in a narrow alley, Toll paused and lifted the knocker.

The door opened at once to frame an English girl in a blue dress with white mobcap and apron. She was blond and buxom. Her blue eyes sparkled from one face to another, then came to meet Saxon's eyes with a look one could not mistake.

"My wife Dorry," he told them. "She and I welcome you, our friends, to our house."

THAT EVENING WAS for Sandy Purbeck the merriest and the happiest he had ever spent. In Dorchester, Massachusetts, he had known happiness; but there merriment had not been thought necessary to it.

Saxon Toll produced a bottle of good French wine for the meal.

"He has been saving it for you," Doris told them. "When the ship brought me in, we went at once to be married. On the way home from the church he bought two bottles of wine. One we drank together for our wedding supper. He said, 'We'll keep the other until my friends the Lenoirs and Sandy Purbeck come to drink it with us.'"

Sandy could not refuse a glass. It was his first taste of wine. The mild ale he had drunk in Boston with Couturier had so far been his only experience of alcohol. Being his first, it emboldened him and, after the bride and groom had been toasted, he raised his glass again and looked at Nicole.

"My greatest hope is that I may be as fortunate as my friend has been."

Nicole flushed as red as a rose, and Doris and Saxon exclaimed their delight. Mrs. Lenoir was not displeased, although she protested.

"It is my husband who must decide. You will have to discuss it with him."

"I will," Sandy assured her, "as soon as I see him. And I—I hope—hope you believe enough in me to plead my cause with him."

"I have liked you since you first came to our house," she replied. "And"—she paused to glance at the girl—"I've suspected she likes you too."

"I do, Maman," Nicole whispered.

"Ah! It is well. But we shall see. Marriage is a serious thing—an affair of importance to be arranged by the man of the house. If Monsieur Lenoir gives his permission after his talk with you, you shall have my blessing—Sandee."

She proved a kindly although strict duenna. When Saxon tried with well-meant but clumsy suggestions to persuade her and his wife to retire and leave the lovers alone, she rose.

"Ten minutes they may have to say good night to each other. At the end of that time I shall expect you, Nicole."

As the others left the room he opened his arms, and she came. At last he raised his head, far giddier with kisses than with his one and only taste of wine.

"Nicole, I love you with all my heart. I know I'm not worthy of you. But there's nothing of which I'm ashamed—nothing about my life I'm afraid to tell your father."

"I know," she told him softly.

Although in the past she had chattered and he been the silent one, she yielded now with compliance of love, seemingly satisfied to listen and agree.

"I wouldn't have dared ask for you—for a girl like you—if I had been hiding anything wrong in my past."

As he spoke he thought about Peregrine. But he could not be blamed for that. He would tell her father, and her father would understand. When she was his fiancée Peregrine could no longer pay court to her or even go to see her. Monsieur and Madame were French and practical. He would explain that while he could not disown his brother, he disapproved of Peregrine to such an extent that he would not have him in his home.

Nicole took his face between both her hands and shook her head as she smiled.

"Do I not know it, my dear—know you have nothing to hide? It makes me happy—and safe—and warm. For I have known girls who gave their hearts away, only to find the man had deceived them—to find another woman who had a claim on him."

"There is no other," he promised her. "I told you all about poor little Ness. She will always be a sweet memory to me. But you—you, Nicole—are reality—and life."

Madame's peremptory call took her out of his arms. He told himself he would lie awake until he saw her next morning. But twenty miles of paddling caught him as he touched his pillow. The leather-lunged watchman in the street shouted the hours unheard by him. When he had dressed and hurried out, he found her at breakfast with all the others. He dared not kiss her before them; but he fixed his eyes on her face as he sat across table from her and ate the good English porridge cooked by Doris Toll.

Afterward he went alone to the wharf to ask for Mr. Hawke at Mr. Lenoir's old office. Peregrine emerged from an inner room and took him outside on the open wharfhead.

"I heard of your arrival and was expecting you. The pretty French girl is along too, I hear."

"She is—and she and I are practically betrothed. It is about her I came to see you."

Peregrine smiled amusedly. "Jealous, are you?"

"It's not a question of jealousy. You've proved you can't be trusted. Mrs. Lenoir told me you'd been to the house—after you promised me not to go."

"I cannot remember promising anything."

"That doesn't matter, since I don't trust your word. But Mrs. Lenoir has told me she doesn't wish you to see Nicole again."

"She as good as told me so that night. I was doing her husband a favor."

249

"As an excuse to see Nicole. Well, don't go near them again. If you do, I swear to you I'll tell Mr. Lord and the elders at Dorchester the whole story about you."

Peregrine's face was bitter.

"In other words, you hold a whip and won't hestitate to use it."

"You may call it that. It amounts to the same thing."

"Very well. There are other girls. Don't be so pious. You may yet have reason to understand what happened to me. If a man once gets mixed up with a slut—"

"I don't get mixed up with sluts," said Sandy.

"Then go ahead and enjoy yourself. Take your girl to meet the brig. She's outside the bar now, waiting for afternoon tide. Of one thing you may be sure: *I* won't be there to bother you. I'm avoiding the Dorchester people arriving on her."

Sandy felt sure of that as he returned to the house. A ship's arrival was an event, and they all planned to go with him to meet and welcome this one. Standing on the wharf and watching the brig drop anchor, Sandy recalled a morning when he had stood there watching the young men of Charles Town volunteer to go out against the pirates. He had hardly known Nicole then; and yet subconscious desire for her approval had caused him to step into line.

She was standing close enough for her shoulder to touch his arm; a fact of which Madame Lenoir, on his other side, was unaware. He looked down at the rowing boat bringing the first load ashore. There was a blond, sharp-featured girl who looked familiar. She was waving a hand and calling his name. With surprise, he recognized her.

"Forbearance White!" he exclaimed.

He stepped forward to meet them as they came ashore. This, Sandy realized, was why the elders had sent him to Charles Town. But he could not see that, just behind him, Madame was watching him sharply and Nicole anxiously.

Forbearance White and an older woman were first to put foot on the wharf. The girl turned toward him with outstretched hands, but the official on duty was barring her way.

"Your names?" he demanded. "Where you expect to settle—and your purpose in coming?"

The older woman answered, loudly enough for all waiting upon the wharf to hear.

"I am Widow Orderly White, coming to make my home at Dorchester-on-the-Ashley. The pastor and elders of the church there expect me. They also expect my niece, Forbearance White, who intends to marry a young man come ahead and waiting for her."

"Name of the man?" asked the officer.

But before she could reply, Forbearance had pushed by them both.

"Here he is—come to meet me!" she cried, and threw both arms around Sandy's neck.

"THE POINT," said Sandy, pacing wildly to and fro in the small front room of the Tolls' house, "is that I knew nothing of this."

"The point," said Madame Lenoir, "is that my daughter

251

has been trifled with and shamed before all Charles Town."

Nicole had been led, white and silent, to her room. Doris had been banished by Madame Lenoir.

"Such affairs," she had decreed, "—*affaires tellement affreuses*—are not suitable for the ears of innocent young women."

"There are no affairs," Sandy shouted. "That's what I'm trying to tell you."

Saxon Toll, permitted to stay, tried to lend him a hand.

"Mrs. Lenoir, as a woman of the world, you must know there are certain women—"

"Ah!" she cried triumphantly. "It is that I know! And it is from that I would protect my daughter."

"I didn't mean that at all. I meant there are women who will do anything to make a man marry them."

"Only if once, through his wickedness, he becomes involved with them. Alas! How I have been deceived! I approved this young man. I thought him earnest—hardworking—good—*un jeune homme très sérieux*. Never did I dream that he was concealing such infamy!"

Sandy had finally rushed from the house and spent the night at a tavern. But he had returned the next day at an early hour. Saxon and Doris condoled with him and tried again to argue with the irate Frenchwoman. But she refused to leave her room and would not let him see Nicole. All he could do was to start back to Dorchester with the new arrivals whom he had been sent to meet, and whom he now thoroughly hated.

He hated them with all his heart: the widow White, who sat gaunt and forbidding; Forbearance, who would not meet his eyes but watched him when he looked away. At Dorchester he went at once to Mr. Lord. The young pastor heard him in amazement.

"Deacon White told me he understood you were to marry Forbearance. That is the reason he sent you to meet her and her aunt."

"He may have understood it, but I did not," said Sandy. "I gave Forbearance no reason to think I cared for her. I have not written her since I left Massachusetts."

Deacon White was summoned. He said his daughter Thankful had told him her schoolmaster loved and awaited her cousin. She had told him the matter was once mentioned in school, and that Master Purbeck had caned a boy who denied it. He knew she was in constant communication with the older cousin to whom she was so devoted. While writing letters, she had often quoted messages of respect and love sent through her by Sandy.

Sandy now knew the younger girl to be a vicious liar and the older a nervous introvert. But between them they had placed him in a bad position. Pastor Lord's face was stern.

"Why did you go to meet this girl if you did not intend to marry her?"

"I didn't know she was coming. Deacon White told me only that it was my turn to go."

"It has been common talk here for weeks that the widow White and her niece Forbearance were the ones expected."

He had not even heard it. Nicole had filled his heart. He tried to explain.

"I am in love with another girl. I hoped to marry her and was thinking only of her."

253

It was plain that pastor and deacon thought he had started to meet a Puritan girl to whom he had plighted troth, but on the voyage had been bewitched by a French hussy. He left them in as great a rage as that which had hold of him when he left Madame Lenoir.

But he knew that his only hope of convincing her was to get pastor and elders on his side. He believed that if they knew the truth, their Puritan conscience would force them to make amends. If they told Mrs. Lenoir it was all a fabric of Forbearance's diseased imagination, she would believe them and again believe in him. If Forbearance and Thankful were allowed to keep on telling that he had begged Forbearance to come and marry him, the village would despise him—and so would Nicole.

He went to Mr. Lenoir and poured out the story. The Frenchman shook his head.

"I like you and would have thought you the last man to—to be caught by a conniving woman. But I cannot have my daughter touched by any scandal."

In these hard days the O'Kellys were his only refuge. Willy had heard the gossip and reported it angrily. From O'Kelly himself down to the youngest child, they gave their faith and their love to Sandy.

"If one of me gurrls," the Irishman said, "should ever lie the suchlike, I'd lay me cattle stick on her until she confessed the truth."

Sandy sat gazing with heartache at the house across the next field. Although it was early dusk a light sprang up within it.

"Mr. Lenoir is lighting his candles early."

" 'Tis the women," said Willy. "They came back an hour ago—just before ye walked in."

"I didn't know. I didn't see them as I came by the parade ground."

"Their canoe came up the creek here, instid of takin' them to the public landin'. 'Tis tied down by me bench, where I keep me own canoe. Miss Nicole knows the spot, and 'twas there she landed."

In order to avoid me, Sandy thought bitterly. The creek mouth offered itself before the village was reached. At high tide a small craft could reach the O'Kelly or the Lenoir house without being seen by anyone in the town.

Willy voiced some of these unspoken thoughts.

" 'Twas but a bit of a canoe, an' two men paddlin' it."

He was by now at the window, leaning out to look at the Lenoir house.

"There's one of the men now, come to the door, Master Purbeck."

Sandy moved to stand by him. He saw the man at the door—and he could not fail to recognize his brother. He tried to control his voice.

"Are the men staying?"

"No. I heard the other one say they must be gettin' back to Saint Giles before mornin'. But Missis Lenoir offered to give 'em supper."

Sandy left, and waited for an hour on Willy's path. When they came, Peregrine was unruffled.

"I'll be with you in ten minutes, Smith," he said to his companion. "This is a chap I've known a long time. Wait for me where we came ashore."

As the furtive-looking man called Smith moved away, he laughed.

"To think of my little brother turning Casanova!"

"Didn't I tell you what I'd do if you saw Nicole again?"

255

"That was before your unfortunate fall from grace. Since you've lost her, don't be a dog in the manger."

"I haven't lost her. I intend to get her back. You've known Forbearance a long time. You know she lied."

"I know all about her. I warned you long ago."

"You did. And I warned you what I'd do if you bothered Nicole."

"I haven't bothered her, I assure you. While I don't flatter myself she's in love with me, injured pride makes her willing to accept attention from another man."

"Her mother dislikes you and distrusts you. I don't see how—"

"That's your trouble. In worldly matters you don't see what's right under your nose. Even if Madame doesn't like me, she's glad—after what you did to her daughter—to have her daughter seen walking and talking with another beau."

Sandy was choking with anger. "You took her to walk?"

"On White Point—where all the town was walking. But the old dragon played me false. She came along too."

"It's your last walk with her," Sandy told him.

He caught his brother's arm in a grip that made Peregrine wince.

"We're going now to Mr. Lord, and tell him the whole story."

"Take your hands off me! If you don't, I'll tell him a story of my own!"

"What are you talking about?"

"About whatever small chance you have of getting back the Lenoir girl. If you unmask me to Mr. Lord and the elders, I'll tell them you've been hiding me for rea-

256

sons of your own. I'll tell them our bargain was that, so long as you kept my secret, I'd not tell I knew long ago in the Bay Colony there was something between Forbearance White and my brother."

THE HEAT OF midsummer lay like a blanket on Dorchester township. In sultry daybreaks the mockingbirds still sang, and the wood thrushes continued to chime like bells in the twilight. But human beings who had been bred in a northern land could not endure it. Many were made ill; all were made nervous and irritable. Small grievances grew poignant.

Sandy, working his orchard and building his fence, only went to the trading post when he needed supplies. More than once, as he started to bow to them, older women had turned their faces away. In church he sat far back with Willy, hungrily watching Nicole's bonnet, escaping as soon as the service was over.

Twice he had sent Willy with letters of explanation and appeal. Nicole had read the first, then told the boy there was no answer. She had refused even to accept the second.

Forbearance and Thankful walked out with arms around each other's waists. Once he had come upon them suddenly, on the path that led past the commons to the O'Kelly and Lenoir houses. Forbearance had stopped short and cried out: "Sandy!" Thankful had glared at him and drawn her cousin away, as if he threatened them with harm.

When Shannon Couturier, in the uniform of a militia captain, rode up to the back of the house, Sandy ran to meet him with a cry of welcome.

"Did you ride all this way just to see me?"

"As a matter of fact I'm on my way from Saint Giles to Newington. I had to see you. I've just been to Charles Town—and talked with Saxon Toll."

The long, hot day drew to its close, and they talked late into the night. When Sandy finished his story, the other man was thoughtful.

"I shall talk to Mr. Lenoir before I leave tomorrow. But, it seems to me, the surest way to vindicate yourself would be to catch those two girls in another lie."

"I wish I could—and prove it to the township! But so far they're doing nothing except playing the part of injured innocence and putting me in the role of villain."

"Sooner or later they'll slip and be caught. I'm out to catch an offender now. That's why I'm visiting all these places. Saxon, by the way, has been elected a lieutenant of the Charles Town militia."

Sandy was glad to hear that, and glad of any news which took his mind from his own troubles. He listened.

"It's the buccaneers again. They haven't come into harbor. They don't need to. They're getting information from someone who knows our shipping. Not only information as to times of sailing, but exact information about cargoes carried by Lord Ashley's merchantmen."

"How can they?"

"Only from Saint Giles. The two clerks there are friends of mine. Their honesty is beyond reproach. I've just been questioning them, and I think I have a clue."

"I recall them," Sandy said. "They rode over here to see me. They seemed frank and likable fellows."

"They are—but not overly bright. They're city bred, fresh from England, and desperately lonely in this wilderness. It causes them to make friends with men unworthy of them."

Sandy said bitterly: "What does it matter? Even if you try to lead a decent life, you get blamed unfairly."

"Cheer up! All this will turn out well. When I leave here I'm going to Newington to see Lady Rebecca Axtell, who is a friend of my mother's. I shall tell the Dame that the elders are doing you a wrong. She is not one to bite her tongue—and I think they'll listen to her."

Sandy thought, with a flash of hope, that they would listen. He had heard of the Dame of Newington but had never met her. From the first, she had been a powerful friend to the young Puritan township. When she spoke, its councilors heard her with respect.

"A delegation from Dorchester is going some day this week to meet with her about matters concerning the school. I haven't been asked to join them, although I'm the schoolmaster. Perhaps they're planning to replace me."

"Nothing of the kind," said Couturier. "Lady Rebecca believes that Dorchester should have a free school patterned after the one in its parent Dorchester. It would be the first in South Carolina, and it's that your townsmen are going to discuss."

When he rode off the next day he left Sandy in better spirits. Shannon had talked with Mr. Lenoir and made the Frenchman confess that he could not believe Sandy

259

Purbeck guilty of double dealing. "But," the sericulturist had confessed, "an affair of the heart is a woman's affair. Nicole is sad and listless. I believe she loves the young man. Still, my wife insists that he is a monster."

If he could only talk with Nicole. If only he could make Forbearance and Thankful confess!

However, he slept better that night and woke feeling more hopeful. He was eating his breakfast when Willy burst through the door—a wild-eyed Willy, panting so for breath he could hardly speak.

"Injuns! They's a ring of 'em—the yellow-painted divils—all roun' the Lenoir house—howlin' they're goin' to burn it!"

Sandy was on his feet and loading the Brown Bess.

"No!" he shouted to Willy. "Don't go back alone!"

" 'Tis no more than women an' children in me own house an' the Lenoirs'. I must be goin'," the small hero told him.

Sandy rammed his powder hard.

"Where are your father and Mr. Lenoir?"

"Gone to Newington with all the other menfolks. Sure, but the red haythen waited to catch us this very time!"

They started together in a run.

"You stop," he ordered Willy, "and knock on every door along the Broad Path. All of the men haven't gone. Tell the ones you find to get their muskets and come!"

But, as he ran on alone, the village appeared deserted.

The party for Newington had made an early start to avoid travel in the heat, he realized. He wondered how many men had gone. Willy would assemble the ones left. What had happened at the Lenoir house since the little Irish boy had made his dash for help?

There was nobody in sight when he passed the O'Kelly home. Doors and windows were shut, but it seemed unmolested.

Then he saw the Indians—about thirty Cusabos—standing fifty feet from the Lenoir house. Without waiting to see more, he dropped to one knee, struck flint and fired.

Due to his haste, the shot went wild. The Indians ran for cover. Still kneeling, he reloaded the musket and took cover for himself behind a mulberry tree. He was now behind the house which fronted upon the creek. The Indians had run toward the water and were, he knew, hiding in the sweet myrtles along the bank. He was determined to get through the back door to Mrs. Lenoir and Nicole.

Dodging from tree to tree, he made his approach. He struck the panel with a fist.

"Nicole—it's Sandy! Let me in!"

She opened the door. "Sandy! I knew you'd come!"

But he had no time to answer that. He was bolting the door behind him.

"Where's your mother? How have you stood them off?"

"Maman's in the kitchen, boiling kettles of water to throw on them. I was talking to them through the window when you shot and frightened them away. They said they'd burn the house if I didn't give them a cow."

A cow? O'Kelly's cow! It came upon him like a thunderclap. He had warned the elders about the Indian incident and begged them to send a cow to the Cusabos as a peace offering, but then in his own distress he had forgotten to find out what they had done about it. But how had the Cusabos mistaken this house for the O'Kellys'?

"I'll go out and talk with them. Is it the same warrior who talked with us on the way to Charles Town?"

"I think so—but I don't know. They are all painted yellow and black and have feathers in their hair. Oh, Sandy, I'm so afraid!"

Madame appeared from the kitchen.

"There is no longer need for fear. The water is boiling, and ready, for the attack."

Sandy handed the long gun to Nicole.

"I'm sure they'll listen to me if I go out unarmed. But, in case they don't, this is the way you light the fuse. . . ."

He showed her, then moved toward the door. She followed him, begging: "Sandy, don't go!"

"Bolt the door after me," he ordered her as he went.

As he stepped out, instinctively bracing himself for an arrow or a thrown hatchet, the long slope down to the creek appeared peaceful and empty. The sun, just over the trees in the east, glittered upon cobwebs spun during the night upon grass and bushes. But those bushes, he knew, hid Cusabo warriors. Would they listen to him—or kill him while he was speaking?

He advanced slowly, with arms outstretched to show that he carried no weapons.

"I come in friendship," he called aloud, "to ask you what you want?"

No answer came from the myrtles ahead. Behind he heard Nicole wailing: "Sandy—come back!"

Halfway to the creek he stopped and raised both hands above his head.

"Let the man who has come for the cow show himself and talk with me. He shall have the cow to take back with him."

The warrior stood up then. "You one time lie. Maybe lie now."

"I didn't lie— But you shall take a cow back with you—if you go peacefully and do no damage."

"Big man beat my brother—why he stay in house? Why he no come out?"

"He's not in the house. This isn't his house. Two women alone are in there."

The savage insisted stubbornly: "This house big man house. He hide maybe."

"He has gone away from the village. This is *not* his house."

"This his house," said the warrior. "I ask white girl. She tell me this big man house."

Sandy had been playing for time, and his plan had worked. Between the trees of the orchard he saw running figures: Willy, the older schoolboys of the town, Michael Bacon, and Richard Stevens. The last two carried muskets, the rest only clubs. The blacksmith came into view, armed with his heavy hammer.

Sandy shouted to them: "Wait! We can settle this by talking." He added warningly: "There are thirty armed warriors here."

Behind their spokesman the warriors rose to confront the white men. They had bows as well as hatchets.

Across the dewy morning grass the two parties faced each other. The white men were being re-enforced by irregular arrivals. Elder Pratt and Deacon White—not strong enough to journey to Newington in the heat—hobbled valiantly behind, with walking canes for their only weapons.

Sandy knew they were all perched upon a keg of gunpowder which would be sparked to explosion by an ill-advised word or movement. He spoke to Bacon and Stevens.

"They've come for the cow—the same reason they followed us down the river. Explain it to Elder Pratt—and keep all the rest of them quiet."

He turned back to the Cusabo. "The men who walk with sticks are chiefs of the village. They listen."

The Indians waited in stony silence. Then the two elderly churchmen moved forward and placed themselves upon either side of Sandy.

"You shall have the cow," said Elder Pratt, "if you take it and go at once."

The Cusabo moved a step toward the Lenoir house.

"Man beat my brother gotta come out. He gotta gimme plenty cow."

Elder Pratt's voice was authoritative and stern.

"There is no man in this house. You have come to the wrong house. I will send a boy to get the cow—if you'll take it and go away."

The warrior's eyes, like dark small stones, fastened upon the old man's face as if to read the truth. In the pause Mr. Pratt spoke again, clearly and fearlessly.

"And if you do not take it and go, the white soldiers will punish you. Their leader is now nearby. He will call them and they will march upon you with guns."

Threat of the militia was a terrible one. The Cusabo still tried to argue, but his voice had lost its assurance.

"Me know bad man in this same house. White girl tell me man beat my brother live here."

Sandy thought wildly that it could not have been Nicole. Elder Pratt asked the question.

"What white girl?"

"One-two white girl I meet 'long path one day. Big one—little one—hold arm round each other. I say: 'Me look for bad man beat my brother. You tell bad man he gimme cow or I burn his house.' White girl point finger this same house. White girl say, 'Bad man live there—big, bad man beat your brother. You come back night—burn bad man house—kill bad people in it.'"

S ANDY COULD NOW look back upon the following scene as a nightmare; a nightmare from which he emerged in happy release.

With stern Puritan justice he had demanded that Forbearance and Thankful be brought to confront the Cusabo. And with Puritan justice, Deacon White had agreed. The warrior who had spoken with the girls identified them. The sight of the band of Indians so terrified them—as Sandy had been sure it would do—that they broke down and confessed.

Ever since Forbearance's arrival they had walked the lonely path to the Lenoir house, in hopes of getting a glimpse of the girl Sandy loved and they hated. And upon these walks they amused themselves by weaving wild tales of revenge upon her. One day they had, in perverted imagination, pushed her into the creek and drowned her. One day a black bear had emerged from Rose Creek swamp and devoured her. They had wished they were not afraid to go into the woods and catch a rattlesnake and hide it in her bed. For through it all Thankful had assured her cousin that the French girl was a witch and had by witchcraft taken Sandy's love from her.

They had been told by young Stevens and Bacon the story of the Cusabo's demand for O'Kelly's cow. When the Indian met them on the path and asked which house was O'Kelly's, the chance seemed to them no more than divine justice. They had not then—and did not now have—the least compunction about consigning the French witch and her parents to death by fire. Their only compunction now was terror of Puritan justice which they knew would come upon them at the hands of the deacon and widow White.

Sandy struck while the iron was hot, with no pity for tears.

"Tell them the truth, Forbearance—if you hope for forgiveness. Just as you made up these stories, did you not make up your story about me?"

Hysterical, she admitted it and screamed her remorse. Deacon White, with a businesslike grip on his cane, at last led his daughter and cousin away.

Sandy looked at Elder Pratt.

"Am I fully exonerated?"

"Completely," said the churchman, "—with my regret for the wrong done you."

When the warriors led the cow away and the villagers dispersed, Sandy looked at Nicole. With her mother, she had stood by and heard it all.

266

Madame said: "You are as I first thought, *un jeune homme très sérieux*. As soon as Monsieur Lenoir comes home, I shall tell him we were mistaken."

Sandy was aching to kiss Nicole, but, being shy and reserved as he was, he could not do it under chaperonage.

"The cause of all this," Madame told them both, "is plain. It is lack of laughter. The wretched young girl—who lived in a gloomy village in a land of ice and ate only English cooking, which has no seasoning—is truly to be pitied. Lacking laughter, which spices life, she became *dérangée*."

That may well be, thought Sandy. He could now afford to forgive. But his one thought was to kiss Nicole —and she read it on his face.

"Maman!" she exclaimed. "The hot water will have boiled away and the bottoms of all your kettles be burned!"

Mrs. Lenoir turned with a shriek and rushed into the house. And Sandy laughed aloud as he caught his almost-lost love in his arms.

And he went back that afternoon for a talk with Mr. Lenoir. It prolonged itself until twilight, for the Frenchman was cordial. With Gallic frankness he regretted the mistake which had kept the lovers apart for several unhappy weeks.

"But she is my daughter, as truly as if by blood. She was my first thought. It is why I did you a wrong."

"I understand," Sandy reassured him. "Nicole's worth waiting for—and fighting for too."

"She is that," said the Huguenot. "She has both courage and laughter. What more can any man ask in a wife?"

Urged by all three, Sandy stayed for a supper whose

food had plenty of spice and whose talk plenty of laughter.

Walking home, as he had done on that same path so often before, he was again happy and at rest. He had begged for an early marriage, and Mr. and Mrs. Lenoir had said they saw no obstacle. Nicole had been allowed to walk to the door with him for a good-night embrace. He had the small home ready for her. The orchard was set and the trees would bear fruit. To see her in his own kitchen making pies and preserves. . . .

A slender figure in uniform was standing by the gate of his newly built fence. Sandy exclaimed at the sight.

"Shannon! I'm so glad you're back!"

Couturier put a hand on his shoulder.

"I'm back with bad news, Sandy. On my way to Newington, I was intercepted by a rider from the militia. Since I saw you yesterday, I've ridden down to Charles Town, changed horses and ridden back again."

To Sandy, who was no horseman, the feat sounded fantastic. And there was warning of trouble in his friend's voice.

He asked: "But, why? Why did you do it?"

"Because I couldn't let anyone else. I had to tell you myself. My militiaman brought me word that a trap I laid had worked. Two men were caught in the act of giving information about Charles Town shipping to pirates."

The night about them was dark as death, and so was Sandy's heart. It had come to him suddenly—before Couturier could finish.

"I turned back to Charles Town with my messenger, to find that one of these men had died of a gunshot wound received when he tried to escape. I saw the other—

268

chained in Charles Town's dungeon. He is known as Hawke—but he's Peregrine Purbeck, your brother whom you thought dead."

ALL NIGHT THEY worked down river in Sandy's light canoe. They had stopped only to call Willy from his slumber and ask him to stable Couturier's horse and give Sandy's note to Nicole.

Why had he not seen it? he was asking himself. Its clues had been before him since, on the folly's beach, he had found a dead campfire and a forked stick cut for a gun rest. That must have been the start of the evil traffic. Peregrine had fled Charles Town for fear of recognition. Upon the island he and his friend called Smith had met the escaped pirates. Instead of reporting them to the authorities, they had fraternized and had listened to offers of Spanish gold in exchange for information.

The man called Smith had ingratiated himself with the young English clerks at Lord Ashley's warehouses. That had been his part of the business. Saint Giles was too near Dorchester for Peregrine to go there openly.

Peregrine's had been the bolder part. It was he who met the pirates on the same folly beach and delivered to them the information: information he himself secured on Charles Town's wharves and information his friend secured at Saint Giles.

But Shannon Couturier had outwitted them both. Shannon told the story while they drove the dugout down river.

"I arranged for my friends at Saint Giles to tell this

man Smith of a cargo of extra-large and fine fresh-water pearls—a cargo which did not exist, but which would be bait for a buccaneer. Then Smith was followed by one of my militiamen, a woodsman from the Edisto who tracks like an Indian. He saw Smith meet Hawke and give him a piece of paper. All we had then to do was follow Hawke—follow him to the same beach where we found the campfire. He built a fire there that night for signal, not knowing that a platoon of militiamen were hidden in the yaupon watching his every move. At dawn a galley was standing offshore and a rowing boat with three men put in. My men held their fire until they saw Hawke hand the paper over to one of the pirates. Then they shot down the three buccaneers and took Hawke prisoner. The list of information, in Smith's handwriting, was taken from the body of one of the dead pirates."

"Smith wasn't there?"

"No. His work was done when he handed the list to Hawke. My men brought Hawke directly back to gaol, and went to arrest Smith at his lodgings. He jumped from a window and ran—and they shot him."

Sandy was thinking it might have been easier for Peregrine if they had shot *him*. A man who traded with Carolina pirates was a pirate to Carolina law. There could be only one sentence for his brother who lay in the dungeon. Sandy had witnessed a trial of pirates. Shooting would have been a cleaner and more merciful death.

But although he saw no way of saving his brother, he had to go to Peregrine.

Saxon Toll met them in the dawn.

"I've been watching for you half the night."

"I told him," Couturier said. "Only he and I know Hawke's true identity."

They took Sandy to the same small house where he had first met Saxon's bride. He tried to control his features and to eat the breakfast she served, for he knew she was ignorant of his awful errand.

"You are so weary you look haggard," she told him. "Go now to your room and sleep. I will not let my husband and Captain Couturier keep you talking."

He was thankful to be alone with his misery. Dropping his boots on the floor and throwing himself upon the bed, he racked his brains for the slightest chance—chance for Peregrine to escape a gallows on White Point. . . .

When he woke hours later he heard voices—the voices of Shannon and Saxon in the lower hall. In the wild hope that something might have developed while he slept, he walked in stockinged feet to the door to call to them. But Couturier's words arrested him.

"You're too big, you ox," he was saying. "He knows how to box, but nobody would believe a man his size could knock you unconscious."

Saxon insisted stubbornly: "It's the only way. A hired gaoler could be made drunk. But the governor's orders are that a man sure to be sentenced to death is guarded constantly by a militiaman."

Sandy caught at the door to steady himself. He knew what the sentence had to be, but the words struck him like a blow.

"Lieutenant Toll," said Couturier's light voice, "as your superior officer I order you to do as I say."

"Captain C'traire," drawled Toll's deeper tones, "order and be damned to you! You command a company of backwoodsmen on Pon Pon. I'm a leftenant of Charles Town militia."

Couturier laughed. "In that case, you are surely sportsman enough to leave the decision to the toss of a coin."

Toll's voice was doubtful. "It's an even chance."

"It's supposed to be," said Couturier. "Do you choose face or reverse?"

"Face," said Saxon.

"I counted on that," Couturier remarked. "For some reason, no man chooses reverse."

There came the ring of gold on the floor. Couturier cried out: "I win!"

"It's other side up," Toll owned grudgingly. "But," he added, "I still feel—"

Couturier's voice was deadly earnest now.

"But however you feel, you know in your heart it's the only chance for Sandy Purbeck's brother."

So THEY HAD some plan. He could not see how it would work if they had a militiaman on guard. But whatever it was, he grasped at it. If they but told him how to approach, he knew how to knock a sentry out without killing him.

He washed his face, pulled on his boots and ran downstairs with hope in his heart.

"Doris has dinner ready for us," Doris' husband told him. "We'll eat and then talk. Shannon has an idea."

It was as he had guessed when he overheard them: the old and only idea of disposing of a guard.

272

"*Captain* C'traire," said Saxon sarcastically, "will be busy all afternoon with His Excellency. No doubt the guv'nor'll make him a general for his skill."

"In commanding backwoodsmen?" Couturier countered.

"No—in tossing coins," Saxon Toll replied.

Their joking, Sandy knew, meant they were hopeful.

Couturier said: "I've got to pick a guard for tonight. My company started today back to the Edisto. But I'm in charge of this affair until I have the governor's permission to turn it over to the Charles Town militia."

Toll still smarted from the loss by the tossed coin. "Be sure you pick a guard no larger than yourself. There's no use to make this thing harder than it need be."

"I'll do my part. You do yours," Couturier told him, and departed.

Saxon's part was to take Sandy to the dungeon near the water front.

"The night guard goes on at sunset," he told him on the way. "He mustn't see you—now or tonight. Remember, it's of the greatest importance that you never come face to face with him. You must hide, and step out behind him and hit him—all at once."

"I can do it—if you show me where to hide."

Saxon showed him a narrow lane between two storage bins.

"This is his beat. He must pass here. You'll have to be crouching. You'll see his legs—then move out behind him."

"Where are the keys?"

"They hang inside, on a spike in the wall. There are

273

two dungeons, and he's alone in the smaller—the one we'll reach first from this door."

The sentry saluted Lieutenant Toll.

"Want a look at the scoundrel who was selling us to the sea hawks?"

Sandy winced. Peregrine had chosen a fitting pseudonym. He heard Saxon replying.

"Yes. My friend here came thirty miles out of the country to see him."

"Come back," the sentry invited, "and see us hang him next week."

Sandy went with Toll through the outer door and faced a brick wall with two other doors. Beside the nearer hung an iron key eight inches long. Toll inserted it in the lock, turned it and drew the heavy bolt. As he opened the door a stench came out to them. It was the odor of filth and airlessness and heat, and—Sandy sensed —the odor of death.

All was dark and utterly still as they stepped inside. Toll locked the door after them, then said: "Speak to him, Sandy—but keep your voice down."

Sandy whispered: "Where are you, Peregrine?"

"I'm over here—to your right from the door—manacled to the wall."

The floor felt slippery underfoot, and a rat squeaked loudly and suddenly.

Peregrine swore. "One of the cursed beasts ran over my face last night!"

Saxon's voice was low and stern.

"Keep quiet! All you've got to do is listen—listen to us if you want to save your neck."

274

"You know there's not a chance. Go away and leave me alone!"

"Hold your tongue! And hold your wrists up for me. I'm going to open the locks of your hand irons now."

Peregrine's whisper was incredulous. "You mean—"

"Not now. Sandy'll come for you just after midnight. Do exactly as he says—or I swear you'll hang. He'll guide you down to the river, and I'll be there in his boat. A Greek galley is standing out in the roads, waiting to clear with the tide an hour before dawn."

"Her master'll take me?"

"He'll take any man he can get his hands on. Most of his crew deserted him here, because he's such a brute."

"Less of a brute than a hangman's noose," Peregrine said. "I'll be ready."

CROUCHED BETWEEN THE bins in the narrow alley, Sandy was now awaiting his chance. Along Bay Street the watch had gone by, shouting: "*Midnight —and all's well!*" All was not well with him, and could not be until he had saved his brother from death and his father's name from public disgrace.

Toll had showed him the quickest way down to the river. Toll would be there with the canoe, to row out to the Greek galley.

Waiting, Sandy reviewed every step taken and every word spoken. It was his way to be thorough, and in this extremity there must be no mistake. When they came out of the dungeon Toll had said to the guard: "Do not enter Hawke's cell. Slide his food under the door. I've just unlocked his irons, and we must take no risks."

The guard had dared to exclaim: "Unlocked his irons, Leftenant?"

"He said the rats ran over his face—and his wrists are sore."

"His neck'll be sorer," said the guard cheerfully.

"That may be. But we're a British colony. We don't torture prisoners, as Spaniards and pirates do."

Twice now Sandy had seen the night sentry pass—only a pair of legs moving in militia pantaloons. The city watch must by now be at the northern boundary, at Market Creek. This was the time to strike—before the watch came back, when the sentry next came by.

He crouched, tense and listening, until he heard footsteps approaching.

As the guard passed, Sandy rose behind him and hurled himself on the man's back, at the same time throwing his left arm over and around the man's mouth to stifle a cry. With the same movement he jerked back the man's head and brought his right fist up in a short, sharp jolt for the chin.

The slender figure went limp against him. Sandy laid him down on the cobblestones and went swiftly through the gaol's outer door.

Peregrine was silent, his spirit broken at last. He followed Sandy down to the river, and they waded ankle-deep through mud to the canoe. In silence Saxon Toll had pulled for the riding lights of the Greek galley.

"We're in luck that the night's starless and moonless," he said at last.

276

Neither one of the brothers replied. The darkness lay on Sandy's heart as deeply as on his eyes. As they nudged under the Greek's bow the deck watch hailed them.

Toll answered him: "We're bringing you a seaman."

The thrown rope slapped on the black hull. Peregrine leaned and caught it and pulled himself to his feet.

"Thanks," he said huskily. "No other brother in the world would have stood by me as you've done."

The only words Sandy could find were: "Good-by, Peregrine."

Then he went back to Toll's house and for twenty-four hours slept the blessed sleep of exhaustion and relief.

When he awoke, his friend told him: "The galley cleared before dawn—before the night sentry was found by the sunrise replacement."

"Did I hurt him badly?"

"He's got a sore chin and a couple of teeth loosened. He says he can honestly swear he never saw who hit him."

"Where's Shannon?"

"With the governor again."

"I'm going right back to Dorchester. Isn't he going with me?"

"Yes. He'll be in later. And as for you, you'd better stay in the house until you're leaving."

"Does anyone suspect me? I'm not worried about myself, but for you and Shannon."

"Nobody knows who Hawke really is, so they have no reason to connect you with his escape. All visitors in the seaport are bound to be suspect; and if he sees you, the sentry we saw yesterday may recall that you've been around the gaol."

"You're right," Sandy agreed; for above all he wished not to bring suspicion upon his friends.

"Talk on the streets is that the buccaneers sent in a longboat with a rescue crew. Another guess I heard struck closer to truth."

"What was it?"

"A wharfman told me he talked yesterday with the Greek ship's mate. He said the mate was out to get a crew by hook or crook. He asked if the laws of this colony allowed felons to be handed over if the ship paid their fines."

The Greek ship was by now far at sea. Sandy refused to let himself think of any hardship which Peregrine might be enduring. It was possible that through hardship he could yet work out his salvation.

Couturier came in wearing a neckcloth of fine white silk above the open collar of his uniform. He spoke a little thickly.

"His Excellency didn't make me a general, but neither did he order me gaoled."

Sandy was staring at the purple and orange bruise which was visible on chin and jaw when his friend turned his head.

"Shannon! It was you? What a blind fool I was!"

"We did our best to blind you, Saxon and I. You did it just as neatly, if not so lethally, as Jamaica's Jungle John. All I felt from the blow was shock—no pain— until I woke up."

"No wonder the governor had you up! How did you explain it to him? The reason I didn't guess was I didn't dream a captain—of an out-of-town company—"

"My company did the work. I've tried to impress that

278

on Saxon. I impressed it on the governor too. I told him I'd sent my men home but had not yet finished filling out all papers and formally transferring the prisoner to Charles Town jurisdiction. Both of those statements were true. I told him, that being so, I felt it my duty to take the night guard's shift myself. That was true—inasmuch as I felt it my duty to a good friend."

Although he was not emotional, Sandy's eyes stung and he found it hard to steady his voice.

"I only hope that—someday—I'll be a good enough friend to—to repay something of what I owe you both."

ALL SANDY COULD think was: *If we make good time, I may see her tonight!*

"For heaven's sake, rest your paddle and let us drift," begged Couturier. "It's high noon. You'll have a heat stroke."

The tide was with them but was too slow for Sandy. His conscience would not allow him to let his friend share the work; for he saw that the Huguenot was stiff and painful from his shoulders to the top of his head. He knew that it had taken cold courage as well as warm friendship to ask and await a blow from a trained boxer who weighed a stone more than his victim.

"I wish Saxon had won that toss of the coin. He's bigger and stronger than you—and has a wife to plaster his jaw."

"He's too big. You might not have knocked him unconscious. And he's no actor; he couldn't have pretended.

I knew that sentry would have to face questioning by the governor and possibly the chief justice. I couldn't take a chance of their breaking Saxon down."

"But you did take a chance. I heard you talking, although I was too distracted to guess exactly what it meant. That coin could have fallen face up."

"Oh, no, it couldn't," said Couturier.

He drew it from a pocket and held it out in the palm of his hand. Sandy shipped his paddle and took it and turned it. There was no face on either side. Both were engraved with reverse symbols.

He grinned as he handed it back. "Better not let Saxon see it."

He knew Couturier had showed it to him in order to reassure him that Couturier had been determined to play the role of sentry, and to help dispel Sandy's remorse for the blow.

Dusk hovered above the river like wings as they passed the wide mouth of Eagle Creek. Here and there a white heron rose and slanted away. The wild white spider lilies rose upon bare stems like ghostly amaryllis from the black mud between stream and bank. The sooner he reached Dorchester, Sandy was thinking, the better would be his chance of seeing Nicole that night. People rose early in the Puritan township, ate their supper meal shortly after sunset, and went to bed not long afterward. Unless Nicole was waiting for him. . . .

As they came to the mouth of Dorchester Creek, a small figure hailed from the bluff.

"Turn in," Willy yelled. "Bring the boat up the creek. I got the horse waitin' for Cap'n C'traire an' Miss Nicole waitin' for you!"

It was all Sandy needed to give him new strength. He shot the narrow dugout into the creek mouth against the outrushing tide and drove on to the low bank by Willy's bench. Nicole rose from it and came to meet him as he dropped his paddle and leapt ashore.

When he looked up from that long embrace Couturier had finished mooring the dugout, and Willy had panted up from his run overland. Couturier came up the bank and kissed Nicole's hand.

"My felicitations. I expect to be asked for best man. And now, if you'll excuse me. . . ."

He turned to call back: "Come along, Willy!"

As they went, Sandy drew her down on the bench close by him.

"In my note I could tell you only that I had been called away."

"I was content with that, Sandy. When you said you had to go, I knew you were right to go."

"Now I can tell you all about it, my darling."

"You need not tell me unless you wish to. I doubted you once. I'll never doubt you again."

He loved her more for her faith in him, but he told her.

She nestled closer in his arms. "He did not deserve it—but I'm glad you did it, Sandy."

"He's my brother still. But I was jealous, Nicole, when you liked him—and coquetted with him."

"The only reason I coquetted with him was that I hoped to make you jealous."

"You succeeded in doing so. From now on, save all your coquetry for *me*."

She laughed aloud at him; and from across the creek a wood thrush chimed an echo like bells.

"My own love—my darling Puritan—are you asking for coquetry?"

"From my wife—yes. You've taught me to like it—taught me that life, like food, is improved by spice."

Then fear seized him suddenly. He had thought he held her, once before, and she had slipped from his arms.

"Will you be happy with me, Nicole? Can you find happiness with a dull Puritan husband?"

"There are things *you've* taught *me* about Puritan goodness and strength. I'll be happy—and safe—with you, Sandy."

"I'll keep you safe, my darling. But all my worldly goods consist of a small house by a river."

"What does it matter how small the house, if there is laughter and love in it?"

"There will always be laughter and love in it, my own dear love," he promised. "And outside will be a wood-thrush song—like your voice—and always a river."

(1)